Fire and Rain

A Wildest Alaska Novel

Pamela Clare

www.pamelaclare.com

FIRE
and
RAIN

PAMELA
USA TODAY BESTSELLING AUTHOR
CLARE

FIRE AND RAIN

A Wildest Alaska novel
Published by Pamela Clare, 2022

Cover Design by © Jaycee DeLorenzo/Sweet 'N' Spicy Designs
Sea Rescue image: icholakov01
Man in shirt: icholakov01
Ocean Spray: miltonia

Copyright © 2022 by Pamela Clare

This is a work of fiction. Names, characters, places, and incidents are products of the author's imagination or are used fictitiously, and any resemblance to actual persons, living or dead, business establishments, events, or locales is entirely coincidental.

All rights reserved.

No part of this book may be reproduced, scanned, or distributed in any printed or electronic format without permission. Please do not participate in or encourage piracy of copyrighted materials by violating the author's rights. No one should be expected to work for free. If you support the arts and enjoy literature, do not participate in illegal file-sharing.

ISBN: 979-8-9854351-6-0

*This book is dedicated to the courageous men and women of the United States Coast Guard, who risk their lives to save others day in and day out with very little fanfare.
Semper Paratus.*

Acknowledgments

Special thanks to Jacqueline Cetrulo for her help and support with the Coast Guard elements of this story. She made such a difference, and I am deeply grateful.

Additional thanks to Michelle White, Mary White, Jackie Turner, Benjamin Alexander, and Shell Ryan for their continual support. I couldn't do this without you. No, I mean it. I really couldn't.

Glossary

DIC — Dependency and Indemnity Compensation
SBP — Survivor Benefit Plan
RTB — Returning to base
SAR — An acronym for Search and Rescue. Pronounced like a word, not like letters.
Duty Room — A room where Coasties sleep when they've got a 24-hour duty shift.
Conn — To give verbal instructions that guide a pilot into position.
Evolution — A term used by most branches of the military. In this context, it refers to the work needed to complete a mission and can probably be used interchangeably with mission.
TrakkaBeam — A big spotlight that helps helicopter flight crews spot people on the water.
Mikes — Minutes. "Thirty mikes out" means "thirty minutes away."
Deck — The deck of a ship. Terra firma. For a helicopter crew, it means on the ground.

Bingo Fuel — The minimum amount of fuel needed to return safely to base.

Prologue

January 11
Air Station Kodiak
Kodiak Island, Alaska

THE SAR ALARM jerked Sean McKenna from a sound sleep. Instantly awake, he got to his feet and left his duty room, already wearing the black thermals that all flight crews wore beneath their survival suits.

The operations duty officer's voice sounded over the loudspeaker. "Now put the ready helo online. Now put the ready helo online."

Justin Koseki emerged from the duty room across the hall and walked with Sean down the narrow corridor toward the locker room. "Get any sleep?"

"Some. You?"

Sean had met Justin a little more than eight years ago at boot camp, and they'd been friends ever since. Tonight, they were both on duty and needed to be ready to take off at a moment's notice.

Justin shook his head, a smile on his face. "I was talking with Eden. She wants to try for another baby."

Eden Alexyev Koseki was Justin's beautiful wife of three years and the mother of his eighteen-month-old son, Maverick.

Sean chuckled. "Weren't you just complaining about the cost of diapers, man?"

Justin grinned. "She wants our kids to be born here in Kodiak so her parents can have time with them before we get transferred away. I'll ask to stay here for as long as I can, but you know how that goes."

Justin had already secured a second tour of duty in Kodiak, but where he served after that was up to the Coast Guard. Most Coastie families lived far from loved ones, moving every two to four years. But Eden had deep roots on the island, with ancestry that included Alutiiq, Russian, Scottish, and French Canadian. She'd never lived anywhere else, and Sean couldn't blame her for wanting to raise her children here.

Justin glanced at him. "When are you going to meet someone?"

They turned the corner and headed down the stairs.

"Dude, do the math. There are twenty-six percent fewer women than men on this island, and if you subtract married women, little girls, and grandmas, the pickings are slim. Besides, you know what they say. If you mess around on Kodiak Island, you'll end up with dependents, a disease, a divorce, or a dishonorable discharge—or maybe all four."

Besides, Sean's life was too unsettled, his job too risky, and his workdays too long to be in a serious relationship. The divorce rate for Coasties wasn't as high as it was for members of the Air Force. Still, he didn't want to settle down with a woman until he had a permanent home, and he'd never planned to be a father. For that reason, Sean had always kept his relationships safe and casual—until he'd transferred to Kodiak. Then he'd found himself without a love life.

Justin laughed. "You're a flight mech. You've got shiny gold wings on your uniform. Women dig wings."

"Too bad I can't wear my uniform into the bars."

"I didn't meet Eden in a bar."

"Not all of us get to show off the way you rescue swimmers do."

Justin had jumped out of the helo at Kodiak's Crab Fest as part of a demonstration to show the crowd what rescue swimmers did. But rather than hooking himself up so he could be hoisted back up to the helo like he was supposed to, he'd swum over to a pretty woman standing with her sisters at the pier and asked for her name and number. He'd been reprimanded, but it had been worth it. Six months later, Sean had flown up from Air Station San Francisco to stand with Justin at his wedding to Eden. Sean had taken one look at the landscape and had requested to be stationed in Kodiak for his next move.

Some Coasties hated Alaska, but Sean loved it. It was a land of extremes—extreme beauty, extreme weather, extreme risk. Living and working on Kodiak Island got Sean's blood pumping in a way that no other assignment had.

They reached their lockers and dropped the banter. Lt. James Spurrier and Lt. Junior Grade David Abbott, the helo pilot and co-pilot, were already halfway into their survival suits.

"What've we got?" Sean opened his locker, began to dress out.

James yanked up the diagonal zipper of his survival suit. "Sector Anchorage got a call from a twenty-eight-foot fishing boat called the Marjorie T. A forty-six-year-old male collapsed suddenly, seized, and is having trouble breathing. The boat is about fifty miles offshore."

"Do they have an AED on board?" As the rescue swimmer, Justin was an EMT and would be in charge of medical care once they got the patient into the helo.

"No defibrillator." James grabbed his flight bag. "The woman who made the call sounded extremely upset and said she didn't have first aid training. The operations duty officer told her how to put him in a recovery position and asked her to check for a pulse. She couldn't tell his pulse from her own."

"Adrenaline will do that." Sean zipped his suit, grabbed the rest of his gear, and walked with the others toward the operations center. "What's the weather doing?"

Here in Alaska, the weather could change in a heartbeat and varied drastically from one area to another. It might be a calm night over Air Station Kodiak but gusting forty knots with zero visibility a ten-minute flight up the coast.

"Clear skies with gusts up to fifteen knots. Water temp is forty degrees."

"Nice." Sean's primary job was to conn the pilot into position and manage the hoist, lowering the rescue swimmer to the water or the deck of the boat and then lifting him and any patients or survivors to safety. High winds made that job a lot more challenging.

They found Lt. Michelle Yamada, a fixed-wing pilot, staffing the operations duty officer post for the night. She'd already calculated their flight path. "There are no land obstacles in your way. It should be a straightforward evolution."

James' gaze was on the map, where the ship's position was clearly marked. "Any amplifying information?"

Lt. Yamada nodded. "The boat isn't moving, so they're getting tossed around by the swells. Apparently, the patient is the only one who feels safe piloting the craft. The woman who called in is the patient's wife. The patient is unconscious and unresponsive. She thinks he has a pulse, but she's pretty upset and confused. I asked a corpsman to join you just in case you need extra medical help. Wade Sheppard is already waiting near the helo."

"Good idea." James pulled on his helmet. "Let's go."

It was a short helicopter flight to the position of the *Marjorie T*, so Sean helped Justin and Wade get the cabin ready for the patient, the three of them preparing for the worst. Sean and Justin had worked dozens of SAR cases together and operated quickly and efficiently. As a corpsman, Wade rarely flew, but he had a higher level of medical training and was allowed to administer medications that Justin could not.

"Once we get the patient into the cabin, I'll defer to you," Justin told Wade, the conversation carried over earphones so that everyone could hear over the din of the rotors.

"Copy that." Wade hung a bag of IV fluids and retrieved an AMBU bag, while Justin got the AED ready. IV tubing. O2. Medications. Pulse Oximeter. Blankets.

An unconscious patient meant a litter rescue, but Sean would wait until Justin had left the cabin to put the litter together. He turned to the window, flipped down his night-vision goggles, and searched the endless ocean for the *Marjorie T*.

Abbott's voice came through the headphones. "I wonder what a small craft like that is doing out here in the middle of the night."

"Good question," James replied. "Something must have gone wrong."

There was no fog, but there wasn't any moonlight either, the darkness broken only by the MH-60 Jayhawk's lights. They had no photos of the *Marjorie T*, and Sean wasn't sure the boat had power or functioning lights.

James' voice sounded in Sean's ear. "You've got door speed."

"Roger that. Opening cabin door." Sean leaned out as cold air rushed in, his gaze on the inky black surface of the swells below.

James tried to pick the boat up on the radio. "Marjorie T, this is Coast Guard Rescue Six-Zero-Three-Eight, do you copy?"

A moment of silence was followed by a burst of static. "Coast Guard, it's the Marjorie T. I can hear you, but I can't see you. Help us!"

Sean spotted the vessel bobbing in the water. "They're at our two o'clock."

"I see them." David turned on the helo's TrakkaBeam, the powerful spotlight illuminating the boat below. "Let there be light."

"Is the big flashlight giving you a god complex, Abbot?" James joked.

"Marjorie T, Rescue Six-Zero-Three-Eight, we're nearing your position. Can you give us an update on the patient, over?"

"He still isn't moving. I think I felt his heart beating."

"Good copy, Marjorie T. We'll circle your position and figure out the best way to reach the patient, over."

Sean made a quick study of the boat and any hazards it might present to a hovering helo. "The boat's really small, and there are a couple of antennas coming off the cabin."

David peered out his window. "Looks like our patient is in the stern."

"I see him." Sean had already made up his mind. "We're going to have to put the swimmer in the water. You good with that, man?"

Justin nodded, his gaze on the boat. "I'll climb on board and assess the patient. Then you can send down the litter."

"Roger that." James circled the boat once more.

Sean got down on his belly to get a good view of the craft and all parts of the helo, then conned James into position. "Ten feet to the right."

It was one of the most critical parts of any rescue. If the helo's rotor contacted any of the boat's antennas, it would be lights out for all of them. He kept giving directions as James brought the helo to a hover about fifteen feet above the water's surface just off the boat's starboard side. "An easy right. Hold."

Justin was already in his harness and fins, so Sean started his safety check. "You ready?"

"Yeah, man. Let's get this guy." Justin sat with his legs dangling over the water.

"Safety check complete." Sean gave Justin a little push. "Swimmer is leaving the cabin."

"Roger."

Justin took the plunge, disappearing beneath the water.

"Swimmer is in the water."

Justin surfaced, gave Sean a thumb's up, then swam with strong strokes toward the boat.

"Swimmer is okay. He's heading toward the Marjorie T." Sean watched as Justin reached the boat's starboard railing and pulled himself onto the craft. "The swimmer is on deck."

With Wade's assistance, Sean got the litter ready and attached it to the hook and hoist line. Then he moved back to the open door, waiting for Justin's signal.

Below, Justin knelt beside the patient, checked for a pulse, then turned to speak to the woman, his words drowned out by the helo's rotors. He looked up, motioned for Sean to send down the litter.

"Swimmer has asked for the litter."

"Begin the hoist," James said.

Sean held onto the line so the litter wouldn't spin in the helo's rotor wash. The litter had almost reached Justin when the cabin door opened and another adult male staggered out, hand over his mouth as if he were coughing.

Justin's voice came over the radio. "Abort! Abort! We need to get everyone off the boat *now*. We'll pick them up in the water. They're cooking meth, and the patient was exposed."

Fuck.

"Abort the hoist! I'm putting some distance between us," James said as the helo moved upward and back. "Prepare to recover our swimmer and survivors from the water."

"Aborting the hoist. Get out of there, Koseki." Sean raised the litter, holding tight to the line as it moved slowly upward.

Below, Justin caught the unconscious man beneath the arms and dragged him toward the railing, shouting to the other two passengers to abandon ship.

Were they arguing with him?

Come on!

James spoke into the radio, updating Sector. "The swimmer says they're cooking meth onboard. We've aborted the hoist and put some distance between us and—"

A deafening blast. Searing heat. Flames.

Almost at once, the shockwave hit the helo, ripping the line from Sean's hand, and hurling him backward. The litter and hook were blown back into the tail rotor. The aircraft pitched, spinning, alarms screaming.

"Mayday! Mayday!" James' voice sounded in Sean's headphones as the helo spun out of control, heading for the water. "This is Coast Guard Rescue Six-Zero-Three-Eight! The Marjorie T just exploded. We're going down! I repeat, we are going down!"

"Justin!" Sean shouted into the chaos.

Then they hit the water with a bone-jarring crunch.

Fire and Rain

EDEN KOSEKI SLIPPED QUIETLY into Maverick's room to check on him, her heart swelling as she watched him sleep. He was completely relaxed the way only a baby could be, his downy hair dark against his pillow. It was hard to believe that this sleeping angel was the same little rascal who'd dumped his cup of milk onto the floor this afternoon—and then cried in protest when she'd cleaned it up.

She drew up the quilt her mother had made for him and then walked out of the room, leaving the door cracked behind her. She needed a hot soak and a good night's sleep.

She walked to the tub and turned on the tap, undressing and tossing her clothes into the bedroom. Then she hung a clean towel on the rack, put her phone where she could reach it in case one of her sisters called, and stepped into the tub, sinking into the hot water with a sigh.

She closed her eyes and let her thoughts drift, savoring the heat and the quiet.

She'd heard the helo lift off about thirty minutes ago and knew that Justin was out there somewhere, trying to save lives. When they'd first met, she'd sat by her VHF radio any time he went out on a case, listening, needing to know he was safe. But they'd been married for three years now, and she'd adjusted to the risks of his job—mostly.

She'd fallen in love with that brave man who'd jumped out of a hovering helicopter and swum through icy water just to ask for her name and number. Danger was part of the package that was Justin. If he could cope with it, so could she.

When she'd met Justin, she'd been working full-time as a pharmacy tech at Safeway. She'd enjoyed that job more than the jobs she'd had as a teen—acting as a tour guide, waiting tables, working at the fish processing plant. When she'd found out she was pregnant, she and Justin had talked about it and decided they had enough money saved up for her to leave work until their kids were in school. Given his long hours and unpredictable schedule, it had seemed the best thing for them as a family. It wasn't as if Eden had any great career ambitions.

She was an Alaskan through and through. What mattered to her was family and spending as much time as she could in nature, boating, fishing, hiking, watching wildlife. For her, a job was just a way to pay the bills, nothing more.

But Justin had always wanted to be in the military. He'd chosen the Coast Guard because he loved the water. Then he'd learned about Aviation Survival Technicians—rescue swimmers—and he'd known exactly what he'd wanted to do.

Her brave, crazy husband.

She found herself smiling as she remembered their conversation tonight and the sexy purr in his voice when she'd told him she wanted to try for another baby.

"Are you saying no more condoms?"

"No more condoms."

"Man, I wish I weren't on duty tonight."

Oh, so did she.

She had grown up as the middle child with four sisters—Natasha, Maria, Katie, and Anya—and she wanted Maverick to have at least one sister or a brother. She also wanted her parents to meet her children before they passed. They were in their sixties, and neither of them was in very good health. Though Justin had promised he would do all he could to stay here on Kodiak Island, she knew that was beyond his control.

Eden brought her hands to rest on her belly, the silver stretch marks from her pregnancy with Maverick barely visible. Would their next baby be a girl or a boy? A part of her hoped it would be a girl so they would have one of each. She would love to watch her newborn daughter wrap Justin around her tiny finger. But boy or girl, it didn't really matter to Eden.

In the distance, she heard the rotors of another helicopter

leaving the station. Was it for the same case, or had they gotten another call?

Justin would tell her all about it when he came home in the morning.

WRAPPED IN A BLANKET, Sean sat in the troop seat of another MH-60, James strapped in beside him as the helo that had rescued them made its way back to base. He was oblivious to the searing pain from his burns and the ache of his broken arm, his mind fixed on those few seconds just before the explosion.

Abort the hoist! Abort! We need to get everyone off the boat and pick them up in the water. They're cooking meth, and the patient was exposed.

Abort the hoist. I'm putting some distance between us. Prepare to recover our swimmer and survivors from the water.

Aborting the hoist. Get out of there, Koseki!

BOOM!

Mayday! Mayday! This is Coast Guard Rescue Six-Zero-Three-Eight! The Marjorie T exploded. We're going down!

If only Sean had shouted to Justin to jump *now*...

If only he'd held onto that hoist line...

After the helo had hit the water, Sean had unhooked himself and helped Wade escape the sinking aircraft. That's how he'd discovered that his right arm was broken and useless. The pain had been excruciating. Sean didn't remember all of it, but they'd both made it out and up to the surface again.

Sean had glanced around, his right arm limp. "Where are Spurrier and Abbott? Do you see Justin?"

Wade turned in the water. "No, I... There!"

James had surfaced fifteen feet to Sean's left.

"Abbott?" Sean had shouted.

Flames had reflected off Spurrier's flight helmet. "Gone."

Jesus.

Abbott was dead, and Justin...

Driven by desperation, out of his mind with pain and grief, Sean had fought to swim through swells and flaming wreckage, searching the surface for any sign of Justin—a flash of orange, his helmet, anything.

But James had caught him in a rescue hold and dragged him away from the flames, slapping a small strobe light to his helmet to make him visible from the air in case they were separated. "Don't fight me, man. It's too late! It's not safe."

Sean had never felt so helpless.

Now, a boat crew and a third helo were searching the water for remains. The Coast Guard would do an investigation and come up with procedures to avoid this in the future. But nothing would bring back Justin or David or the people whose lives they'd died trying to save—to say nothing of the multi-million-dollar aircraft that now lay at the bottom of the Gulf of Alaska.

"Petty Officer McKenna!"

Sean's head jerked up. Had he blacked out? "Sir?"

"I think he's in shock." But Wade wasn't speaking to Sean.

Trey Nash, the rescue swimmer on this flight, turned to Wade and James. "Apart from the blanket, he says he's fine and has refused treatment."

Sean wanted to insist that he was okay, but he couldn't keep his teeth from chattering.

James spoke clearly. "McKenna, you are to do whatever Trey and Wade tell you to do. That's an order. Do you understand?"

"Y-yes, sir."

Wade leaned closer. "I'm going to give you some morphine and get you in the litter so we can transfer you as soon as we land."

The jab of a needle.

After that, it was a blur of shivering, pain, and voices.

"... second-degree burns on the exposed part of his face ..."

"He's got a right humeral shaft fracture. I splinted it when he was unconscious."

"Between the meth and the burning ship, we can't rule out chemical exposure."

"We should be on deck in zero-five mikes."

Then he was on a gurney, rolling toward a waiting ambulance, the dark sky above him. Before he drifted into unconsciousness, one thought crystallized in his mind, the pain it caused worse than any injury.

How in God's name was he going to tell Eden that the man she loved was dead?

Chapter One

April 15

Sean McKenna gritted his teeth as Ryan, his physical therapist, ended today's appointment with deep-tissue torture on his right shoulder.

"I know it's painful, but one day you'll be grateful."

"If ... you ... say so."

He was right-handed, so it was going to be nice to have the use of his dominant hand again. But the fracture of his humerus had caused soft-tissue damage to his right shoulder that had required surgery, and his shoulder was sore and stiff. At least the bone was healed and he was rid of the brace and sling.

"Okay, that's enough for today." Ryan turned to a small refrigerator and drew out an ice pack. "You ice it while I print out those exercises for you to take home."

"Thanks." Sean took the ice pack, pressed it against his shoulder.

Three months had passed since the night of the incident. During that time, Sean had been on medical leave. His facial burns, though extremely painful, had been only partial thickness burns and so had left minimal scaring in the form of pale blotches that no longer grew a beard. But broken bones and injured muscles took longer to heal than blisters—or emotions.

Not a day passed when Sean didn't wish he'd handled things differently. If only he'd gotten that basket back into the cabin before the explosion. Or shouted earlier for Justin to abandon the rescue and jump. Then Justin and David might *both* be alive.

Those choices haunted his nightmares, making it hard to get a full night's sleep.

Investigators had identified the three people from the *Marjorie T*, a local family. All three had prior drug-related arrests. The last Sean had heard, an informant had told police that they owed a lot of money to some drug dealer. Police believed they'd been cooking meth to sell as a way to pay off that debt. Now, investigators were after the dealer.

Ryan returned with a handful of printouts, each describing a new exercise. "We went through all of these today. Keep doing what you're doing, and you'll be back on active-duty status soon."

"Thanks." Sean stepped off the exam table and took the printouts. "Same day and time next week?"

Ryan nodded. "See you then."

Sean put on his shirt and jacket and left the clinic. The sky was overcast, a cold breeze blowing from the east, carrying the scent of rain. He walked to his gray Subaru Forester, climbed inside, and drove toward Justin and Eden's place on Aviation Hill, a government housing area for Coastie families just off the base.

Coast Guard investigators had released their report on the incident this morning, and he wanted to make sure she had a copy. Investigators had determined that the flight crew was not at fault and that all procedures had been followed. They had also concluded that the Coast Guard needed protocols to keep crews safe from potential floating meth labs in the future.

Are you doing this for Eden's sake or for yourself?

On the night Maverick had been born, Sean had promised Justin that he'd watch over Eden and Maverick as if they were his own family should anything happen to Justin. He'd was doing his best to keep that promise, and delivering this report was part of that.

The report hadn't assuaged Sean's sense of guilt. Close to a minute had passed between Justin's realization that they were cooking meth and the explosion that had killed him. A minute was more than enough time for Sean to yell into his radio for Justin to jump and for Justin to hit the water. If he'd been below the surface when the ship had blown...

Sean also had a box of belongings from Justin's locker and from the duty room he'd stayed in that night that he needed to return to her. James had put it all in his back seat, but Sean kept forgetting about it. He hoped the contents of the box and the memories they stirred wouldn't make Eden's day harder. But how could they not?

Sean made a left off Rezanof Drive onto Aviation Hill Loop Road and turned onto Beach Circle, parking in the driveway of the tidy duplex where he'd spent so many weekends and evenings. He drew a deep breath and picked up the printout of the investigation report, reminding himself that he was here to help Eden and not to unburden himself. Then he climbed out of his vehicle, walked up the steps to the front door, and knocked.

When Eden answered the door, Sean could tell she'd been crying, her eyes puffy and red. She wore an old KHS Bears T-shirt over faded jeans, her long, dark hair hanging free. Sean had always found her beautiful, her mixed heritage giving her matchless features—high cheekbones, full lips, big eyes of hazel-green. He'd always told Justin that he'd married the most beautiful woman on the island.

She motioned for him to enter, speaking softly. "Maverick is asleep."

Sean stepped inside, closing the door behind him.

Eden smiled. "You're not wearing the brace. How does your shoulder feel?"

"Stiff. Sore. It's nice to have my right hand back."

"I bet. You're almost healed. The scars on your jaw are almost gone, too."

"Almost." He followed her toward the kitchen table, where official papers were spread everywhere. "You've been busy."

"The Casualty Assistance Calls Officer was here this morning going over the last of the paperwork with me." She ran a hand through her hair, leaving it tousled. "I've been trying to figure out my finances, make the right decisions. Social Security is taking forever. It's so much to deal with all at once. It's just ... hard."

The quaver in her voice as she said that last word hit Sean in the chest. "Can I help? I'm pretty good with Coast Guard lingo and budgets and the like."

Like Justin, Sean had filled out all the necessary forms so the Coast Guard would know what to do with his remains and his military benefits in case he was killed in the line of duty.

Eden gave him a sad half-smile. "You didn't come here to help me fill out paperwork."

"I brought the report from the crash investigation." He set the document on the table. "I thought you might want a copy. I can summarize it if you don't want to read it."

Eden's brow furrowed, her arms crossed over her chest. "Thanks. I'd like that."

"The report states that the flight crew wasn't to blame for the crash or Justin's and David's deaths. The report also states that the Coast Guard needs to come up with protocols for dealing with potential meth labs on watercraft."

Eden nodded, her expression unchanged. "What's their plan for that—teaching flight crews how to read minds? Meth radar?"

"I have no idea."

She met his gaze, some of the tension on her face easing. "Does this mean you'll stop blaming yourself now?"

Her question took him by surprise. He had apologized to her for Justin's death, but he had never shared his gnawing sense of guilt or dumped his pain in her lap. She had enough on her shoulders without dealing with his emotions, too. But apparently, she'd seen through him.

Confronted with her frank question, he was honest. "It was my job to get him safely back on board the helo so he could come home to you. I ... failed. If I could trade places with him, Eden, I would. In a heartbeat."

Her lips curved in another sad smile, tears glittering in her eyes. "There was nothing you could have done. I'm glad you, Wade, and James survived."

Her kind words seemed to cut his soul, leaving his own grief and guilt raw.

Before he could think of what to say, she wiped her tears away. "I'd appreciate your help if you have time. It's all so overwhelming."

He swallowed. "I'd be glad to."

She walked to the stove. "I'll make coffee."

EDEN CHANGED MAVERICK. "Uncle Sean is here. Do you want to go say hello?"

Maverick looked up at her through his father's brown eyes. "Sawn."

"Yes, Uncle Sean is here." She lifted him off the changing table, set him on the floor, and handed him his favorite blankie. "He's helping me with some work. Are you hungry?"

His little hand around her finger, she walked with Maverick to the dining room.

Sean looked up, smiled. "Hey, there, buddy. Did you get a good nap?"

Maverick gave Sean a shy smile, half hiding behind Eden's leg.

"I'll just get him a snack." Eden settled Maverick in his highchair and went to get some graham crackers and a sippy cup of milk. "He says your name now, you know."

"Is that true? Can you say my name? Who am I?"

When Maverick simply stared at Sean without speaking, Eden laughed. "He's making me look like a liar."

"That's okay. He's just waking up. I know the feeling, little dude."

Eden set the graham crackers and milk on Maverick's tray and pointed to Sean. "Who's that? Can you tell me who that is?"

But Maverick had popped the cup into his mouth.

Sean pushed a notepad across the table toward her. "I think I've put it together here if you want to go over it."

"Thanks." Eden sat in the chair closest to Maverick, tucked her hair behind her ears, and looked down at the notepad.

Sean pointed with the pencil. "The five-hundred thousand from the life insurance and death gratuity—you wanted to put that into savings, right?"

"I *hate* that term—death gratuity." Something in Eden snapped. "What does that mean, anyway? A gratuity is what you give a server who brings your meal quickly and gets your drink order right. A *death* tip? Come on! Where's the dignity in that?"

Surprised by the force of her own rage, she stopped, drew a breath, and found Sean watching her through sympathetic blue eyes.

"I'm sorry. That wasn't directed at you." Rage spent, she was now on the brink of tears. "I... I would rather have Justin back than any amount of money in the world."

"Hey, don't apologize." Sean rested a big hand on hers for a moment, his touch warm and comforting. "You're right. It's a stupid term. The military specializes in those—and acronyms."

She reached for a tissue, dabbed her eyes, smiling despite herself. "Justin called it military alphabet soup."

Sean nodded, a sad smile on his face, and Eden knew he'd heard Justin say that, too. "He was a fun and funny guy—the best."

Eden had always enjoyed watching Justin with Sean together. They were both tall, strong, and good-looking, but that's where the similarities ended. Justin had had brown eyes and dark hair that he'd kept short, while Sean had blue eyes and dark blond hair. They looked nothing alike, and yet they'd been kin since the day they'd met.

"You were like a brother to him."

Sean's gaze dropped to the table. "He *is* a brother to me. He's just ... *gone*."

For a moment, Eden simply stared at Sean, his words describing her feelings in a way that no one else seemed to understand. "Yes. He's still my husband. He's just *gone*."

She knew her friends and relatives meant well, but their attempts to comfort her had as often as not left her wanting to scream.

Your tears will dry, and you'll meet someone new and fall in love again.

Everything happens for a reason.

I guess God needed a very brave angel for some special purpose.

She didn't realize she was crying again until Sean spoke.

"I can come back later if this is too much and you'd like to be alone."

She reached for another tissue, shaking her head. He was always so considerate, and he'd done so much for her already. "No. Sorry. I just... I just miss him."

"So do I."

Of course, Sean missed him, too. Sean had known Justin longer than Eden had, and the two had been inseparable. Sean had eaten dinner at their place as often as not. He'd gone camping, skiing, hunting, and fishing with them. She'd seen tears on his cheeks at Justin's memorial service.

She cleared her throat, got up to toss the two tissues in the trash, doing her best to put the broken, hurting pieces of herself together. "More coffee?"

"No, thanks. I'm fine."

She sat once again and focused on his neat handwriting. "Let's try this again."

"It's smart to set that five-hundred thousand aside for emergencies or a house or Maverick's future. You'll be getting monthly DIC, plus Social Security, plus his SBP money. Together, that's a little more than thirty-five hundred a month pre-tax. You have to pay taxes on the Social Security and the SBP, but not the DIC. I'm not a tax person, but my guess is that you'll have a net of about twenty-six hundred each month. It's not a lot, but you get to remain in base housing for now, right?"

Government housing was free, and she was allowed to remain here for a year from the date of Justin's death. But did she want to stay?

"I can stay for now, but I'm not sure I want to."

Fire and Rain

His brow furrowed, and he cocked his head as if curious to hear her reasons.

She tried to explain. "Everywhere I look, I see Justin. His shaving stuff. His uniforms. His kayak. His clothes. His fishing gear. I still have his toothbrush. Sometimes having him all around me is comforting. Sometimes it's torture. Being so close to base, I can hear rescue helicopters take off, and it makes me think of that night, of hearing him fly away, not knowing he would never come back."

"I'm so sorry, Eden. That must be hell."

She nodded, her grief so heavy it threatened to sink her.

"I understand if you'd rather move."

"I don't know what I want. When I think about finding a place in town, I get completely overwhelmed. Moving with a toddler. Going back to work. Leaving our home and so many memories behind. I was happy here." She reached for another tissue. "I know I'm contradicting myself. I probably sound crazy. Whether I stay here or move, it all feels impossible."

Sean leaned closer, met her gaze. "You don't sound crazy at all. You don't have to do anything you're not ready to do. Whatever you decide, you *won't* face it alone."

She sniffed, nodded. "Thank you. You've been so good to us."

His eyes filled with shadows, but he smiled. "Hey, you're family, right?"

SEAN CHOPPED the tomato and tossed it into the salad while Eden washed Maverick's hands, a job that seemed to require loud protests from Maverick. She'd asked Sean to stay for supper and then confessed she would have to order pizza—again. Something in the way she'd said it told him she was sick of fast food. So, he'd run to the store and come back with a roast chicken, mashed potatoes, and salad fixings.

It wasn't five-star gourmet, but it was better for them than pizza.

Maverick was the first to reappear, the indignity of having his hands washed forgotten as he ran on tiny bare feet through the house like a knee-high escaped convict.

Eden followed, carrying a small towel, a look of mixed annoyance and humor on her face. "Let me dry your hands, Mavie, and then we'll have supper with Uncle Sean."

Sean set the salad on the table with the rest of the meal, laughing to himself as Eden caught the little rascal around the waist and did her best to dry his hands. "You're good at this toddler wrangling business."

"Practice." Eden scooped up her son and carried him to his highchair. "I'm not sure why he hates to have his face and hands washed. You'd think it was torture."

Then she saw the table. "You set the table, too."

"Don't look impressed. I've eaten here often enough to know where things are."

"True." She sat next to Maverick, while Sean sat across from her where he'd usually sat, leaving Justin's chair empty. "Thanks so much for everything today."

"You're welcome."

They talked about small things while they ate. The recent eruption of the Shevaluch volcano in Russia that had grounded aircraft in the Aleutians for a day. The beginning of tourist season and the stream of yellow school buses that ferried them around town. The latest bear sighting on base.

Sean looked at Maverick and had to laugh. "Hey, little man, are you going to eat the mashed potatoes or just wear them? You know when you get messy like that, your mommy has to wash your face again."

Maverick laughed as if Sean had just said something hilarious.

Eden shook her head, a smile on her pretty face. "I used to worry that he was going to starve to death unless I put the food into his mouth. But he keeps growing and gaining weight, so some of it must be getting into his tummy."

Parenting was outside Sean's wheelhouse, but that made sense to him. "If he keeps going through the diapers, he ought to be okay, right?"

Eden laughed. "And he does. I've been reading about potty-training. I had hoped to have him out of diapers before the next baby..."

The smile fled her face. There would be no next baby—not with Justin as the father.

"There are no words, Eden. I'm so sorry." That reminded Sean. "I just remembered. I need to get that box of Justin's things from my car. I keep forgetting to bring them in."

Those hazel-green eyes went wide for a moment. "Oh. Right."

Sean wished he knew how to make this easier for her, but he didn't. "You deal with Mr. Potato Face, while I do the dishes. Then I'll get the box."

"Okay." She seemed to swallow her grief as she stood and got Maverick out of his highchair. "Let's get you in the tub and then into your pajamas."

"My bwankie."

"No, you can't have your blankie in the tub. It will get wet. But you've got your whale and your duckie, right?"

"Duckie!" Maverick darted toward the bathroom.

Sean could only imagine what it had been like for Justin to watch these little domestic moments unfold on his nights at home. He had loved Eden so much and been so proud to be her husband and Maverick's father. But he would never see the ending of the story he'd begun with Eden, and she and Maverick had no choice but to go on without him.

Shifting his thoughts, he made short work of the dishes and then went to wipe down the table. But when he came to the highchair, he wasn't about to spend an hour cleaning mashed potatoes out of every crack and crevice. God, kids were messy!

He grabbed the highchair, carried it outside, and set it down on the driveway. Then he hooked up the garden hose, turned it on, and sprayed off the highchair. He left it to sit on the porch while he went inside to grab a towel.

He had almost finished drying it when Eden stepped outside, Maverick in her arms, drinking from a bottle and wearing fuzzy yellow pajamas with feet.

She gaped at him, clearly amused. "Did you spray that down with the hose?"

Was that so strange? "Hey, it worked."

Just then, an H-60 Coast Guard helicopter passed overhead. They both looked up and watched it fly by in silence.

Sean carried the highchair back inside. "I'll get that box."

They spent the next hour going through the things from Justin's locker. Eden pulled out a slightly bent photo from the night Maverick had been born. In the image, she smiled at the camera, newborn Maverick in a blanket on her bare chest, Justin bending low so that his face was next to hers. "He was so happy that night."

"It's the happiest I've ever seen him." Sean had been in the waiting room, pacing the floor. "He kept that taped to the inside of his locker. He said it reminded him of his reason for being a rescue swimmer. He wanted to save lives so families could stay together."

The tragic irony hung in the air between them, Eden's eyes filling with tears.

Then Sean had to tell her. "You're the last thing he talked

Fire and Rain

about before we got on the helicopter. He said you wanted another baby, and there was a big smile on his face. He loved you, Eden, you and Maverick. You two were his entire world."

Eden smiled through her tears. "Thanks for telling me that. And thanks for bringing me his things—and for helping with the money stuff and dinner."

"You got it." But Sean thought he might choke on her gratitude.

If he'd done a better job, her husband would be here tonight instead of him.

Chapter Two

April 25

SEAN LOWERED THE LITTER, holding fast to the hoist line so the helo's rotor wash wouldn't send it into a spin. Then he saw it—smoke. It wafted out of the small boat's cabin, and there was a strange odor to it. He wasn't sure how he knew the smell was meth, but he did.

He warned the others. "The cabin is in flames. They're cooking meth, and it's going to blow. Aborting the hoist."

But Justin hadn't noticed. He continued to administer first aid to the unconscious patient then turned to talk to the passengers. Was his radio malfunctioning?

Sean shouted into his mic. "Justin, abandon the rescue! The boat is on fire. It's going to blow. We'll retrieve you from the water."

The helo's rotor fanned the flames, black smoke rising high into the air now.

"I'm putting some distance between us and that blaze." James veered off, adding another twenty feet to the helo's altitude.

Below, Justin was still talking to the passengers.

"*Abandon ship!*" *Sean shouted again.* "*Jump! Get out of there!*"

Justin glanced upward, the TrakkaBeam bathing him in light and reflecting off his helmet. Somehow, Sean could see his features clearly despite the distance and the glare.

Then the ship exploded just as Sean had feared it would, surprise on Justin's face as flames consumed him.

"Justin!" Sean sat upright, covered in cold sweat, unsure whether he'd shouted the name or whether that had been part of his dream.

Fuck.

He threw back the covers, got up from his bunk, and walked to his bathroom, where he splashed cold water on his face, the sound of the blast still ringing in his ears.

Damn it.

He reached for a hand towel and met his gaze in the mirror, hating the haunted look he saw in his eyes. The dream hadn't been accurate. That's not how it had gone down that night.

In reality, the boat hadn't been on fire, and he'd only shouted at Justin to get off the boat once. Justin had been dragging the patient toward the railing and talking with the other passengers before the explosion. Sean had never made eye contact with him, not even for a moment, a thought that filled him with desolation.

No chance to say goodbye.

Back on his bedside table, his alarm sounded.

Good fucking morning.

He walked back to his bed, turned off the alarm, then hit the shower, wishing the hot water could wash the lingering emotions of the dream down the drain. It was bad enough dealing with those memories during his waking hours. Now, he was getting twisted versions of that night in his nightmares.

That was the third time he'd dreamed about the explosion this week. And no matter how the scene played out, Justin died.

Post-traumatic stress.

The Coast Guard required its members to get counseling after incidents involving injuries or fatalities. He, James, Wade, and even Lt. Yamada had been required to go through a few evaluation sessions and be cleared before they returned to active duty. If they knew he was having nightmares now...

He dried off and put on his ODUs—operational dress uniform—and walked over to the galley for breakfast. A thick fog lay over land and water, the scent of rain mingled with the reek of rotting seaweed.

Life in Kodiak.

Inside the galley, he saw Wade sitting with Trey. James Spurrier ate breakfast with a few other pilots, all lieutenants or lieutenants junior grade. Lt. Yamada sat alone, reading a newspaper. Some of the newer enlisted guys from the shop crew were seated together—Chris, Samantha, Matt, Amanda, Rock, and Kai.

No one had noticed him yet, so Sean filled up a plate with scrambled eggs, hashbrowns, sausage, and sliced fruit and carried it with a cup of hot coffee toward an empty table, preferring to eat alone. But before he could sit, Trey and Wade motioned to him to join them.

Shit.

He didn't feel like talking with anyone, but he couldn't ignore them. He walked to their table and took a seat. "Hey."

"Must be nice to have the use of your hand again." Wade passed him the salt and pepper.

"Thanks. It is."

"I saw you've got your fitness eval later today." Trey stirred sugar into his coffee. "Do you think you're up for it?"

"I doubt I'll be able to finish the upper-body portion." Fifty pushups followed by chin-ups and pull-ups was going to be hard for his shoulder. "I'm pretty sure this is just to see how far I still have to go."

"If anyone can do it, you can. You've come a long way already. When we lifted you out of the water, I thought you might be looking at a medical discharge, but..." Trey's words trailed off, as if he realized this might not be Sean's idea of great breakfast conversation.

"The Medical Evaluation Board is sure I'll be back on active duty soon." Sean took a drink of coffee, then started on his breakfast.

Wade changed the subject. "What's Crab Fest about? Is it a good time?"

He'd arrived in Kodiak last summer.

Trey answered. "You're going to love it, man. The whole town turns out—not to mention tourists. It's like a county fair meets a celebration of everything that is awesome about Kodiak. It's a great place to meet women."

"Are you going?" Wade asked Sean.

"I went once. I've been on duty most years and couldn't." Sean didn't want to hang out with crowds right now. He felt like an outsider these days, as if some part of him was no longer in sync with everyone else.

Apparently, realizing he didn't feel much like talking, Trey and Wade moved on and began planning a day of mountain biking for their next shared day off, talking about the best trails and looking at maps on Trey's phone.

Sean finished his breakfast. "See you guys later."

He carried his tray with its dishes to the bins, then left the galley and made his way toward the rec center. He wanted to stretch and do some PT before the fitness test. It wouldn't change the outcome, but it might keep him from reinjuring his arm.

Eden dragged through the morning, doing her best to be cheerful around Maverick. He deserved a mother who was focused on his needs rather than lost in her grief. She didn't want him to see her in tears all the time. But today was *hard*.

Last night, she'd dreamed about Justin. He'd been here, alive and happy, with her and Maverick. They'd sat in the kitchen talking and laughing the way they had so many other days. So many precious days. And for the brief time of that dream, the shadows around Eden's heart had lifted. She'd been indescribably happy to be with him, so relieved to see him alive again—only to be slammed by loss the moment the dream had ended and she'd opened her eyes.

It had felt like losing Justin again.

She had struggled to get through breakfast without crying. She'd called her mother and asked her to please come and help with Maverick for a few hours. Eden needed a shower. Maybe the three of them could go for a short hike on Old Woman Trail to forage—anything to dull the ache in her chest.

She settled Maverick on the floor with his little Lego Duplo blocks. "Want to build a dump truck?"

"Copta."

Justin had gotten this Lego set for Maverick because the pieces could be used to make a helicopter. Naturally, that's what Maverick wanted to build first.

"Show me how to make the helicopter." Eden willed herself to focus only on her son.

Maverick took the block she offered and put it together with the one he held in his left hand. "Got it."

She smiled. "Yep. You got it."

He knew what he was doing, and slowly the helicopter came together. But what fun was a helicopter unless you made it fly? When it was done, Maverick stood and held it up, blowing raspberries to make the whir of the rotors.

"Look at it go." Eden had been twenty when her father was killed in a car crash, and she couldn't imagine growing up without him. She'd give anything to know how much Maverick understood. Had he noticed that his father no longer came home, no longer ate meals with them, no longer read to him, played with him, or gave him baths?

Stop. Don't do this to yourself.

Eden heard a car engine and saw her mother turn into the driveway. She got to her feet and groaned to see that her cousin Mila Crane had come, too. She'd asked her mother *not* to bring Mila again, not after the way she had behaved last time she was here. She'd had the audacity to tell Eden that she was *wallowing* in grief rather than trying to heal.

Eden couldn't handle Mila—not today.

She got to her feet. "Baba is here, Mavie."

But Maverick's attention was riveted on the little helicopter.

Eden opened her front door. While Mila finished a phone call next to the car, Eden's mother hurried up the steps and walked inside.

"Why did you bring her?" Eden whispered. "I can't deal with her today."

"I told your Aunt Evelyn that I was coming, and I guess she told Mila. What was I supposed to do? Tell her you don't want her here?"

"Yes!" Eden loved her mother, but she didn't have much of a backbone when it came to her sisters. "Mom, I can't do this. Damn it."

Mila ended her call and walked up the stairs in three-inch heels, a big smile on her bright red lips. "Hey, Eden."

Eden held the door for her, not bothering to return the smile. "Mila."

Mila held up a shopping bag. "I bought some new clothes for your little man."

Born three years apart, Mila and Eden had played together as kids and had gotten along—provided Eden did everything Mila's way. Things hadn't changed much since then. Mila was now a mother of two school-aged kids. Her husband, Charlie, worked on an off-shore oil rig in Prudhoe Bay, earning enough money that she was free to spend her days volunteering in the community—and meddling in other people's lives.

Eden shut the door.

"Is that your helicopter?" Her mother sat on the floor next to Maverick.

"Daddy fwy copta."

That's what Eden used to tell Maverick any time they played with these blocks. She closed her eyes, fighting a rush of grief. "I haven't had a shower today. Can you watch Maverick?"

"Of course!"

Eden walked to the bathroom, locked the door behind her, and turned on the water. Then she undressed, stepped into the spray, and let the tears come.

I can't do this without you, Justin. It hurts too much. When will it get easier?

She leaned against the wall and wept until the hot water ran out. Only then did she realize that she hadn't washed. She quickly shampooed and conditioned her hair and washed her face and body, the cold somehow calling her back to herself. Then she turned off the water and dried herself with a warm towel.

A quick glance in the mirror told her she wouldn't fool anyone. Her mother and Mila would see her red eyes and know she'd been crying. Her mother would understand, but Mila...

Who cares what she thinks?

Towel wrapped around her naked body, Eden walked out of the bathroom and hurried across the hall to her bedroom, where she found the light on and Mila taking Justin's clothes out of the bedroom closet.

For a moment, Eden stood there, mouth open, stunned.

Mila saw her and smiled. "I thought I could help you sort through this. I can take it all to St. Mary's—unless you can think of a better place. I'm not sure what to do with his uniforms. Does the Coast Guard have a place to recycle them?"

Eden's face burned with rage, her pulse thrumming. "Put it back—all of it. Now! You have no right to touch his things or go through our closet."

Mila looked surprised. "I'm just trying to help. You'll need to do this eventually. It's been three months, so—"

"If I wanted your help, I'd ask for it. The man I love is dead!" Tears rushed into Eden's eyes. "You don't get to tell me how to handle my grief. Put his things back. Now!"

"Okay. Fine." Mila began to hang Justin's clothes back in the closet. "You can't keep this stuff forever."

"It's not your business what I do with his things. Quit trying to run other people's lives." Eden dressed in the bathroom then found her mother sitting wide-eyed on the sofa, the new clothes Mila had bought Maverick folded neatly beside her.

Her mother looked up at her through pleading eyes, her voice a whisper. "She means well. She bought Maverick some really cute clothes."

"I didn't ask her to do that," Eden whispered back. "What right does she have to go through Justin's things? Next time she tries to tag along, just say *no*. I mean it. I don't want her in my house."

"I'm really sorry, Eden. I know this is hard. I went through the same thing when your father died. Do you want us to go? We came to cheer you up."

"I need support, not cheering up. The man I love is *dead*.

My life will never be the same. If you want to help, ask what I need. Don't let her barge in and take over."

Why was that so hard to understand?

Mila walked into the living room. "Aunt Lydia, I think we should go. I'm not sure Eden is really in the mood for company today."

In the mood for company?

Eden fought to keep her teeth together.

Eden's mother got to her feet, bent down, and kissed Maverick. "Baba's going now, sweet boy. I'll see you again soon."

A few moments later, Eden watched them drive away, feeling both angry and guilty, the day darker than it had been before they'd come.

SEAN SAT shirtless on a bench in the men's locker room, cold pack on his aching shoulder and bicep. He'd made it through the fitness assessment and had surpassed the minimum requirements—but not without pain.

The locker room door opened, and Captain Walcott entered, clipboard in his hand.

Sean stood.

"As you were." Captain Walcott glanced at the clipboard. "I was just reading through the results of your assessment. You did well—better than I expected."

"Thank you, sir."

"You're having some pain now?"

"Yes, sir."

The captain nodded. "When you're done here, stop by my office."

"Yes, sir."

Captain Walcott turned and left.

Fire and Rain

Ten minutes later, Sean knocked on his office door. "Reporting as asked, sir."

"Yes. Please, take a seat." Captain Walcott glanced down at his clipboard. "I've spoken with the Critical Incident Stress Management Team and medical. They say you've put forth substantial effort and are healing well. What are your thoughts about returning to duty?"

Sean had anticipated this question, and he thought he knew the answer Walcott wanted. But he couldn't lie. "I know what it takes to control the hoist line and to pull a two-hundred-pound man on a litter inside the cabin. I don't believe my arm is sufficiently strong again to do that job without risk to me or to the people we rescue. Not yet."

For some reason, Captain Walcott looked pleased. "I appreciate the honesty of your answer, and, after talking with your team, I agree. We don't want you to reinjure yourself, and we don't want your arm to fail during a critical moment in an evolution."

"No, sir." Sean didn't want that, either.

He didn't want any more deaths on his hands.

"As you know, I recommended you for advancement before the incident. Your scores from Leadership and Management School were outstanding. You've nailed your RPQs and your EPME. You'll sit for the exam next week, and I expect you to do well."

Sean had to fight to keep the smile off his face, remembering his conversation with Eden about military alphabet soup. RPQs were Rating Performance Qualifications, while EPMEs referred to Enlisted Professional Military Education. Then he remembered that he and Justin had planned to take the exam together, and any urge to laugh vanished. "Yes, sir."

"In the meantime, I'm putting you back on active duty, but not on a flight crew. Leavitt is about to take a month of leave—three weeks of paternity leave and a week's vacation. I'd like you to take his post while he's out. We'll see how well the shoe fits."

Dalton Leavitt was one rank above Sean, an E6—petty officer first class. He went out with flight crews when needed, but he played more of a training and managerial role in the shop, helping new AETs master their qualifications.

Captain Walcott went on. "Some of the newer guys are pretty green, and none of them has your electrical engineering degree. You know the electronics on the helos as well, if not better, than anyone here. This will give you a chance to strengthen your leadership skills while we wait for the outcome of your exam. It will also give that arm a little more time to heal. You'll start tomorrow. Report to Leavitt at zero six hundred hours."

"Yes, sir." Sean stood.

"These past three months have been hard for all of us here at Air Station Kodiak, but they've been especially hard for you, and, of course, Koseki's widow and child. You've handled it as well as anyone could."

"Thank you, sir." The captain's words made him feel like a fraud.

The *incident* was the first thing on his mind every day and the last thing on his mind as he fell asleep at night.

"You should know that our investigators and drug interdiction team are still working with local, state, and federal law enforcement to arrest anyone associated with the Marjorie T and meth smuggling here on the island. They won't give up."

"I'm glad to hear it." Sean wanted anyone associated with any potential meth ring to be arrested, though nothing would bring Justin or David back.

"One last thing." Captain Walcott looked up at him, brow furrowed with curiosity. "I've always wondered why you chose to enlist. With that degree and your aptitude, you could have gone to OCS and started your career as an officer. You could still go to OCS if you wanted."

Sean had no interest in Officer Candidate School. "I wanted to be part of a flight crew, sir. It seemed to me that an officer's commission would take me out of the sky and land me in an office. I'm doing my dream job—or I was until the incident."

"True enough. Very well. We'll see you early tomorrow."

"Yes, sir." Sean left the captain's office and walked back to the locker room to get his gear, overwhelmed by a need to get away.

He carried his gear back to his room, put on a pair of hiking boots, and got his daypack together—water, rain gear, bear spray, energy bars. Then he headed out, climbed into his vehicle, and drove the short distance to the trailhead behind the Loran Building. He shouldered his pack and started up the trail to Old Woman Mountain.

Sean had already gotten his workout for the day, so he set out at an easy pace, willing himself to let everything go. The crash. His sense of guilt. The dream. As he moved uphill, mud squishing beneath his boots, fresh air filling his lungs, some of the tension left him.

Overhead, a pair of eagles soared against a blue backdrop. Though the fog from this morning had mostly lifted, the light had a misty quality about it, a breeze blowing from the east, the air carrying the scent of spruce, salt spray, and moist earth. Around him, everything was green, and some plants were in flower.

Not that Sean knew much about the flora. He could tell a Sitka spruce from an alder and a birch, and he could identify fireweed by its bright purple flowers, but that was about it. A Boy Scout he was not.

He came to a bend in the trail and spotted a dark-haired woman walking through a meadow off to his left, a basket on her arm. It took a moment before he realized it was Eden and that she had Maverick with her. She knelt, picked something from the ground, and showed it to her son, who took it from her and sniffed it.

Sean hesitated, unsure whether he'd ruin the moment for Eden if he said hello. Then again, he couldn't very well head up the trail without saying something.

"Out for an adventure?" He kept walking slowly.

If she wanted to talk, she'd let him know. If she just waved at him, he'd continue on his way without bothering her.

Eden turned, waved—and walked toward him, Maverick beside her.

Chapter Three

Eden found herself smiling as Sean left the trail and walked through the meadow toward them. "Out for a hike?"

"I thought I'd get some fresh air."

After what had happened this morning with Mila, Eden had needed the same thing. "It's a good day for that."

His gaze shifted to her basket. "Are you out for a picnic?"

Eden tousled Mavie's hair. "We're foraging."

"Foraging." Sean repeated the word as if he'd never heard it.

She held up her basket. "We're harvesting wild foods for supper—whatever we can find. The mountains are better than Safeway. There are all kinds of good things here for food and medicine—nettles, fireweed, fiddlehead ferns, claytonia, salmonberry shoots."

Sean knelt, looked at the shoot in Maverick's hand. "What have you got there?"

"Sambewwy." Maverick held it up.

Sean took it, sniffed. "What do you do with it?"

Eden laughed at his expression. "I usually pickle them or use them in stir-fries."

Eden showed him the patch of salmonberries she'd found and harvested a few more shoots, which she let Maverick place in a paper bag. "I don't pick many shoots in any one area because that means fewer berries. I come back for leaves in a few weeks and for berries later in the summer. I make the berries into jam. You've eaten it."

"I have?" He chuckled. "Can I help?"

She was hoping he'd ask. "I'd like that."

They moved across the meadow. Eden showed both Maverick and Sean how to find and identify the edible plants, sharing the knowledge she'd been given, tucking the harvested leaves and shoots into different paper lunch sacks for easier sorting later.

"Always use gloves to harvest nettles."

"You can tell wild onion because its leaves are flat and because it smells like onion. If it doesn't smell like onion, it's not wild onion but death camas."

"Once you know which plants grow in which environments, you know what to look for in a sunny meadow or the edge of a stream or the forest."

They moved toward the edge of a damp, forested area where Eden found claytonia, watermelon berry sprouts, docks, and one of her favorites—fiddlehead fern.

Maverick stuck a fiddlehead in his mouth, grimaced at the texture of the chaff.

Sean nodded. "My thoughts exactly, little dude. You can eat this?"

Eden couldn't help but laugh as she took the fiddlehead from Mavie. "You remove the chaff first. I put them in the dryer inside a sleeping bag sack and run it on the fluff cycle until the chaff is gone. Have supper with us tonight. I'll make nettle pesto."

She hadn't planned to say that. The words had just popped out.

One eyebrow arched. "Nettle *pesto*? Okay. You're on."

Sean carried Maverick on his shoulders as they made their way back down the trail to the parking lot. Then he climbed into her vehicle, Maverick falling asleep on the short drive home. While Eden carried Maverick inside and put him in his crib to finish his nap, Sean carried her basket. She found him standing in the kitchen, peeking into each of the bags.

"Where did you learn all of this? Is it one of those Kodiak things?"

"More of an Alaska thing." Eden put on gloves, scooped the nettles, and dropped them into a colander to rinse them. "My Alutiiq grandmother taught me, but my ancestors survived this way. My mother and I used to forage a few times a week when I was a little girl. Nature provides—if you know what you're doing."

He glanced around the kitchen. "Can I help?"

"Want to get some salmon out of the fridge to grill?"

While he fired up the grill, Eden steamed the nettle leaves and then put them into cold water. Then she ran them through a food processor with walnuts, garlic, and lemon juice, adding olive oil until she had the consistency she wanted. When that was done, she handed a small bowl of the pesto to Sean along with a basting brush. "To coat the salmon."

He sniffed, eyebrows shooting up. "You got it."

In thirty minutes, she had pasta with nettle pesto and a salad of wild onion, claytonia, docks, and watermelon berry shoots sitting on the table with a lemon dressing. It had been so long since she'd cooked a real meal, and something about it made her feel more like herself.

Clinging to that feeling, she got out a bottle of chilled chardonnay and two glasses and set them on the table, too. Maverick was awake now, talking to himself in his crib, so she changed him and got him into his highchair while Sean finished with the salmon. Soon, the three of them sat around the table.

"Here we are again, hey, Maverick?" Sean smiled. "But this looks much tastier than a Safeway chicken."

"I hope you like it. Everything but the pasta, olive oil, and lemon was harvested here."

He seemed impressed. "The salmon, too?"

Eden spread her napkin on her lap. "Justin caught that last time you two…"

It was like being ambushed. One moment, she'd felt almost normal, and the next…

Shadows flitted through Sean's eyes. "Our last fishing trip for winter kings."

Eden swallowed the lump in her throat, poured the wine. "Yes."

Sean raised his glass. "To Kodiak."

"To Kodiak."

SEAN SET his glass aside and served Eden salmon. He'd seen the color drain from her face when their conversation had naturally brought them around to Justin. He'd felt it too—that pang in the heart. "Will Maverick want some?"

"I'll give him some of mine." Eden took a few small pieces of salmon from her own plate, along with pasta and a little salad. "He's not crazy about the greens, but he loves salmon and pasta."

As if to prove his mother's point, Maverick picked up a piece of fish and mashed it into his mouth with a flat palm.

Sean couldn't help but chuckle. "That was efficient. You really do love salmon, don't you, buddy?"

"Oh, he does—even roe."

Fire and Rain

"Smart boy." Sean speared some of the salad. "Here goes. Kodiak weed salad."

There was an explosion of crisp flavors on his tongue, a tang of succulent leaves, lemon, and something that tasted like cucumber but wasn't.

Eden laughed softly. "You look surprised."

He chewed, swallowed. "That's really good."

"I'm glad you like it. Try the pesto."

He took a bite of the pasta next, the earthy taste of nettles blending with the walnuts, olive oil, and pasta. "Delicious."

The pesto tasted even better on the grilled king salmon. And for a moment, Sean ate with gusto, completely forgetting his manners. He glanced up to find Eden watching him, the hint of a smile on her lips. "Sorry."

"Don't apologize. I'm glad you like it."

He dabbed his lips on his napkin. "What else do you harvest from the hills?"

"All kinds of berries—salmonberries, cranberries, lingonberries, thimbleberries, blueberries, huckleberries, spruce buds. There are medicines, too, like devil's club, yarrow, and willow."

"And your grandmother taught you all of that?"

She sipped her wine, nodded. "My mother's family mostly, though my father had some Alutiiq ancestry, too."

"And Russian, I believe, and a bunch of other stuff."

She smiled. "The population of Kodiak Island isn't that big. When new DNA washes up on the beach…"

That made Sean laugh. "Justin used to say you were your own United Nations."

Sean regretted his words the moment they were out of his mouth, but he was relieved to see the smile still on her face.

"I like that I can talk with you about him. Some people don't want me to mention him at all. It's as if he's been erased or something."

"I'm sorry. They're probably trying to avoid their own grief." Sean listened as she told him about a visit from her mother and cousin Mila earlier in the day.

"I found her stacking his uniforms on the bed. She wanted to know if the Coast Guard recycles them. I lost my temper, yelled at her to put them back, and told her never to touch his stuff again."

Sean might have said something stronger. "How did she take that?"

"Mila did what I asked but was snippy about it. After that, she wanted to leave, which was fine by me. I know my mom felt bad about it, but she let Mila come when I asked her not to. She texted later to apologize. Still, I can't help but feel guilty."

"You get to decide who enters your home, Eden. Your family needs to respect your wishes, especially now. How hard can that be?"

Maverick was clearly fed up with sitting in his highchair and arched his back, struggling to get down, pesto on his face. "I go *dowwwwn*!"

"Hang on, Mavie." Eden stood, grabbed a washcloth, and cleaned his face and hands before removing his bib and setting him on the floor.

He took off on his little feet, running nowhere in particular, free at last.

"Do you think I'm taking too long?" Eden set the washcloth in the sink. "Mila said I shouldn't wallow in Justin's death."

"*Jesus*." Sean muttered under his breath, instinctively reaching to take Eden's hand. "No, of course not. Justin was your husband. It's only been three months. You two were crazy about each other. Everyone knows that. Maybe Mila's forgotten what it's like to have a husband she loves. He works in Prudhoe Bay you said?"

Eden nodded. "They only see each other a few months every year. When they're together, they seem happy, but..."

"Ignore her." Sean squeezed Eden's hand, then let go. "She doesn't get to decide what you think or how you feel."

"Three months doesn't seem like a long time to me when I thought Justin and I had the rest of our lives to spend together."

"It's not long at all." Sean could empathize. "I didn't love Justin the same way you did, obviously, but three months doesn't feel like a long time to me, either."

Eden lifted her gaze to meet Sean's. "Thanks. You always make me feel better."

Her words unleashed a surge of guilt. If he'd done his job that night...

Sean helped Eden clean up, while Maverick played with blocks on the living room floor. "I should be getting back. I've got an early morning tomorrow. I'll be helping to train the new AETs while my arm and shoulder finish healing."

Eden looked up at him, eyes wide. "Oh, gosh. I'm so sorry. I didn't even ask you how it went today. You had your fitness eval, right?"

"I passed, but I know I'm not strong enough to operate a hoist line—not yet. I'll be working in the avionics shop for a while."

"Are you okay with that?" She closed the dishwasher, started the cycle.

"For now."

She turned to him, dishtowel in her hands. "Can I ask you a favor?"

"Of course."

"Crab Fest is coming up. As much as I'd rather avoid it, I don't want Maverick to miss out. He was just a baby last year. This year he's old enough to go on some of the kiddie rides. Would you mind coming with us and just being there? It's a lot to ask, I know, and you'll probably be bored out of your mind. None of my sisters can make it."

Kodiak Crab Festival was where Eden and Justin had met.

He understood. "I'd be happy to. And Eden? When I'm around, you can talk about Justin as much as you like, okay?"

She smiled. "Thanks. You're a good friend."

May 4

SEAN GOT UP EARLY to take the SWE—the Servicewide Examination. He'd been a little nervous going in, but once he'd gotten into it, time had passed quickly. After he turned in his exam, he made his way to the Avionics Shop, where he'd been working for the past week.

There'd been an early morning SAR flight for a boat taking on water. The helo had just returned when Sean started his watch.

James, who'd piloted the helo, walked up to Sean, helmet in his hand. "It's good to see you back, man."

"Dalton Leavitt is about to take paternity leave. I'll be filling in for him while my arm and shoulder finish healing."

"Look at these guys. Is it my imagination, or are the AETs getting younger every year? They look like kids, man."

Sean chuckled. "I had the same thought."

Spurrier glanced over his shoulder to the helo the new AETs were towing into the shop. "The radio was spotty toward the end of this flight."

"Might be electrical noise. Any trouble with any of the displays?"

Spurrier shook his head. "Just the radio."

"We'll isolate the problem and get it fixed."

"I knew you would." Spurrier headed toward the lockers to change.

Sean got some tools together and walked over to the new guys. "Listen up. Today, we're going to get some practice troubleshooting. The pilot reported problems with the radio on this last flight. That can be caused by electrical noise. Who can tell me what electrical noise is?"

When no one spoke up, Sean chose someone. "Rock, what is electrical noise?"

Rock shifted uncomfortably, his gaze on the floor. "Electrical noise is when electrical signals get into circuits where they don't belong."

"That's essentially correct." Sean gave the group a more detailed explanation and got to work, showing them how to use an oscilloscope.

He let them find the problem and then helped them fix it, giving everyone a chance to get hands-on experience. When the repair was completed, he inspected their work, answering their questions and stressing how important it was for them to do their jobs perfectly.

"Samantha, what happens if you make a mistake and the instruments fail in flight?"

"Someone could get hurt."

"Someone could *die*—not just that helicopter's flight crew, but also the people they've been sent to rescue."

Samantha's expression softened. "You were on the helo that crashed, weren't you?"

He felt every gaze on him, waiting for his answer. "I was, and I'm damned lucky to be alive. Two good men died that night. One of them was my best friend. His wife and child will never see him again. You do *not* want to be the reason a member of a flight crew doesn't come home to his family."

Leavitt, who'd been at a prenatal appointment with his

wife, walked up behind Sean. "Listen to Petty Officer McKenna. When that SAR alarm goes off, you need to know you're sending the flight crew out in an aircraft that's in perfect working order. If that's too much responsibility, you don't belong in avionics."

They finished the repairs, and then it was time for lunch.

Dalton walked with Sean to the galley. "How did they do this morning?"

"They have a lot to learn. Were we ever this green?"

"I'm sure I was, but not you, man, not with that degree of yours."

The day's menu was fish and chips with a side salad and brownies. Sean couldn't help but think of the salad he'd had yesterday and how much tastier it was than iceberg lettuce and shredded carrots. "Have you and your wife ever foraged here?"

"*Foraged?*"

"I ran into Eden Koseki last week. She was out with their son foraging for wild greens and shoots. She invited me over to have dinner and try it out."

"No, we've never foraged. It sounds gross." Leavitt poured dressing onto his salad. "Is the stuff she eats really food, or is it just weeds, like dandelions?"

"I'm not sure there's a hard line between weeds and edible greens." Sean tried to remember the names of the greens. "Claytonia. Watermelon berry sprouts. I can't remember everything she picked. Best salad ever. She made nettle pesto to put on the salmon."

"Nettle *what*?"

"That's what I said. She really knows the plants here on the island. She learned from her mother and grandmother, and now she's teaching Maverick."

"How is she doing, really?"

"Things are hard. She's doing as well as can be expected."

"It really makes you think, doesn't it?"

Fire and Rain

"What do you mean?"

"Our job. It's not without danger. It's not often that something goes wrong, but when it does, the people we love most suffer."

An image of Eden's tear-stained face came to mind, and Sean found himself grateful that he was still single. "That's true no matter what you do for a living. You could drive a school bus or work in a grocery store and still die on the job."

That didn't seem to reassure Dalton. "I'm not sure it's a good idea to have a baby now."

Sean chuckled. "It's too late to change your mind."

"Tell me about it. They're inducing Angela tomorrow."

"Tomorrow? I hope it goes well."

"Thanks." Dalton talked about the preparations they'd made and the things he still wanted to do before the baby came. "One thing we don't need is baby clothes. The other Coastie wives gave us so much baby stuff that we won't have to buy anything until this boy is five."

"It's a boy then?"

Dalton grinned. "Yeah."

"Congratulations, man. That's great. I'll be thinking of you both."

The conversation shifted to the shop, with Sean bringing Dalton up to date on what they'd done this morning.

Dalton seemed satisfied. "You're a natural at this."

Sean wasn't so sure. "Do you ever regret advancing?"

Dalton looked up from his plate. "Not at all. I like the pay increase. I could probably fly more than I do if I wanted to, but I spent years as part of a flight crew. I'm okay with keeping my feet on the ground these days."

They finished eating and walked back to the shop, where Dalton checked the work they'd done this morning. Sean went over each person's performance, offering tips and suggesting study assignments. He was just ending his shift when the SAR alarm went off.

"Now put the ready helo online. Now put the ready helo online."

Sean shifted gears. "Come on, folks! Let's move!"

Chapter Four

May 28

EDEN PARKED in the elementary school parking lot. "Are you ready to see the parade, Maverick? There are going to be firetrucks."

Sean unbuckled his seatbelt. "You get the toddler, and I'll get the tactical gear."

"Tactical gear? Roger that." Eden laughed and opened the lift gate so Sean could get the stroller and diaper bag.

She hopped out and got Maverick out of the back seat. "We're going to have such a fun time today, Mavie. We're going to go on rides and play games and get balloons."

She hoped it *would* be a good day. It was hard to imagine being here without Justin, but she didn't want Maverick to miss out on the fun. More than that, she needed to face this. For as long as she lived, there would be reminders of Justin around every corner, on every beach, and up every trail. She'd told herself she could handle it, especially with Sean there. She trusted him, knew that he understood.

Sean took out the stroller, locked it in the open position,

and plopped the diaper bag in the back. "Your ride is ready, buddy."

Eden settled Maverick in the seat and took the handles. "The parade route is just ahead on Mill Bay Road."

They walked the short distance, part of a trickle of people heading to see the parade.

Sean glanced at the sky, light reflecting off his mirrored aviators. "I can't believe it's not raining. It always rains for Crab Fest."

It *was* a beautiful, sunny day, but Eden knew that could change. "Don't jinx it."

There was a thin line of spectators on both sides of the road, so it wasn't hard to find a place to stand.

Sean glanced around. "I was expecting more of a crowd."

Eden laughed. "Everyone else is *in* the parade."

They stood near the end of the parade route, so there was a bit of a wait for the fun to begin. Maverick got restless, tried to climb out.

"You need to stay in your stroller, Mavie. The firetrucks will be here soon. Watch for them down the street."

Maverick leaned over the front of his stroller and craned his little neck. But when he saw nothing, he tried once again to climb out.

"Want to sit on my shoulders?"

"Uncle Sean says you can sit on his shoulders." She lifted Maverick out of the stroller and handed him to Sean.

Sean settled Maverick on his shoulders, held onto his little legs, and gave him a few playful bounces that made him laugh.

The sound was a balm to Eden's soul. She had mostly stayed home since January. And though her two older sisters, Natasha and Maria, had brought their kids to play with Maverick, Eden knew that couldn't make up for being with a mother who was always sad.

Fire and Rain

When at last they heard the first squawk of a siren, Maverick's eyes went wide, and he pointed. "See, Mommy?"

"I see! That's a police car. See the flashing lights?"

Behind the police vehicle marched the Coast Guard Color Guard, flags fluttering in the breeze, the crowd going respectfully silent as they passed. They were followed by a National Guard personnel carrier. And then, at long last, came the firetrucks.

Maverick's eyes went wide, and he pointed, almost bouncing on Sean's shoulders. "Fietwuck! Fietwuck!"

"I see it." Eden smiled at his excitement. "It's big, isn't it?"

Sean grinned. "The kid likes firetrucks."

The lead truck gave a blast of its siren, and Maverick laughed with delight.

Eden loved seeing him happy.

Then came the island's many Little League teams, its Scout groups, and its high school sports teams, the roller-skating club, and the local hockey league.

"You weren't kidding when you said the rest of the town was in the parade."

"We're just getting started."

A motorcycle club, engines revving. Moms with Mowers doing a choreographed routine. A local dog training school with a bunch of pups. A float for the Kodiak Area Native Association with Alutiiq dancers. The Maritime History Museum float. The Kodiak Military Museum float. That guy on the unicycle who came every year.

Bringing up the rear was the Coast Guard's big fire engine with the cherry-picker.

Maverick was beside himself. He pointed. "Fietwuck!"

Sean turned to Eden. "I can arrange for him to come on base and see the engine. There's no reason he can't look at it close up and maybe climb inside."

Eden's heart constricted. "Justin was going to set that up."

He'd never gotten the chance.

"I'll handle it."

"Thanks." She smiled. "For a man who doesn't want kids, you're good with them."

With the parade over, they walked back to Eden's SUV, loaded up, and drove the short distance toward Kodiak Harbor.

Eden glanced over at Sean. "Now the real fun begins."

"Bring it."

SEAN HANDED the ride operator the required number of tickets, while Eden settled Maverick in what looked like a tiny cartoon helicopter. There weren't many rides for tots on the midway, but this one was perfect for Maverick.

He smiled up at his mother. "I fwy copter! Daddy copter!"

"That's right. You're going to fly in a helicopter like Daddy." Eden bent over the helicopter to buckle him in. "Don't stand up, okay, Maverick? Hold on."

The operator's gaze lingered on Eden's butt as if he were imagining what lay beneath her jeans, and Sean fought the urge to punch the bastard.

Chill out, man.

"You fly helicopters?" The operator's breath reeked of cigarette smoke.

Sean didn't feel like explaining his relationship to Eden or Maverick or sharing details of his job. "I'm a Coast Guard flight mech."

"Cool, man."

Eden finished buckling Maverick into his seat and came to stand on the other side of the fence beside Sean. The operator closed the gate and started the ride.

The flight of tiny helicopters and airplanes began to spin,

carrying precious cargo in slow circles. Maverick let out a squeal of laughter that didn't stop, his face bright with excitement. The other children were smiling and laughing, too, and Sean found himself wondering what it must be like to be at the age when everything was new.

Sean hadn't spent much time around small children, but he had to admit there was nothing like that laughter. "You've got a little thrill-seeker on your hands."

"Don't I know it." Eden took some photos with her phone. "I love seeing him so happy. I try not to cry in front of him. It's been hard to be the mother he needs."

"You're too hard on yourself. From where I stand, you're a hero."

She looked up at him, doubt in her hazel eyes. "You really mean that?"

"Hell, yes, I do."

"Thanks."

Around and around Maverick went, still laughing. But when the ride stopped, his expression fell. "Go!"

The operator opened the gate so parents could collect their children, but when Eden tried to take Maverick out of his seat, he shrieked and tried to twist away from her.

"Can he go again?" Sean took the tickets out of his pocket.

"There's no line, so fine by me." The operator took the tickets.

Maverick rode three more times before Eden insisted they go. "There are more rides, Mavie. Let's find the carousel."

The rides for small kids were mostly grouped together, so the carousel wasn't far away. At the sight of the brightly painted horses, Maverick forgot about the helicopters.

Sean handed over the tickets and watched while Eden rode the carousel with her boy, holding him on the back of a bright green and purple pony. She pointed at something out in the harbor and smiled, looking happier than he'd seen her in months.

God, she was beautiful. Truly beautiful. Hadn't he always told Justin he'd married the most beautiful woman on the island?

Knock that shit off now. Don't think about Eden like that even if it is true.

After the carousel, they all climbed aboard the Spin the Apple ride, which Sean remembered from his own childhood. Using the wheel in the center, he gave their apple several good spins, which made Maverick squeal. And then it was time for lunch.

They sat in the shade of the dining tent, two plates piled high with crab legs, melted butter, and lemon wedges and one with hot, fresh fry bread.

Sean moaned, the crab melting on his tongue. "God, I love Kodiak."

"Fresh from the ocean last night." Eden dipped some crab meat in butter and fed it to Maverick, who sat in his stroller, mouth open like a baby bird.

"I didn't expect to see you here."

Sean looked up to find a woman with shoulder-length dark hair standing at the end of the table, two school-aged kids behind her—a boy and a girl.

Eden's expression darkened. "Mila."

So, this was Mila. She was pretty and polished, with bright red lipstick, eye makeup, and salon nails, and a big, glittering diamond ring. But no amount of gloss could hide the hard glint in her eyes.

Sean disliked her instantly.

Eden gave Maverick another bite of crab and looked past her cousin to the children. "Hey, Nick. Hey, Lina. Are you two having a good time?"

"We went on the Star four times!" Nick turned to his

sister, a grin on his face. "Lina thought she was going to be sick."

Eden shifted her gaze to Lina. "That can happen on these rides. Maybe you should let your tummy settle before you—"

Mila interrupted Eden, turned to Sean. "I'm Mila Parson, Eden's—"

"Eden's cousin. I know."

Mila tried to pretend she was pleased by this, but Sean didn't miss the way her gaze jerked to Eden for a moment, as if wondering what Eden had told him about her. "And you are...?"

Eden answered. "He's Sean McKenna, Justin's best friend."

"Oh." Mila's perfectly shaped eyebrows rose, and she surveyed Sean with renewed interest. "You're the one who survived."

"Yes." Sean followed Eden's example and spoke to the kids, unwilling to be drawn into a casual conversation about the worst night of his life with a stranger. "Flying on a helicopter can make a person sick to their stomach, too."

Lina looked surprised. "Really?"

"Yeah. The wind can be pretty rough sometimes."

"Have you ever fallen out?" Nick asked.

"Of a helicopter?" Sean shook his head. "No. We're strapped in."

"So, are you two...?" Mila pointed first at Eden and then at Sean.

"Eating? Yes." Sean took another bite of crab and saw Eden fight not to laugh. "Have you had your fill of crab legs yet?"

The kids shook their heads.

Mila gave a wave of her hand. "They'll have that for supper. They're selling eight for two hundred dollars, so I'm going to buy a bag. Come along, kids. Auntie Eden and her *friend* don't want to be interrupted."

When Mila had gone, Eden looked over at Sean. "God, she gets on my nerves!"

Sean grinned. "I have no idea why."

EDEN HANDED Sean her keys so he could unlock the door. She lifted a sleeping Maverick out of his car seat and carried him inside to his crib, where she removed his shoes and pants and covered him with his favorite blankie. Then she walked out to the living room to find Sean standing in the kitchen, leaning back against the counter, phone in hand.

He slipped his phone back into his pocket. "I think we wore the little man out."

"He had a great time today. We both did."

"And I got to meet your cousin Mila."

Eden laughed. "I loved how you handled her nosy question. Did you see her face?"

He shook his head. "I was trying not to make eye contact."

"She's not used to people standing up to her." Then Eden remembered. "I promised you a cup of nettle tea."

"Right."

She set a pot of water on the stove to boil and put dried nettle leaves with dried mint into the diffuser of her teapot. "You're not still skeptical, are you?"

"About your skills with nettles?" He chuckled. "Absolutely not."

"My grandmother has been drinking this tea all of her life, and she's going to be a hundred in four or five years."

"Wait." Sean gave her a puzzled look. "She doesn't know how old she is?"

"She says ninety-six. But my mother and aunties say she's ninety-five. She doesn't have a birth certificate."

"Wow."

While they waited for the water to boil, Eden got down two mugs and a jar of honey and shared her grandmother's story. "Her family came from Afognak. She grew up living the old ways—seal hunting, gathering plants for food and medicine, and fishing. Then she met my grandfather. In her lifetime, she went from a traditional subsistence lifestyle to living in a house with electricity, driving a car, and traveling by airplane. Can you imagine that?"

Sean shook his head. "My great-grandfather had a farm in Illinois. He grew up with horse-drawn wagons, barn-raisings, and kerosene lanterns. He used to talk about how incredible it had been to watch men walk on the Moon. He died when I was still little, but I remember thinking he was ancient. To experience that kind of change in a single lifetime..."

"How does a person keep up with that?" The kettle whistled, and Eden poured the steaming water into her tea pot and carried the pot to the table to steep. "I hope you like—"

She tripped over something and dumped hot tea and wet nettle leaves down the front of Sean's shirt. "Oh, God!"

He gasped, shot to his feet, and caught her, the front of his T-shirt soaked.

She set the teapot on the table and darted back to the kitchen. "I'll get a cold cloth. God, I'm so sorry! I hope the burns aren't bad."

"I'm fine."

Eden stuck a washcloth under cold water, looking over her shoulder to see Sean pick up one of Maverick's toy trucks.

He set it on the table. "You could have broken an ankle."

"I should have been more careful." She hurried back to Sean with the cold washcloth. "This should help. I'm really sorry."

He slid the washcloth beneath his T-shirt. "It's not bad. No blisters."

"Let me at least wash your shirt. I'll get you one of Justin's to wear home."

"It's no big deal, really."

"I can't let you wear that back to base."

He drew the T-shirt over his head and handed it to her. "If you insist."

An unexpected frisson of desire shot through her, and Eden couldn't help but stare. His tanned skin was red where the tea had scalded him, but that's not what held her gaze.

Firm pecs with flat, tan nipples. A six-pack. A trail of light brown curls that disappeared beneath his jeans. Years of pulling people on litters into helicopters had left him with well-developed triceps and biceps. But there were scars, too—small surgical scars where they'd repaired his right biceps and shoulder.

Distracted, Eden reached out, ran her finger along one of the scars. "Does it still hurt?"

"Sometimes."

Eden caught herself. "I'm sorry. I ... uh... lost my train of thought. Mom brain."

"You were going to wash my shirt."

"Oh! Right." Cheeks flaming, she turned and hurried toward the laundry room, hoping he hadn't noticed her staring. "I'll just drop this in the washer and grab you a clean, dry shirt."

"Eden, you don't have to do that. I can wash it myself. I don't want you to—"

"It's no trouble." She was already halfway down the hall and needed to get away.

What the hell was that?

She'd seen Sean shirtless plenty of times. Out fishing with Justin on Justin's boat. At the beach. All those times the men had played football at the park. She and some of the other Coast Guard wives had whispered together about how ripped he was, how handsome his face was. But Eden had never reacted like this.

You're just tired. It's been a long day.

Yeah, no. Even she couldn't believe that.

She dropped his sodden shirt in the laundry basket and walked to the bedroom, where she found herself standing in the closet, looking at Justin's T-shirts.

All at once, guilt assailed her. Justin hadn't yet been gone for five months, and she was getting turned on by another man? And his best friend on top of that.

What is wrong with you?

She drew a breath, tried to pull herself together. Sean was waiting, and Maverick would surely wake up soon. She looked at the T-shirts, picked one of her favorites, and carried it back to the kitchen, certain Justin wouldn't mind Sean taking one of his shirts.

She found Sean standing in the kitchen, rinsing the cloth she'd given him in the sink. "I'm pretty sure it will fit. You can keep it. I think Justin would be happy to know you're wearing it."

"Thanks." Sean took the shirt. "I used that cloth to wipe up the tea. I hope that's okay."

Eden saw that the table was clean and dry. "Thank you."

Sean glanced down at the image of the humpback whale fluke on the front of the T-shirt. "I remember this one. Are you sure?"

Eden nodded, her emotions tangled as he drew it over his head. "More tea—or have you had enough boiling water for one day?"

It was a pathetic attempt at humor, but it made him laugh.

He glanced at his watch. "I hate to run, but I really ought to get going."

She couldn't help but feel disappointed—and relieved. "Early shift tomorrow?"

"I'm on duty tonight."

"And you spent the day with us instead of sleeping?"

"It's okay. I had a good time. I'll get some dinner from the galley, head to barracks, and try to get a few hours of sleep."

"Thanks for coming with us—and for helping me with Maverick. I'm not sure I'd have been able to face it alone." She hadn't stayed around for the Coast Guard rescue swimmer demo, but no one could expect that of her.

"You're welcome." Sean's gaze met hers, and he smiled—a smile Eden felt down to her toes. "You're a badass. You didn't have to go at all, but you did. I respect that. Thanks for a fun day. Call if you need anything, okay?"

"Okay."

With that, he said goodbye, leaving Eden to grapple with her emotions.

Chapter Five

May 30

SEAN SAT on the edge of the pool, fins on his feet, goggles covering his eyes. He had just come off a busy night shift and wanted to get in some laps before he hit his bunk. He had the place to himself. But he wasn't alone.

Over here, Koseki!

Justin dove, swam with the pool brick through deep water, Trey, Rob, and Scott, doing their best to get the brick away from him. They caught up with him, swarmed him, the four of them wrestling for control under water.

Sean saw his chance, drew a breath, and swam below them, almost to the bottom of the pool. Justin let the brick drop, and Sean snatched it, using his fins to propel him toward the cones that marked the goalposts. He surfaced and scored a goal just as the others caught up with him.

Justin surfaced, grinned, gave him a high five. "The AET who outswims the rescue swimmers."

The pool room was full of memories for Sean, echoes all around.

How many times had he and Justin played brick ball here? How many fitness assessments had they done together here? How many laps had they swum? How many sessions of water egress training?

Sean slipped into the water, drew a breath, and started to swim, using exertion to clear his mind. There was no pain in his shoulder, and the stiffness wore off after the first couple of laps.

Down and back and down again.

Okay, McKenna, I'll race you—five hundred yards and the loser buys dinner.

You're on, Koseki.

Sean kept swimming, pushing himself, but the memories kept coming.

Sean buckled into his seat. He was in the back this time, Justin in front.

"Bottoms up!" Justin turned to him, and the two exchanged a fist bump before the lights went out and the vehicle flipped, plunging them into the water.

Sean unbuckled his belt, felt his way toward a window, popped it, and swam to the surface. He glanced around for Justin and saw him on the other side.

Down and back and down again.

"Fish on!" Justin reeled in his catch, rod bending. "Come on, fish!"

Sean grabbed a net and positioned himself to scoop up the salmon once Justin got it to the surface. "I see it. It's a big one—a king. Don't let it get away!"

"I'm working on it." Justin reeled it in bit by bit until, at last, it came close to the surface, silver scales glittering.

Sean dipped the net, caught the line, and Justin pulled it onto the boat. "That is one big winter king. That must weigh at least twenty-five pounds."

Down and back and down again.

"Abort! Abort! We need to get everyone off the boat and pick them up in the water. They're cooking meth, and the patient was exposed."

"Aborting the hoist. Get out of there, Koseki."

Sean surfaced, grabbed the side of the pool, his heart slamming in his chest.

What the *hell* was wrong with him?

The answer came to him in a single word.

Eden.

He'd seen her reaction when he'd taken off his shirt—and had felt an answering pull. Her touch had scorched him, made his blood go hot. He'd found himself wanting to drag her against him, to kiss her, to peel the clothes off her body so he could touch her sweet curves.

No fucking way.

He couldn't do that. Eden was Justin's widow. Yes, he'd always found her attractive. What straight guy wouldn't? But he'd never been tempted to think of her sexually—until yesterday. He hadn't been able to take his mind off her since, his thoughts drifting to fantasies of kissing her, caressing her, tasting her.

And that's why you're torturing yourself?

As painful as they were, memories of his friendship with Justin were easier to handle than knowing he had betrayed that friendship, at least in his head.

The lights came on, and Captain Walcott walked in. "McKenna? Are you okay?"

"I'm fine." Sean lifted himself to sit on the side of the pool. "I thought I'd get in some laps before turning in."

He dreaded trying to sleep, knowing what was waiting for him in his nightmares.

"How's the shoulder?"

Sean rotated it a few times. "It's good, sir. No pain. My shoulder feels strong."

Captain Walcott nodded. "Glad to hear it. Pending a green light from medical, I'm returning you to the flight crews. Leavitt's paternity leave is ending. Apparently, his mother-in-law arrived from New Mexico to help with the baby last week, and Dalton can't wait to get back in the avionics shop."

Sean grinned. "Understood."

Captain Walcott seemed to study him. "Are you sure you're up for this? What you went through was a Coastie's nightmare. The Coast Guard can make use of your skills in many ways. You could join an Aids to Navigation Crew."

Sean appreciated the offer, but trudging through seagull and seal shit to service lighthouses wasn't his idea of a challenge. He removed his fins and goggles and stood, water streaming down his body to puddle on the concrete. "I'm eager to get back in the air, sir. Every time a helo took off without me, I felt like I ought to be going, too."

Captain Walcott nodded. "That's how I felt when I quit serving as a pilot. We'll get you in for a final medical eval, and I'll add you to the flight crew duty rotation."

"Thank you, sir."

"Get some sleep. You all had a busy night last night."

With three back-to-back SAR missions, the line crew had run full throttle.

"Yes, sir." Then Sean remembered. "Justin's son Maverick is almost two, and the kid is crazy about firetrucks. I told Eden I'd try to arrange for him to see the big cherry-picker. Who do I need to see to work that out?"

"It's fine with me. Check with Lt. Corey Mitchell, chief of Fire and Rescue, just to make sure the time works for them. Let's do all we can for Eden and her boy."

"Yes, sir." Sean retrieved his towel and headed toward the men's locker room for a hot shower, promising himself that he wouldn't cross any lines with Eden.

It was a promise he intended to keep.

Fire and Rain

EDEN WALKED with her grandmother on a forest trail across the highway from Fort Abercrombie State Historical Park, a warm breeze making the leaves above them rustle, the air sweet with the scent of earth and growing things. The trail was mostly flat, which made it easier for her grandmother, who was frail and had balance issues.

This foraging walk had been her grandmother's idea. She'd asked Eden's mother to watch Maverick so the two of them could have some time together. Eden was happy to get away for a while, and she loved spending time with her grandmother. So far, they'd found claytonia, fresh salmonberry leaves, docks, and wild garlic.

"There." Her grandmother pointed with her cane. "Those look like some good docks."

"You have sharp eyes." Eden walked to a patch of docks and filled a small paper bag with the tender leaves.

"These old eyes are still good enough to see a thing or two."

Uh-oh.

Eden recognized that tone of voice.

"I have two granddaughters who are hurting."

So, this was about Mila.

Eden didn't want to endure a lecture about how Mila had been trying to help, but she would never say a cross word to her grandmother. And so, she said nothing.

"Mila was wrong in what she did. Yes, your mother told me." Her grandmother gestured with her cane. "More docks."

Eden crossed to the other side of the trail and picked more docks. "Mila has been bossy since we were little girls, but we're not children now. She does a lot of hurtful things."

"Mila has always been jealous of you, *aa'icagaq*." Her grandmother used Eden's childhood nickname, which meant *little cute one*. "That doesn't make up for the wrong she has done, but it's true."

"Jealous? Of me, Baba?" Eden found that hard to believe.

Grandmother pointed to something in the middle of the trail ahead of them and laughed, exposing her few remaining teeth. "What's the story behind that?"

In the middle of the trail ahead sat an old running shoe. It was covered in moss and had a small sapling growing through it. It had clearly been there for a very long time. But that's not what held Eden's attention.

"Why would Mila be jealous of me? She has a lot more money than I do. She and Charlie own a nice house, cars, and lots of jewelry. She's on every board and committee in town. She's an important person here in Kodiak. I don't understand."

"Let me explain." Grandmother walked to a bench and sat.

Eden sat beside her, basket in her lap.

"You both grew up to be beautiful women. That is true. Mila has more money. That is also true. But you are rich in things that money cannot buy."

It seemed to Eden that money bought pretty much everything. "Such as…?"

"A good heart. A kind soul. You know how to love and how to give of yourself. Others are drawn to you because of those things. But Mila doesn't believe that she is enough. She puffs herself up not to make herself seem better than others, but to keep herself from feeling that she is lower than everyone else."

Eden had a hard time believing that. "But she's *so* smug and irritating. She thinks her way is the only way, and she's always been like that."

"She doesn't know how to feel safe without controlling everything. You see the world through the richness inside you, and because of that, you always have enough. Mila only knows what she doesn't have, and she fills that emptiness with things that the world admires—money, jewelry, clothes. But those things cannot bring her happiness."

Her grandmother's insights almost made Eden feel sorry for Mila. And for a time, the two of them sat without speaking, the breeze and birdsong the only sounds.

Eden broke the silence. "How long did you grieve for your first husband?"

Her grandmother had been married to an Alutiiq man before she'd met Eden's grandfather, but he had died in a kayak accident not long after they'd married.

"It was quite hard in the beginning because we were so young, and it was unexpected. I mourned for him and missed him every day. But when I met your grandfather, that grief lifted bit by bit, until I saw that I was being given a second chance. We were married a year later."

"Why didn't you remarry after Deda died?"

Her grandmother chuckled. "I was sixty-five, and I had my children and grandchildren to keep me busy. My time for being married had passed."

Eden decided to come out with it, knowing her grandmother wouldn't repeat what she said to anyone. "There's another Coastie, who's been helping me since Justin died. He and Justin were best friends. I like spending time with him, and he is *very* good-looking. I'm attracted to him, and I think he feels the same way."

"You know this man well? Is he a good man?"

Eden nodded. "He was like a brother to Justin and spent a lot of time at our house. He went fishing, camping, and hunting with us. He's been so kind to Maverick and me."

"Good." Her grandmother took her hand, her brown eyes warm. "Who can say what is right for another? Life is short, and it does no one good to be lonely. Justin loved you, and I think he would want you to be happy. Honor his memory by living a full and happy life."

"Being attracted to another man makes me feel guilty, as if I'm betraying Justin."

Her grandmother patted her arm. "Justin is gone, but you still have life ahead of you. Finding a new man doesn't mean you've forgotten the old. Never turn your back on love, Eden. You're old enough for a bit of hanky-panky."

Eden gaped at her grandmother, a devout Russian Orthodox woman.

But her grandmother only chuckled. "I gave birth to nine children. Do you think I don't know what goes on between men and women?"

Eden laughed. "Of course, you do."

"Come. It's getting close to lunch time. We should go."

"Don't you want to forage for more greens?"

"You can keep what we found. They're hard for me to chew."

They walked slowly back down the trail, Eden savoring every step. She didn't have much time left with her grandmother, and each moment was precious. They reached Eden's SUV, and Eden helped her buckle up in the front passenger seat. Then she climbed in and drove to her grandmother's house.

She shared a bowl of soup with her grandmother, then settled her in her recliner, put a blanket over her, and kissed her cheek. "Rest well, Baba. And thank you."

Her grandmother squeezed her hand. "I'm proud of you, *aa'icagaq*."

"And I'm proud to be your granddaughter."

By the time Eden reached the front door, her grandmother was asleep.

Fire and Rain

June 1

SEAN WALKED toward a waiting H-60 with James, Trey, and Zeke Carlson, who'd just transferred in from Air Station Astoria in Warrenton, Oregon.

"That is the helicopter." Trey was having fun teasing Sean. "It's a rotary-wing aircraft with a maximum range of four-hundred forty-five nautical miles."

Sean flipped Trey the bird. "Hey, Trey, what's this?"

"Listen, man, you've been out for a long time. I'm just trying to help in case you've forgotten anything."

James turned to Zeke, a grin on his face. "Don't listen to Trey. Sean is a top-notch flight mech—one of the best I've worked with during my career."

"Thanks, Spurrier." Sean chuckled. "I'm blushing."

"Don't say that," Trey teased. "That big head of his will only get bigger."

They boarded the H-60. Sean put on his helmet and buckled into his seat, which was closest to the door. Pre-flight check. The whir of the rotors. And they lifted off for a training flight to give Zeke the lay of the land.

"What makes flying in Alaska different from anywhere else is the weather," James told Zeke. "There will be times when you're flying in zero-zero conditions—total whiteout, no horizon. When the weather's bad here, it's the worst kind of bad."

"Sounds like fun," Zeke answered.

Only half-listening to the conversation, Sean watched land give way to ocean, sunlight glinting off the rolling swells. It had been almost five months since he'd been on a helo, five months since he'd flown over the water. God, he'd missed it.

"How does it feel to be airborne again?"

It took Sean a moment to realize James was talking to him. "It's better than breaking in new AETs."

James laughed. "Don't let the captain advance you."

"Rescue Six-Oh-Four-Two, Air Station Kodiak, copy."

"Air Station Kodiak, Rescue Six-Oh-Four-Two, good copy."

"Sector forwarded a report of a man on a salmon seiner with severe trauma, including possible fractures and a head injury. The vessel, the Kodiak Star, is in Outer Chiniak Bay, north of Cape Chiniak."

And in an instant, their training flight became a rescue mission.

The information as it came in wasn't good. A wire cable had snapped, and the boom had collapsed, dropping the heavy power block onto the victim, who was unconscious, unresponsive, and bleeding from one ear.

Sean helped Trey prepare the cabin for a critical patient and then set up the litter with a backboard and a C-collar. They'd been flying over Inner Chiniak Bay when they'd gotten the call, so it wasn't long before the boat came into view.

"You've got cabin door speed," James told him.

"Roger that. Opening cabin door." Sean sized up the vessel. "There isn't much room. There are a lot of cables and antennae coming off the superstructure. With the boom down, our best bet might be to approach from the bow and lower the swimmer to the port side of the boom."

"Roger that."

Sean conned James into position, keeping an eye on those antennae and the loose cable that was swinging in the helo's rotor wash. Then he turned to Trey, the two of them working through the safety check and connecting the hook to Trey's harness.

"Safety check complete. Swimmer is leaving the cabin." Holding the hoist line, Sean gave Trey a nudge and began to lower him fifty feet to the ship's deck.

Sean took care not to let Trey slam into the railing, holding tight to the hoist line to keep it steady. "Swimmer is on deck. Retrieving the cable."

While Trey did an initial assessment on the patient, Sean retrieved the hook, connected it to the litter, and waited for Trey's signal. As he watched Trey work, Sean's pulse took off unexpectedly, images of Justin bent over the patient on that terrible night flooding his mind.

Aborting the hoist. Get out of there, Koseki.

Sean sucked in one breath and another until the panic of the flashback had receded.

Get your shit together, man.

Trey gave him a thumb's up.

"Swimmer has requested the litter."

"Roger that. Begin the hoist."

Sean lowered the litter to the deck, watching while Trey worked with the crew to get the patient onto the backboard, into the C-collar, and then into the litter. He kept James apprised of their progress. "Patient is in the litter. Hoisting the patient. Patient is off the deck. Patient is halfway up. Patient is outside the cabin."

He took hold of the litter and pulled the patient feet-first into the cabin, relieved not to feel pain in his shoulder. "Patient is in the cabin."

"Roger that."

Quickly, Sean unclipped the litter. "Sending the hook down for the swimmer."

A few minutes later, Trey was back inside the cabin.

James' voice came through Sean's earphones. "Patient is onboard. We are RTB."

The pressure was on Trey now as he cut the patient's sleeve with scissors, inserted a large-bore IV, and opened the fluids wide. "Pupils are dilated and unresponsive. Let's hook him up to O2 and get his vitals."

They didn't have time to do much more for the patient, as

the helo had a tailwind. In what felt like only a handful of minutes, they were back at base, Kodiak EMS standing by with a gurney. Sean helped Trey get the litter onto the gurney, and the two of them escorted the patient to the ambulance, handing him off to EMS. And then their job was done.

Sean was on his way back to the lockers when James caught up with him.

"I had one hell of a hard time on my first rescue after the crash. When it came time to bring the helo into a hover, I got a full-on adrenaline rush. But you didn't falter today, not for a second. Great work. I'm really glad to have you back, man."

"Thanks." Sean didn't deserve James' praise, but he didn't say so. "I'm glad to be here."

Chapter Six

EDEN TOOK the tiny bundle into her arms, her heart melting. She'd brought a meal and a gift for the new parents and couldn't pass up a chance to hold their month-old baby. "Hi, there, little Noah. Aren't you cute? He's adorable, Angela—and so tiny. How much did he weigh?"

Angela smiled down at her sleeping son. "He was seven pounds twelve ounces at birth. He lost a little weight in his first week, but he has gained it back. He was eight pounds two ounces at his checkup this week."

"Maverick weighed an ounce under eight pounds. It's hard to believe that he was ever this little. Look at those tiny fingers. Are you breastfeeding?"

Angela nodded. "It's going well now, though it was tough at first."

Eden remembered those days. "Sore nipples are no fun."

"How are *you* doing?"

"I'm better. Some days are harder than others." Then Eden had to say it. "I'm sorry I didn't stop by sooner. The last thing Justin and I talked about the night he died was having another baby. I needed to wait until I was sure I wouldn't start crying the moment I saw Noah. I don't want to spoil your joy with my problems."

She'd said it, and she hadn't shed a tear.

"You don't need to explain." Angela's gaze was soft with sympathy. "I can't imagine how hard this has been for you. You should do whatever you need to do to take care of yourself and Maverick."

"Thank you." Eden didn't want this to be about her. "Are you getting sleep?"

"Some. When Dalton was on leave, he handled one of the night feedings so I could sleep. Now that he's back at work, he needs his rest."

"He's back at work now?" Eden had heard the shower running when she'd arrived and had assumed Dalton was in the bathroom.

Angela lowered her voice. "My mother drives him crazy. He was happy to go back to work. I don't want my mom to miss out on bonding with Noah, but I loved being home together just the three of us—a true babymoon."

Eden knew how complicated families could be. Then it hit her. "Wasn't Sean McKenna filling in for Dalton?"

Angela nodded. "Dalton said he was only too happy to rejoin the flight crews."

"He's back with the flight crews." Eden mindlessly repeated what Angela had just told her, her thoughts scattered by an unexpected rush of adrenaline.

"Dalton was surprised, too. He thought Sean might want to stay on the ground or transfer to one of the Aids to Navigation crews after what happened, but..."

Sean was flying again, risking his life on SAR missions. He hadn't told Eden he was back in the air. She'd thought he was still safe in the avionics shop. She hadn't heard from him since they were together at Crab Fest.

Does he owe it to you to tell you what he's doing?

No, of course, he didn't, but she cared about him.

An older woman entered the living room, her short gray hair in neat, damp curls. "I'm Brenda, Angela's mother."

Eden did her best to snap out of it, her heart still racing. "I'm Eden."

"Eden is the one I told you about—the one who grew up in Kodiak. She brought beef stroganoff for us for supper tonight."

Brenda's lips formed an O of comprehension, her gaze fixing on Eden once more. And Eden knew that Angela had told her about Justin's death. "How kind. Thank you. You have a little one, too, don't you?"

"Yes." Eden fixed a smile on her face. "Maverick will be two in August."

"That's such a fun age." Brenda looked down at her sleeping grandson. "Why don't I make us a nice cup of tea, and we can chat?"

"Thanks, Mom. That would be great."

Brenda brought the tea, and the three of them settled into a conversation, mostly about Brenda's life in New Mexico—the church where she sang in the choir, her interest in genealogy, her hobby of collecting and furnishing dollhouses.

Eden did her best to listen attentively, even when Brenda's long descriptions of her family tree and her various dollhouses left Eden fighting not to yawn.

Angela did her best to change the subject. "I bet you have a very interesting family tree, Eden, with Alutiiq, Russian... and what else?"

"Scottish and French Canadian. That's most of it."

"What's Aloot..." Brenda stopped short.

"Alutiiq." Eden finished the word for her. "It's Sugpiaq—Native Alaskan."

"Oh! You're part Eskimo."

Angela looked apologetically at Eden. "No one uses that word anymore, Mom."

"Well, I can't keep up with all of that stuff, so whatever." Her mother gave an impatient wave of her hand then stood and carried the teacups to the kitchen.

"Sorry!" Angela mouthed.

"It's okay," Eden mouthed back. In her arms, Noah began to fuss. "He's probably hungry. I should get going. I need to run to the store and pick up Maverick from my sister's."

Eden handed the baby back to Angela.

"Thank you." Angela got ready to nurse. "And thanks for bringing dinner."

"It's a favorite family recipe. I hope you enjoy it." Eden got to her feet. "It was nice to meet you, Brenda."

"Lovely to meet you, too, dear."

Eden walked out to her SUV, grabbed her phone, and typed out a text for Sean.

```
Are you working as a flight mech again?
```

She looked at the message for a moment and then deleted it.

Sean's life wasn't her business.

June 3

SEAN FINISHED HIS WORKOUT, showered, and wrapped his towel around his hips. Bag of toiletries in hand, he walked over to the mirror to shave the spots on his face that still grew hair. Today, he was meeting Eden at Fire and Rescue so Maverick could see the cherry-picker. He'd heard via Captain

Walcott that Lt. Mitchell had something special in store for the boy.

He lathered his jaw and ran the razor over his stubble, ignoring the trill of excitement in his chest at the thought of seeing Eden again. This was about Maverick. There was nothing going on between him and Eden. And that moment when she'd stared at his bare chest? He had only imagined the desire in her eyes. It had probably been distress as she saw the redness of his skin where the tea had burned him. These complicated emotions came from shared grief and mutual concern, nothing more.

Do you believe the shit you're telling yourself?

Sean met his gaze in the mirror, his face half covered by shaving cream.

Yeah, I didn't think so.

It didn't matter how he felt. Emotions could be controlled. He couldn't allow himself to feel anything for Eden but concern and friendship.

He finished shaving, rinsed his face with hot water, then dried off and put on his blue ODUs. He wasn't on duty today, but he didn't want to show up in another department on base wearing jeans and a T-shirt. He tied his boots, grabbed his phone, and left the barracks for the short walk to the firehouse.

It was a sunny, warm day, the sky clear and blue. A bald eagle soared overhead, looking for a meal. From somewhere nearby came children's laughter.

Even before he reached the firehouse, Sean could see they were ready for Maverick. The big cherry-picker sat outside, gleaming red in the sunlight, balloons in the Coast Guard colors tied to the driver side mirror. He found himself smiling as he imagined Maverick's reaction.

Fietwuck! Fietwuck!

Sean arrived a few minutes early and found Lt. Mitchell

on the far side of the cherry-picker, wearing his ODU ball cap, his eyes hidden behind gold aviator-style Ray-Bans. He was talking with one of his crew. Sean waited until the conversation ended and then shook Mitchell's hand. "Thanks for hosting this today. It's going to mean a lot to Maverick."

And his mother.

"Hey, we're happy to do it. The Coast Guard is a big family. When I think about that boy never knowing his father, it really gets me. We'll do what we can to help keep his father's memory alive."

"You went all out. The balloons are a nice touch."

"We've got more in store for him than balloons." Lt. Mitchell looked past Sean. "I think they're here."

Sean turned to see Eden park her SUV, ignoring the way his pulse picked up a notch. Then she stepped out of the vehicle—and Sean stared.

Damn.

Eden wore a sleeveless sundress in hot pink, its neckline dangerously low, the hem well above her knees, sandals with heels on her feet. She smiled and waved to Sean before opening the rear door to get Maverick out of his car seat.

Against his will, Sean's gaze fixed on the sweet curves of her ass as she bent over, the hem of her dress creeping perilously high. When she stood upright again, she had Maverick in her arms. She pointed to the cherry-picker, said something to him.

Sean managed to unroot himself from the place where he'd stood staring, and walked to meet them, focusing on the boy. "Hey, buddy."

Maverick smiled at him, pointed. "Sawn, Fietwuck!"

Eden smiled. "I told you he could say your name."

"So, you weren't lying after all." Sean was amazed at how calm he sounded. "That's right, little man. Today, you get to see the big firetruck."

Fire and Rain

Eden stepped toward him, standing so close now that he could smell the clean scent of her skin. "Thanks for doing this, Sean."

"You don't need to thank me, Eden. I was happy to set it up." He took Maverick from her, lifted the boy onto his shoulders. "Let's go see the firetruck."

Not only did Maverick get to see the firetruck, but he also got to climb inside it and go for a ride around the area in front of the firehouse, sirens blaring. Then Lt. Mitchell put him in a tiny harness, clipped the two of them into the basket of the cherry-picker, and had his crew extend it so that Maverick rose high in the air.

Eden waved up at him. "Hi, Maverick! Look at you!"

Sean took out his phone and snapped a few photos of mother waving to son and then a few shots of Maverick, zooming in to get the delighted expression on the boy's face. "That's a toddler living his best life."

When Maverick was on the ground again, the fire crew gathered around him, some wearing ODUs, others in turnout pants.

"This is for a brave boy who loves firetrucks." Lt. Mitchell handed Maverick a brightly wrapped gift.

Maverick looked up at Eden, confused.

"Go ahead, Maverick. It's for you. Open it."

Maverick plopped down onto his bottom and tore into the wrapping paper to reveal a little Coast Guard firefighter uniform, complete with helmet. His face lit up, and he held it up for his mother to see. "See, Mommy?"

Sean saw tears in Eden's eyes and had to swallow the lump in his throat.

She smiled, blinked the tears away, helped him settle the helmet on his little head. "Look at you, buddy!"

Then she turned to Lt. Mitchell and his crew. "Thank you

for this. It means so much to me—and you can see how happy you've made Maverick."

"You're welcome, ma'am. It was our honor to have you and your son here today." Lt. Mitchell turned to one of his crew. "Grab the balloons."

Ten minutes later, Sean tied down the balloons in the back of Eden's SUV, while she buckled Maverick into his car seat and set the uniform and helmet beside him.

Sean closed the liftgate and walked over to Eden. "Are you okay?"

She smiled, her hazel eyes warm. "I got a little choked up when Mavie opened his present, but I'm fine. Thank you for arranging this."

Sean reminded himself about controlling emotions. "You're welcome. You know I'm happy to help. I took some photos. I'll email them to you."

"Thanks." Eden climbed into her vehicle, rolled down the window. "I'm taking advantage of the good weather to go fishing. I hope to catch a yelloweye for fish tacos. Want to come along?"

That's a bad idea.

Sean had spent a lot of time on the *Sea Nymph*, Eden's cabin cruiser, and he had so many good memories—including memories of Eden in a bikini. Given the direction his thoughts had taken lately where she was concerned, he needed to keep his distance, not throw fuel on the fire.

He looked into her hazel eyes. "I'd love to."

EDEN SAVORED the rush of flying over the water. The ocean was her happy place. Ever since she was a little girl, she'd loved being on the water. She'd learned to pilot a boat as a teen, and the *Sea Nymph* had been Justin's wedding present to her.

Fire and Rain

Today was the first time she'd taken the boat out since Justin's death. As much as it made her miss Justin to be aboard the boat again, it also felt like coming home.

She'd left Maverick with her sister Maria, hoping to spend some time alone with Sean. She had no idea where she wanted this to go. All she knew for certain was that she cared about Sean and liked spending time with him. She found him sweet, funny, kind—and incredibly hot. She hadn't been able to get the image of his bare chest out of her mind. But she couldn't say what she wanted or where she hoped any of this would lead her.

Did she want to date him? Did she hope to sleep with him?

She felt a flutter in her belly, and her pulse picked up.

Was that a yes? Or was grief playing tricks on her?

He stood beside her looking sexier than any man should in khaki shorts and a blue T-shirt with a Haida sea turtle on the front. "Whale, eleven o'clock."

"I see it." Eden cut back on the throttle. Humpbacks often napped just below the surface with only their small dorsal fins showing. Careless boaters killed thousands of whales each year. "You've got good eyes."

He chuckled. "Believe it or not, Uncle Sam pays me to watch the water. You should see them from the air. You can see their entire bodies beneath the surface. It's incredible."

"I bet." She piloted the boat carefully through the water to the other side of Long Island, stopping at one of her favorite fishing spots. "We'll drop anchor here."

"I'm on it." Sean walked to the bow and tossed the anchor overboard.

She stepped out from behind the console, inhaled the fresh sea air, and looked around them. Sea lions lounged on an outcropping of rocks. An eagle perched on a tall Sitka spruce, surveying the water. On their starboard side was open ocean, where she could just see a huge cruise ship making its way to port.

With the boat bobbing gently in the water, they got to work, baiting their hooks with sliced herring and small bits of squid left from her uncle's fishing trip this morning. They cast their lines, Eden on the starboard side and Sean on the port side.

Since they'd been talking about his job...

"I hear you're working as a flight mech again." She tried to sound casual, as if she were asking him about the weather.

He glanced over at her, his eyes hidden behind his aviators. "That's what I signed on for. I love my job—most of the time."

Eden fought to keep her temper in check. "Justin loved it, too—right up to the moment it killed him. I've never understood how you guys can survive a helicopter crash and then climb aboard a helicopter again like it's no big deal."

He set his rod in the rod holder, crossed the boat, and did the same with hers. Then he drew her down on the bench beside him, his gaze level with hers. "What's wrong, Eden?"

Her emotions were too jumbled to explain, so she kept her inmost thoughts to herself. "I can't help but worry about you. Every time you go out, you're taking a risk. I felt safer knowing you were on the ground."

An eyebrow arched, and he grinned. "So, you care about what happens to me?"

"Of course, I do! Joke about it if you want to, but I'm serious. I don't know what I would have done without you these past five months. I ... I care about you, Sean."

"I'm sorry." He drew her against him, held her close. "I shouldn't tease you about it. I'm grateful for your concern, and I care about you, too."

She sank against him, held onto him. It felt so good to be

Fire and Rain

in his arms, his body hard against hers, his strength encircling her.

He tucked a finger beneath her chin and lifted her gaze to his. Then his brow furrowed, and his gaze dropped to her lips. Excitement and desire made her pulse pound, and for a moment, she was certain he was about to kiss her. She leaned closer, all but offering him her lips.

Then he lifted his gaze once again, his blue eyes looking into hers. "I promise I won't take chances with my life. I came close to dying once, and I don't want to repeat that experience. But I'm a flight mech. That's what I do—at least for now."

Disappointment lanced through her at the kiss that hadn't happened, her blood still running hot. She willed herself to smile. "I know."

Chapter Seven

It took all of Sean's will to let Eden go. "Let's get you that yelloweye."

Heart still racing, he turned away from her, walked back to his rod, neither of them speaking.

What the hell? You almost kissed her!

She had *wanted* him to kiss her. She had lifted her lips toward his, her body pressing against his with its soft curves. He'd seen desire in her eyes, had watched it become disappointment when he'd pulled away.

But she couldn't truly want *him*.

Justin had been gone for only five months. Eden wanted Justin, not him. She was probably missing a man's touch. Sean couldn't blame her for wanting to assuage her grief and loneliness. But if he'd kissed her, he would have led them both on a path to remorse. She would surely regret it, and Sean would hate himself for taking advantage of her vulnerability and loneliness—and for betraying Justin's friendship.

It was your job to keep Justin safe, and you failed. And now you want to sleep with his widow? What kind of bastard are you?

Fire and Rain

Sean had known it was a bad idea to come out on the boat with her, but he'd thought they would have a toddler for a chaperone. He hadn't known Maverick wasn't coming until he'd met Eden at the marina.

Sean knew he ought to say something to Eden to make it clear they could never be more than close friends. Or maybe he should just let it go, pretend it hadn't happened. He didn't want to embarrass her.

A harbor seal popped up about twenty yards off the port bow, its black eyes, dark nose, and round head giving it the look of a gray bowling ball.

"Hey, buddy."

"He was over here a moment ago. They're curious—and he probably hopes to steal our catch." There was a brightness to her voice, as if she were trying to hide her hurt.

Shit.

"Seals do that?"

Was he going to keep pretending nothing had just happened?

Apparently so.

"Right off the hook if they can."

"Damn." Sean looked the seal in the eyes. "You stay away, man."

"I got a bite."

The seal disappeared beneath the surface.

"I think the seal is headed your way." Sean glanced over his shoulder, saw Eden busy reeling in her catch, her rod flexing. "Looks like you got a good-sized one."

"Might be a halibut."

He felt a tug on his own rod. "I've got a bite, too."

A few minutes later, two good-sized halibut lay in the fish box.

"I guess the seal didn't want to steal our catch after all."

"I see why." Eden pointed to the black dorsal fin of an orca about a hundred yards to starboard. "The seal heard them coming and didn't want to be lunch."

They stayed for another hour, Sean catching a nice cod and Eden getting the yelloweye rockfish she'd wanted. But a bank of storm clouds was moving their way, gusty winds making for choppy seas. It was time for them to go.

They'd just rounded the southern tip of Long Island when a call came over the boat's VHF radio.

"Pan-pan. Pan-pan. Pan-pan. This is the Sunfish. We've got four people onboard about a mile south of Woody Island. Our motor died, and we're getting tossed around pretty bad."

Eden turned to Sean. "That's not far from here. We need to help them if we can."

Sean took the handset. "Sunfish, this is the Sea Nymph. What's the size of your vessel, over?"

"We are a twenty-foot cuddy cabin. I'm afraid these swells are going to flip us or drive us onto the rocks."

"Switch to Channel Sixteen." That was the channel the Coast Guard monitored. "We're headed your way. Let's see if we can haul you into the harbor. In the meantime, if you've got survival suits, put those on now."

While Eden piloted the *Sea Nymph* through the growing swells, Sean talked with the man to get more information about his situation and location, identifying himself as a Coastie. Then the Coast Guard joined in and said they were sending a boat.

"Sea Nymph, did you say you're with the Coast Guard, over?" a voice asked Sean.

"Yes, sir. I'm Petty Officer Sean McKenna, and I'm a flight mech."

"They're in good hands. You'll probably reach them before we do."

That's how it worked in Alaska. Everyone knew how treacherous the ocean could be. It didn't take long for a person to become hypothermic and die in these waters. When someone was in trouble, everyone tried to help.

It took less than fifteen minutes for the other vessel to come into view.

Eden pointed. "There they are—one o'clock."

"I see them." Sean waved to the four men aboard the small boat, then conned Eden into position, lining up the *Sea Nymph*'s stern with the other boat's bow. It wasn't easy, as the smaller craft rocked and turned helplessly in the water.

When they were lined up and in range, Sean motioned for the men to toss him the towline. He caught it and tied it to a bit on the transom of the *Sea Nymph*. "We're ready. Ease us forward, and let's see how this goes.

In the distance, he saw the Coast Guard vessel. It came within a hundred yards and followed them, just to make sure everyone got safely home.

Twenty minutes later, they entered the calmer water of Kodiak Harbor, leaving the Coast Guard boat behind.

Eden brought the men close to the boat take-out, knowing they'd want to service their motor. Then Sean untied the tow cable and let it go, inertia carrying the other boat safely to the edge of the water.

"Thank you!" the men called to them, waving.

Eden turned the *Sea Nymph* around, heading toward the marina to dock, her face flushed with excitement. "I've never done that before. It got my adrenaline flowing."

The awkwardness that had stretched between them seemed to be gone now.

"You did a fantastic job. If you were nervous, you didn't let it show."

She smiled up at him, her dark hair blowing in the wind. "I had one of the Coast Guard's finest with me."

He grinned. "Have I mentioned that I'm an airman and not a seaman?"

Eden laughed. "Now he tells me."

June 6

EDEN SETTLED Maverick in the living room with his blocks and loaded the breakfast dishes into the dishwasher, half listening to the local TV news. A fatal car accident on Monashka Bay Road. A minor temblor centered near Adak. Survivors of a small plane crash near Port Lions rescued by the Coast Guard.

Sean.

She couldn't get him out of her mind—or forget how good it had felt to be in his arms, his body strong and hard. The way he'd looked at her, desire in his eyes...

It still gave her belly flutters.

Why hadn't he kissed her? She was certain that he'd wanted to, but he had stopped himself. Did he still think of her as a married woman? Did he believe he was betraying Justin somehow? Was it the guilt he felt about Justin's death?

Maybe you misread him. Maybe he's not attracted to you in that way.

The few women he'd dated since arriving in Kodiak had all been tall blondes without children. Eden was none of those things. What did he think of her now? Would he avoid her, put distance between them?

Belly flutters turned to a knot of worry.

She hadn't heard from him since their fishing trip Friday. Not that she'd expected him to call necessarily. She knew he'd had at least one duty shift during that time, and she was sure he must be busy. It was peak fishing and tourist season, after all, and the weather had been rough all weekend with rain and forty-knot winds. She'd heard helicopters lifting off close to a dozen times since the storm began.

She dried her hands and walked into the living room to watch the weather report.

"We'll get sunshine this afternoon as this storm breaks up, with temperatures climbing back into the sixties by tomorrow."

Good.

She and Maverick could spend time outdoors tomorrow. In the meantime, she needed to get him dressed and head over to the base gym for his swimming lessons. She and Justin had been teaching Maverick to swim before Justin's death, but she hadn't been to class since.

"Are you ready to go swim, Maverick?"

He stood, block in his hand, as if trying to remember what that meant. Five months was probably an eternity to a toddler.

"Let's get you dressed." She held out her hand, smiled when he took it.

A half an hour later, she and Maverick arrived at the pool. A half dozen mothers and kids waited on benches for the lesson to begin. She knew most of them. They welcomed her, hesitancy in their eyes as if they didn't know what to say.

"It's so good to see you again." Kristin, whose husband was assigned to one of the boat crews, had a daughter close to Maverick's age. "How are you doing?"

Eden kept her answers light. "I'm doing better. We need to catch up on our swimming lessons. How are you?"

"I'm doing great. We're transferring to Miami in a few weeks. I can't wait to get back to warm weather and sunshine. Where are you planning to move?"

"I was born and raised on Kodiak Island, so I'm staying here."

"Oh. Wow! I didn't know that." Kristin switched topics.

"How is Sean McKenna? I saw the two of you at Crab Fest together."

There was a note of undeniable interest in Kristin's voice.

Eden kept her facial expression neutral. "He's doing well. He was Justin's best friend, so he's stopping by to help when he can. I asked him to go with us to Crab Fest. That's where Justin and I met, so it was hard. Sean was kind enough to make the time."

Kristin leaned closer. "If I weren't married, I'd snap him up. He's *hot*."

Eden didn't know whether Kristin was fishing for gossip or not, but she was spared having to respond by the timely arrival of Scott, the swim instructor.

In swim trunks and a swim shirt, he walked straight to Eden. "Welcome back, Eden. Hey, Maverick. Are you ready to get back in the pool, little buddy?"

Maverick pointed. "Swim pool."

Then mothers and children were allowed to get into the water.

Eden couldn't help smiling when she saw how much Mavie remembered. He could still tread water and turn in a circle by himself. He could also float on his back with a little support.

"Look at you, Mavie. You're a fish!"

Just like your daddy.

And it hit her again—how much of Maverick's life Justin would miss. Her heart sank, a hard lump in her throat.

The thought stayed with her for the rest of the swimming lesson. It stayed with her while she and Maverick ate lunch. It stayed with her while she showered away the chlorine and Maverick took his afternoon nap.

On its heels came another thought.

Was she truly interested in Sean, or was she just lonely?

If only God could return Justin to her. She would take

him back in a heartbeat, her brave, wonderful man. During the years they'd been together, she'd never wanted another man, not even Sean. He had been a good friend to them, like a brother.

But Justin wasn't coming back, and Sean...

Eden was twenty-eight. As much as she still grieved for Justin, she didn't want to spend the rest of her life alone. She wanted to share her life with a man. But not just any man. She wanted Sean.

How could one person have so many conflicting emotions?

June 8

Sean walked to the gym, grateful to have finally gotten some sleep. It had been one hell of a weekend. Since Friday, he'd flown on eight SAR missions, all of them on the water. At one point, they'd had every helo on station in the air, and they'd had to bring in flight crews that were on their day off. He was certain it must have been just as busy for the boat crews. In the end, their missions had been successful, and that's what mattered.

He left his gym bag in a locker, grabbed a towel, and walked to the weight room. Trey and Wade were there, along with Dalton and some of the new AETs, classic rock coming from the speakers.

Trey saw him first. "Hey, man, did you get some sleep?"

"Yeah." He'd had another nightmare, but he didn't say that. "You?"

"I'm good to go."

Sean couldn't remember if this was an upper body, core, or legs day, but since he had time, he decided to do a full-body workout, starting with upper body. Since he didn't have a spotter, he chose the machines over free weights. He'd only been here a few times since getting his arm out of the brace, and he couldn't shake the sense of loss. He and Justin had always tried to work out together, spotting for one another, and being here without him…

It gave him just an inkling of what life must be like for Eden.

Sean set the weight for the bench press machine, pushing himself to muscle failure, his mind on Eden—again. He hadn't called her since they'd gone out on her boat, mostly because he hadn't had time. When he hadn't been in the air, he'd been handling the basics—meals, showers, and shut-eye. Still, some part of him seemed frozen in time, stuck in that moment when she'd raised her lips to his—and he'd turned away.

What kind of an idiot are you?

He was the kind of idiot who tried to do the right thing.

"Hey, McKenna, I heard you on the radio on Friday," Trey called to him. "You rescued some mariners, man. Are you thinking of moving to the boat crews?"

Sean chuckled. "Not a chance."

"He rescued some mariners?" Dalton turned Sean's way.

Sean got up from the machine, shook out his arms. "I was out fishing with Eden Koseki and the call came in over the radio from a small boat that had lost its engine. We were nearby, so we got their location and towed them back to the harbor."

James walked in, acknowledged them with a nod, and walked to one of the treadmills. He looked like he hadn't slept in a week.

Dalton's expression changed. "You were with Eden? You're spending a lot of time with her. Foraging. Dinner. Crab Fest. And now fishing?"

Sean moved to the triceps press machine. "I had no idea you were so interested in my schedule. Are you writing my unauthorized biography or something?"

Trey and some of the AETs laughed.

Dalton didn't. "It just seems like you spend a lot of time with her."

Sean set the weight, then lowered it, needing to be mindful of his shoulder. "She's my best friend's widow. We're like family. What am I supposed to do—avoid her?"

Sean heard the anger in his voice, his temper fueled by a sense of guilt. He sat and pushed his way through a set. He'd never gotten together with Eden for any sexual reason. But the attraction was there.

Oh, hell, yes, it was.

But if people were talking about him and Eden...

Dalton didn't let up. "No, but you don't want people to get the wrong idea."

"You weren't close to Koseki or his wife, and you weren't on the helo the night Koseki died. What's it to you?" James set the treadmill. "Maybe you should mind your own business."

Sean finished his set, stood, and moved to the next machine, making brief eye contact with James, who looked exhausted, lines of stress on his face.

There were no more questions from Dalton after that, and Sean finished his workout in peace. He headed to the locker room and found Wade dressing out. He looked worse than James. "Late night?"

"We've had an outbreak of scarlet fever on base."

"Scarlet fever?"

"Yeah. The daycare center and some staff at the rec center have come down with it. I've treated a dozen people since last night, mostly small children."

"Damn." Sean stripped, grabbed a clean towel. "What are

you doing here? You should be in your bunk getting some sleep."

"I want to swim a few laps and burn off some stress before I hit the rack." Wade pulled up his swim trunks, then met Sean's gaze. "I never thanked you for pulling me out of that helicopter."

"I didn't do much." Sean could barely remember that part of it.

"You helped me unbuckle, got me in a rescue hold with your left arm, and pulled me out of a sinking helo when I could barely think straight. I'd call that something." Wade shifted uncomfortably. "I still dream about it sometimes—the explosion, the crash."

"So do I." Sean hadn't admitted that to anyone, but he didn't want Wade to think he was alone. "I don't remember all of that, but you're welcome. You handled it well."

"Thanks." Wade grabbed a towel and headed off for his swim.

Before Sean stepped into the shower, he took out his cellphone and shot Eden a text just to make sure she and Maverick were okay. He still hadn't gotten a reply by the time he'd dried off and dressed. So, he called her.

No answer.

He left a voice message. "Hey, Eden. It's Sean. Just checking in to see how you and the little man are doing. Give me a call when you get a moment."

He told himself she was probably out foraging or visiting her grandma or one of her sisters, but an odd sense of misgiving had taken hold. Unable to shake the feeling, he walked to his vehicle and drove up the hill toward Eden's house.

Chapter Eight

EDEN STRUGGLED to stand so she could put on a pair of jeans. She couldn't remember the last time she'd felt so sick. Her throat hurt so much she could barely swallow. Her stomach hurt, too, and she had a terrible headache.

Mavie was sick, as well. When he'd first started running a fever, she'd thought it was just a cold or maybe another ear infection. She'd made an appointment to see his pediatrician today, but by last night he was vomiting, crying, and refusing to eat. His face had become bright red, too—probably from his fever.

She'd woken up in the middle of the night with a fever of 102 and the worst sore throat ever. She'd taken acetaminophen and had dragged extra blankets onto her bed to stay warm, Mavie snuggled beneath the covers beside her. Neither of them had gotten much sleep. She'd thought for a moment of calling her mother or one of her sisters to help this morning, but she didn't want anyone else in the family to catch this.

Fighting dizziness, she sat on the edge of the bed and slipped on her jeans before getting onto her feet and searching for her bra and a T-shirt. She'd just pulled the T-shirt over her head when someone knocked on her door. She wasn't expecting anyone and needed to get Mavie dressed for their trip to the doctor.

The knock came again, and she thought she heard a voice. "Eden?"

Was that Sean?

Leaving Maverick on her bed, she walked into the hallway, feet bare, and made her way toward the front door, trying not to pass out. She peeked out the front window, then opened the door. "Hey."

"You look terrible."

"I bet you say that to all the girls."

He didn't laugh. "What's going on? Where's Mavie?"

"He's sick. We're both really sick. You probably shouldn't be here."

"To hell with that. We need to get you to the clinic. Is he in his crib?"

"My bed." She sank onto the sofa, head throbbing, her throat so painful. "I have an appointment for Mavie, but I'm really dizzy."

Sean knelt before her, touched a hand to her forehead. "You're burning up. I think you've both got scarlet fever. It's going around the base. Wade Sheppard told me this morning. Apparently, it spread via the rec center."

"Scarlet fever? We went to swimming lessons two days ago."

"You stay here. I'll get Mavie. Then I'll help you get your jacket and shoes, and I'll drive you to urgent care."

Eden felt like crying. "Thank you."

"That's what friends are for." Sean disappeared toward the back.

Not wanting to be a burden, Eden stood, slipped her bare feet into hiking boots, and grabbed her warmest winter parka even though it was a sunny day. By the time Sean returned carrying Maverick, she was back on the sofa, head spinning.

"Where are your car keys?"

She had to think. "They should be in the kitchen in a basket next to the fridge."

He walked into the kitchen. "Got them. I'll take Maverick out, get him into his car seat, and then come back for you."

Eden shook her head. "I'm good. Just take care of Mavie."

She stood and followed them, her palm splayed against the wall for balance. By the time she reached the steps down to the garage, Sean was there.

"I've got you, sweetheart."

Had he called her sweetheart?

He helped her into her seat and then climbed into the driver's side. Then the garage door came up, and Sean backed her SUV out of the driveway.

Eden leaned back in the seat. "Can you turn on the seat warmers?"

Sean glanced at her, his brow furrowed with concern. "Sure thing."

In the back, Maverick began to cry.

Sean looked back at Maverick in the rearview mirror. "I'm so sorry you're sick, buddy. We're going to the doctor right now. They're going to make you feel a lot better."

Eden reached back and held Mavie's hand until they reached the urgent care.

Sean parked. "Wait here."

Eden wasn't sure why she was waiting—until Sean returned with a wheelchair. He opened her door. "No arguments. You can sit and hold Maverick, and I'll wheel you both in. I told them what's going on. They want you to go straight to a room."

"Okay." With Sean beside her, she climbed out and sat in the chair.

A moment later, he placed Maverick in her lap, and inside they went.

Eden kissed her boy's forehead, held him close. "We'll take good care of you."

Once inside the facility, a woman in scrubs led directly to an exam room. The doctor who saw them knew about the outbreak on base. He did rapid strep tests. In ten minutes, he diagnosed them both with scarlet fever.

"You see the rash on Maverick's tummy and cheeks?" He pointed. "That's the hallmark of scarlet fever. I can give you both penicillin injections, or you can take pills and Maverick can take liquid Amoxicillin. I'd recommend some prophylactic antibiotics for you, Sean. Unless you plan on heading to the base clinic today, I've got some samples I can give you. I wouldn't normally do that, but the Coast Guard is an essential part of the Kodiak community."

Eden chose the injection, but she didn't want to put Maverick through that.

In less than an hour, they were back in the vehicle, anti-nausea meds and antibiotics for Maverick and pills for Sean in a paper bag in Eden's lap.

"Thank you, Sean. Thanks for showing up when you did—and for driving us. I could have managed, but it would have been a lot harder."

He glanced over at her, smiled. "Are you kidding? You could barely stand. With that kind of fever, you shouldn't be behind the wheel. I'm happy to help."

He parked the vehicle in the garage, carried Maverick inside, then helped Eden the rest of the way into the house. He took her coat, hung it on the coat tree. "Get into your pajamas and back in bed. I'll give Maverick his first dose of meds."

There must have been surprise on her face because Sean chuckled. "Did you think I was just going to drop you off and head back to the barracks?"

Fire and Rain

"I guess I did. I mean ... we're not your problem."

Serious now, he looked into her eyes. "You're never a problem, Eden."

SEAN DIDN'T REALIZE how much effort went into getting a toddler to take his medicine. He found himself cajoling, clowning around, and saying ridiculous things to get Maverick, who clearly felt awful, to open his mouth and drink. "I know it's no fun with a sore throat, little guy, but this will make you feel better."

When that didn't work, he changed tack, making siren noises. "Hey, look, it's a firetruck. It's trying to come inside."

Maverick finally opened his mouth and took the medicine.

"Good job, Maverick!" Sean held out his closed fist. "Fist bump."

Mavie gave a little smile and rapped his knuckles against Sean's. "Fiss bump."

"Right on." Sean put the bottle of amoxicillin in the refrigerator and rinsed the measuring spoon for use again later. "Well done, little dude."

"You got him to take his medicine?" Eden stood there in a lavender sleeveless sleep shirt and bathrobe, her slender legs bare, her lush breasts unencumbered by a bra.

Do not stare at her breasts. Don't even look in the breastular region.

Sean kept his gaze on her face and lied. "Yeah. No problem."

"Uh-huh." Eden clearly didn't believe him. "I'm going to give him more acetaminophen, and we'll go take a nap."

Maverick was okay with the acetaminophen, but he didn't want to take a nap. He flopped on the floor in front of a *Thomas & Friends* video. Sean made tea while Eden covered her son with a blanket then curled up on the sofa beneath a throw.

He handed her a cup. "I added honey and lemon for your throat."

"Thanks." She took a sip, and he could tell it hurt her to swallow. "How did you know to come here?"

He sat on the other end of the sofa. "I just had a bad feeling. I sent a text, and you didn't answer. Then I called, and you still didn't answer. That made me worry."

"I'm sorry to worry you, but I'm really glad you came. I lost my phone. I heard it buzz but couldn't find it. It's somewhere in my bedroom."

"I'll find it." Sean walked to the bedroom with his phone, dialed the number, and followed a faint buzzing sound to the head of the bed. The phone was there between the headboard and the mattress. He walked back to the living room and handed it to Eden.

"Thanks." She sipped. "How was the weekend? It sounded busy."

Sean told her about the eight cases he'd flown on—a trawler hard aground, two boats taking on water, one with engine trouble, two with malfunctioning bilge pumps, one boat taking on water from a hull leak, and an injury on a crabber.

Eden yawned. "Sorry. It's not your stories. I just didn't sleep much last night."

"Go lie down, get some sleep. I'll grab a book or something and watch over the munchkin."

"Are you sure?

"Of course."

She pushed off the throw, and Sean stood, offering support in case she felt dizzy again. She wrapped the throw around her shoulders. "Thanks, Sean."

Fire and Rain

Then she walked down the hallway and disappeared inside the bedroom.

Sean walked over to check on Maverick, who was focused on the talking trains on the television. "I used to watch Thomas the Tank Engine, too, you know."

Maverick pointed to the TV. "Thomas."

"I see that." Sean walked over to the bookshelf to grab something to read.

A history of the Coast Guard. A biography of George Washington. Another about Winston Churchill.

Didn't you read anything fun, Justin?

A photo.

It was a small photograph of him and Justin the day they'd graduated from boot camp. How long ago that seemed now. They looked so young—just boys dreaming of heroism and adventures, wanting to save the world.

He put the photo back on the shelf. Then he noticed the other half of the bookshelf. These were Eden's books. Most had covers in pastel shades—pink, purple, and blue. One was about pregnancy, and there were a couple about parenting. But the rest...

Sean read the authors' names—Kaylea Cross, Toni Anderson, Katie Reus, Zoe York, Grace Burrowes. He pulled one off the shelf at random, turned it over to see its cover.

Whoa.

Talk about beefcake.

The front was an image of a ripped guy with no chest hair, the surf behind him. He looked ready to fight—or fuck. So, these were the kinds of books Eden enjoyed. Come to think of it, Justin had mentioned her love of romance novels once or twice.

She reads romances when I'm away. When I get home, I get the fringe benefits—if you know what I mean. And I think you do.

The DVD ended, so Sean inserted the next one. "Are you ready for more Thomas the Tank engine?"

His cheeks red, Maverick said something about Thomas that Sean couldn't quite understand. He knelt, touched a hand to the boy's forehead. "I'm going to get you a drink of water, okay?"

When he came back with the water in a sippy cup, Maverick sat up and drank, and Sean felt oddly accomplished. He'd never been responsible for a small child before. But this was going well.

With Maverick settled again, Sean took the book he'd picked out—the one with the ripped guy on the beach—and began to read. But he'd gotten only a few pages before Maverick walked up to him.

"Poopy."

Shit.

Sean set the novel aside, stood, and lifted Maverick into his arms, getting a whiff of his dirty diaper.

Whew.

He didn't want to deal with this, but he wasn't about to wake Eden for a dirty diaper. "Okay, buddy. Let's do this. How hard can it be to change a diaper?"

EDEN WOKE BRIEFLY when Sean laid a sleeping Maverick in bed with her. She drew her son beneath her covers.

"I'll bring you more water." Sean picked up the empty glass on her nightstand. "How do you feel?"

She winced as she swallowed. "My throat hurts, and I'm so cold."

"When did you last take anything?"

She had to think. "Before we went to the clinic."

When Sean returned, he had two tablets of acetaminophen and water. "Here."

She sat up, took the pills, and set the glass back where it had been. "Thank you."

"Just sleep. I'll be here when you wake up."

When Eden awoke the next morning, her sore throat wasn't as bad, and she felt hot—and hungry. She'd gotten up for a short time yesterday evening for more acetaminophen, and some chicken noodle soup that Sean cooked from a can. She'd had strange dreams, but she couldn't remember anything specific.

She heard Sean's voice and knew Maverick must be with him. She sat up, got to her feet, and smiled when she heard Maverick laugh. She couldn't believe what Sean had done for them over the past twenty-four hours. Yes, she could have managed on her own, but it would have been so much tougher.

Feeling weak as a kitten, she slowly walked to the kitchen to find Maverick picking at a plate of scrambled eggs, while Sean sat next to him, urging him to eat.

Sean saw her and stood. "Hey. How are you feeling?"

"Weak, but better."

"You sit. I'll make some tea."

She sat. "Good morning, Mavie. Did Sean make you some eggs? You look like you're feeling better."

Maverick put a hand to his throat, his cheeks still flaming red. "Owie."

"Your throat is still a little sore? Mine, too." She touched his forehead. "You're not as hot as you were. Gosh, it's probably past time for your next dose—"

"Relax." Sean set the kettle on to boil. "He's had four

doses now—three yesterday and one this morning when he woke up. I changed him a few times, too. I don't know what you usually do with the poopy diapers, so I carried them out to the trash."

Eden gaped at him. The man who avoided relationships and swore he'd never be a father had done what a husband would do. He'd done what Justin would have done if he'd still been alive. "I can't believe you did all this—and I slept through it."

"You were pretty sick and exhausted. It's good that you slept."

"Did you sleep at all?"

"Yeah. I crashed on the sofa. I've slept here before, you know. Maverick crawled out of your bed and woke me up at about seven. He and I are good buddies, right?"

Maverick held out his little fist. "Fiss bump."

Sean gently knocked knuckles with Mavie. "That's right."

Eden's heart melted. "I wish I had that on camera."

Sean made breakfast for himself and Eden, too, and they ate together. "I got an email from the commander this morning. Sixteen kids and five adults have come down with scarlet fever so far. They're asking people to stay on base if at all possible. They don't want it spreading in town."

"Good idea."

Sean reached out, ran his thumb over her cheek. "Your face is as red as Maverick's now."

A jolt of awareness shot through her, her face hot where he'd touched her. "I ... I really don't know how to thank you for all of this."

A brown eyebrow arched. "I'd have to be a complete jerk to go home knowing how sick you were. I care about you, Eden—and little Maverick. And, hey, now I can say I'm a veteran diaper changer."

She couldn't help but laugh. "I should get you a T-shirt that says that."

Sean chuckled. "I'd wear it."

"I always thought Justin was a little jealous of you, the single guy who could do whatever he wanted when he wasn't on duty. Now look at you—changing diapers, giving toddlers their medicine, making breakfast for the toddler's sick mother."

Sean took her hand. "Justin was never jealous of me. He never said anything about feeling weighed down by you or Maverick. He told me all the time how lucky he was to have married you. You and Maverick were his world."

Eden hadn't realized how much she'd needed to hear those words. She swallowed the lump in her throat. "Thanks."

"You had something special with him, and I'm sorry it ended."

She squeezed his hand. "I know you are. So am I. And Sean, it's *not* your fault."

He released her hand, got to his feet. "I'll do the dishes."

"Do you mind watching Maverick while I take a shower?"

"Go for it."

Eden showered away the last twenty-four hours of sickness, touched by what Sean had told her. She dressed in a T-shirt and leggings and found Sean and Maverick on the floor, playing with blocks, that little helicopter coming together once more. She sat on the sofa, watching them play. Then she saw it—one of her romance novels sitting on the coffee table with a bookmark stuck in it.

She picked it up. "You've been reading my romance novels?"

"Just the one." He gave her a knowing and very sexy look. "It's super sexy. I mean... wow. It's good, too—suspenseful, smart. I'm not sure what I expected from a romance novel, but I'm enjoying it."

Eden wanted to ask him what he thought of certain scenes but stopped herself.

When the helicopter was complete, Sean got to his feet. "I need to get back. Do you need anything else before I go?"

She shook her head. "I think we're on the mend.

He grabbed his jacket and gym bag and put on his running shoes. "You'll call me if you need anything, right?"

"I will." She stood on tiptoe and kissed his cheek. "Thanks again—for everything."

"You got it." Then he walked over to the coffee table and picked up the book. "Do you mind if I borrow this?"

"You want to borrow one of my romance novels?"

"Well, yeah." He gave her an incredulous look. "I have to know what happens with Sierra and Beckett."

"By all means. Just don't dog-ear the pages."

He feigned offense. "I'm not a heathen."

Then, with a smile that made her pulse skip, he said goodbye and was gone.

Chapter Nine

June 9

Sean's next duty shift didn't start until evening, so he took advantage of the time to clean his quarters in preparation for the routine barracks inspection. When that was done, he grabbed his laundry bag, detergent, and fabric softener and headed to the laundry room, his thoughts on Eden as he shoved dirty socks, boxers, and ODUs into the washing machine.

She'd been surprised to find out he'd given Maverick his medicine and changed his diaper, her gratitude palpable. It hit Sean again how much she'd lost—not just the man she loved but the father of her child, the man who would have been beside her through sickness and hard times. Now she would have to face those times alone.

No, not alone. Sean wouldn't let that happen.

What exactly are you going to do about it?

Given that the captain was pushing to advance him to E6, the Coast Guard would almost certainly transfer him to a new station. He'd end up in Cape Cod, Atlantic City, or Puerto Rico—too far away to do anything to help Eden and her boy.

Her entire family lives here. She has four sisters. She and Maverick will be fine.

The moment the thought crossed his mind, he rejected it. He'd been the one to help her through the paperwork relating to Justin's death. She'd asked *him* to go with her to Crab Fest. He'd stayed with her when she was sick.

So, you think she needs you. Is that it?

A part of him shouted *yes* in answer to that question. Then another thought struck him, hitting him square in the chest.

If you'd done your job, Justin would still be here. She wouldn't need you at all.

Fuck.

Swamped by a mixture of grief and guilt, he poured the detergent and fabric softener into their dispensers and slammed the washer door.

"I hate laundry too, but go easy on the machine, man." Trey walked in behind him with a basket of dirty laundry.

"Right. Sorry."

"Haven't seen you for a couple of days." Trey dumped his laundry in the machine, not bothering to sort it. "Did you meet some island hottie and mess up her sheets?"

"Eden and Maverick had scarlet fever. She could barely stay on her feet. I took care of Maverick so she could sleep."

"Holy shit. Scarlet fever? I heard that's going around base. Are they going to be okay? What about you?"

"They were both doing a lot better this morning. The doc who saw them gave me prophylactic penicillin so I wouldn't catch it."

"You're a regular Florence Nightingale. I'll call you Flo from now on."

Sean shook his head. This was the sort of thing that caught

on and stayed with a man through his career. "No, really, don't."

"Okay, Flo, whatever you say."

"Not funny, man."

"Are you kidding, Flo?" Trey called after him. "It's hilarious!"

Back in his quarters, Sean got busy cleaning, trying to keep his mind off Eden but quickly realizing that was a losing battle. Images from the past twenty-four hours slid one after another through his mind. Eden so sick she could barely stand. Eden asleep, Maverick in her arms. Eden laughing when he'd asked to borrow her book.

The day he'd spent at her place hadn't been the least bit romantic. It had involved sickness, a grumpy toddler, and dirty diapers. But somehow it had felt... *right*.

Sean had never given a thought to being a father. He wanted a lover as much as the next man, but he'd chosen to focus on his career instead. There was a freedom to fitting everything he owned into a few duffel bags and moving from place to place—no attachments, no obligations, no worries beyond the job.

But taking care of Eden and Maverick yesterday had brought him a kind of satisfaction he hadn't known before. They had *needed* him. *She* had needed him. And some part of him had responded.

You want her.

Sean threw himself into scrubbing his shower stall, trying to ignore the direction his thoughts had taken. When that was done, he walked down the hall to the laundry room and tossed his wet laundry into the dryer. Then he went back to his quarters, stripped, and climbed into the shower, his thoughts drifting back to Eden.

You want her.

Hell, yes, he did. But he'd be lower than a snake's asshole if he moved in on his best friend's widow. What kind of man did that?

Even as he rejected the idea, he couldn't keep her out of his mind. Lush curves. Slender brown legs. Big hazel eyes. And those lips...

His body responded, his cock going hard, arousal heavy in his groin.

He gave in, stroking himself to a quick climax, the release intense.

Afterward, he dried off, dressed, and sank onto his bunk, guilt setting in. He was stronger than this. He was better than this.

He was in trouble.

He had a few hours before he went on duty, so he reached for the copy of *Fractured Honor* he'd borrowed, hoping to distract himself with Sierra and Beckett's story. Maybe they could take his mind off Eden.

AFTER A LIGHT SUPPER, Eden packed Maverick in the car and drove the two of them down Aviation Hill and onto base. She craved fresh air but wasn't yet feeling up to anything strenuous. Given that it was now low tide, it was the perfect time for one of her favorite pastimes—beachcombing.

She passed the air station and wondered what Sean was doing right now. She was so grateful for his help—and more than a little surprised he'd stayed. The man who didn't want to be a father cajoling Maverick into taking his medicine and changing poopy diapers?

He helped because he's Justin's best friend and a good guy, not because he's interested in you. When he could have kissed you, he turned away.

Fire and Rain

That thought brought her mood down a couple of notches.

She parked as close as she could to the water, got Maverick from his car seat, and retrieved their two buckets—a little orange plastic pail for him and a five-gallon bucket for her. "Are you ready to go beachcombing, Mavie?"

He pointed toward the water. "Sheshell."

"We'll find seashells and maybe sea glass and who knows what else." Her grandmother had once found a piece of ancient walrus tusk.

Wearing rain boots, they walked slowly along Jewel Beach, Eden teaching Maverick the names of things, the ocean lapping at their feet. Maverick stopped every few feet to look at something, collecting small treasures and putting them in his pail as she had done at his age. Cockle, clam, and mussel shells. A stick worn smooth by the water. A rusted bottle cap.

Eden looked for sea glass, picking it up as she went—bits of green, white, and occasionally blue glass worn smooth by the sea. She probably had ten pounds of sea glass in the garage at home. She'd always wanted to make something with it—jewelry, maybe, or a mosaic.

Maverick pointed to several ochre sea stars left behind a large rock by the outgoing tide. "Mommy, see?"

That was his way of asking her to explain something he'd seen or found.

"I see! Look at those sea stars. We don't want to bother them. They're taking a nap so they can be rested when the tide comes back in."

Maverick looked up at her through innocent brown eyes. "Naptime?"

"Yes, it's naptime for the sea stars."

They moved on, the fresh air and sea spray exactly what Eden needed after being so sick. The beach was her favorite place. There was something about the rhythm of the surf and the lapping of the waves that seemed like the earth breathing, the retreat of the water an inhale, waves spilling over rock and sand an exhale.

When Justin had been alive, she'd come here almost every day, but she hadn't been here since his death. It had been too hard to face this place. Jewel Beach had been their spot, their special place. For that reason, it was full of bittersweet echoes.

Justin had kissed her for the first time just over there. He'd gotten to one knee and proposed on a sunny September day there where the land jutted into the sea. She'd told him she was pregnant when they'd stood together at the far end over there. He'd been with her a week before Maverick was born when she'd found her favorite piece of sea glass—the big cobalt blue piece. She'd taken that to be a sign that they'd live a long and happy life together.

She'd been wrong. Out there, fifty miles offshore, he'd died, consumed in a flash by flames. It hit her in a way it hadn't before that the water lapping at her boots was his grave.

Oh, Justin!

She looked out over the water, let grief wash through her. She wanted to tell Justin that she missed him. She wanted him to know she and Maverick were okay. She also needed to tell him that she had feelings for Sean.

Did she want his blessing, his permission to move on, his approval to have feelings for another man?

Maybe.

Eden knew Justin couldn't hear her, but she spoke to him anyway. "Sean has been good to us. He blames himself for your death. I know he does, even if he won't come right out and say it. I care about him, Justin. He's—"

Something in the surf caught her eye as it rolled over her boot—something red. She bent over and caught it before the waves could take it again.

Red sea glass.

Red sea glass was rare, the color most beachcombers hoped to find.

It was small, not much bigger than a dime. She washed the sand away and held it up—and saw that it was shaped like a heart.

The breath left her lungs, and her throat went tight, tears filling her eyes. She closed her hand around the precious bit of glass and looked out to sea. Maybe she was crazy, but it felt like a message. For a bit of red sea glass to wash over her boot while she was speaking to Justin, and one shaped like a heart at that—it couldn't be a coincidence.

Justin loved you, and I think he would want you to be happy.

Her grandmother's words came back to her, happiness, grief, and hope tangling inside Eden's chest. How could she feel so many emotions at one time?

Nearby, Maverick poked at the float from a long piece of bull kelp. "See?"

She turned her attention back to the present, red sea glass gripped tightly in one hand. "I see. That's bull kelp. That bulb helps it float."

In the distance, she heard the whir of an approaching helicopter, the orange and white of a returning H-60 already visible.

Mavie looked up, pointed. "Copta."

"Yes, that's a helicopter just like your daddy used to fly in." She took Maverick's little hand. "It's time to go home."

The tide was turning.

THE BOOK HELPED DISTRACT Sean for a time. He was quite caught up in Sierra and Beckett's story. Then it turned steamy. Scorching hot. He found himself imagining Eden reading the sex scenes and getting turned on—until he'd remembered Justin telling him that he'd been the beneficiary of her reading habits.

Shit.

Wishing he had time to finish the story, he marked his place in the book, set it aside, and went to the cafeteria for dinner. Then it was time for the change-of-shift briefing. The weather had been calm, so it had been a quiet day—apart from a medevac for a fisherman who'd cast his line and caught himself in the eye with his hook.

Sean went back to his quarters to get ready for his duty shift but had barely pulled on his thermals when the SAR alarm went off.

In the hallway, he ran into Trey, who was also on duty, and the two of them walked together toward the lockers.

"Hey, Flo, you left your clothes in the dryer."

"Shit!"

"Not to worry. I grabbed your stuff and put it all in your duffel bag. It's on the table."

"Thanks." Sean would get it when he got back from this case.

Trey dropped the teasing and lowered his voice. "Have you talked to Spurrier lately? He seems... I don't know... Stressed or distracted."

"He's probably just tired. He flew a lot of SAR missions this past week."

Hell, they all had.

"Do you think the accident could be affecting him?"

Sean remembered what James had told him about the adrenaline rush he'd gotten flying his first mission after the crash. "We've both flown with him since, and I haven't noticed any difference in his performance."

"I haven't either. It's more when we're back on deck. He keeps to himself and seems grumpier than usual. He's just ... not himself."

"Piloting a helicopter that crashed into the ocean at the cost of two crewmen's lives would change anyone."

"You seem okay."

"I live with the memory of what happened every day, man."

They reached the lockers to find James and Zeke dressing out and discussing the new SAR case.

James brought them up to speed. "We've got an injured surfer stranded on an unnamed spit of rock about a mile offshore from Fossil Beach. A fixed-wing pilot spotted him clinging to some kind of navigation marker and called it in to Sector. High tide will cover those rocks and wash him out to sea. We'll have a forty-knot headwind, and there's rain expected in the next hour. We've got an hour and ten minutes before the tide is in, but he'll be submerged long before then. Let's move."

"Roger that." Sean dressed out quickly and hurried to the helicopter.

They moved efficiently through their safety check and took to the skies, heading toward Fossil Beach. While James radioed Sector for amplifying information about the surfer's injuries, Sean studied a map, trying to get some idea of where this was. The Coast Guard maintained aids to navigation, so the marker ought to be listed.

"There's nothing on the map—nada, zip."

James' voice came over Sean's headphones. "Sector says he's got a strobe. No one has had contact with him, so no one knows how badly injured he is or how long he's been there. The pilot who reported him said there are no cliffs to worry about."

Trey added his two cents. "If he's been out there for a while, he's got to be hypothermic and dehydrated."

While Trey assembled what he'd need for an IV and took

out a Wiggy's hypothermia bag, Sean got the basket ready for the hoist and moved into position.

"You've got door speed," James said.

Sean opened the cabin door. "Cabin door open."

"Roger that."

Sean watched for the outcropping and the surfer, grateful that it wasn't yet dark. "Switching my NVGs on."

Though they were called night vision goggles, they were infrared, revealing heat signatures in daytime just as well as at night.

"Is there any chance he might have been dragged to sea already?" Trey asked.

James answered him. "We've got a full tank, so we'll keep searching until we hit bingo fuel levels."

Sean searched the surface of the water. "I don't see any... Wait. There he is at our three o'clock. He's getting knocked around hard by the waves. There's barely anything left of that outcropping. We need to move fast."

While James circled around and brought the helicopter to a hover nearby—he didn't want to blow the surfer into the water with rotor wash by hovering directly above him—Sean and Trey devised a strategy. Sean would lower Trey in the basket, and Trey would help the surfer climb in. Then Sean would send down the hook to retrieve Trey.

"Let's do this." While Trey climbed into the basket, Sean did the safety check. "Safety check complete. Swimmer is in the basket."

"Begin the hoist."

"Roger that." Sean pushed the basket out of the cabin. "Swimmer is leaving the cabin."

He kept a hold of the hoist line, lowering Trey to the water near the surfer. "Swimmer has reached the survivor."

Trey climbed out and helped the surfer, who was limping, to climb in.

"The survivor is in the basket." Sean operated the controls to raise the basket, keeping an eye on Trey, who was now the one stranded. "Survivor is outside the cabin."

He grabbed the basket, dragged it into the cabin. "The survivor is in the cabin."

Shaking and weak, the surfer crawled out and sat, terror in his eyes, tears on his face. "I-I th-thought I was d-dead."

"Not today, buddy." This was why Sean loved his job. "We'll get you warmed up and back home again."

One hoist later, Trey was back in the cabin and working on the survivor.

James radioed ops. "This is Coast Guard Rescue Six-Oh-Two-Three. We have the survivor on board and are RTB."

Chapter Ten

June 11

EDEN CHECKED her reflection in the mirror, the sight of herself in this little black dress with nails and makeup unleashing bittersweet memories.

Damn, babe, you look hot. Don't zip it. What do you say I unwrap you like a Christmas present and make us fashionably late?

With her eyes closed, Eden could almost feel Justin's lips against her throat as he'd undressed her. He'd made love to her, the two of them arriving breathless and a half an hour late to the Air Station holiday party. That was the last time she'd worn this dress. It was also the last time she'd dressed up, apart from Justin's memorial service.

Then it hit her.

It was exactly five months today since Justin's death.

It felt like an eternity.

Today was also her older sister Maria's thirtieth birthday, and Eden had left Maverick with her mother so she could celebrate with her sisters at the Hangout Bar & Grill. The

Fire and Rain

Hangout was the pub where Coasties mingled with locals, and it, too, held a lot of memories. Eden hadn't been avoiding the place, exactly, but she'd known that going there again would be hard.

Val Larsen, the pub's owner, kept a Wall of Heroes with portraits and newspaper clippings about Coasties from Kodiak who'd died in the line of duty. Eden had been there when Val had nailed up a framed photo of Justin and had tearfully accepted a toast in his honor. But she hadn't been back since.

She finished dressing, grabbed a warm jacket, and set out. The Hangout was only six miles down the road from base, so it took just a few minutes to drive there. It was a Saturday night, so they'd made an early reservation, hoping to beat the weekend rush and ensure that Maria got her clam chowder before it was sold out.

As Eden pulled into the parking lot, she recognized Natasha's, Anya's, and Katie's trucks. She parked beside Katie, grabbed her handbag, and walked up the ramp to the front door. A flyer on the door told her that the Outriggers, a local cover band, was performing tonight. Eden had gone to high school with Lynette, the drummer.

She walked inside to find the stage empty and her sisters waiting for her. They waved when they saw her, and she hurried over to their table, trying not to let herself get sucked down by memories. "Hey!"

Maria got to her feet and hugged Eden. "You look gorgeous. But how can you live closest to this place and get here last?"

"I love that red dress." Eden hugged her back then took her seat. "I had to drive Mavie to Mom's place. Baba was there, and we got to talking.

Her sisters let out a chorus of "Ahhs," no further explanation necessary.

A server brought their menus. "You all look so much alike. You must be—"

"Sisters," they said, almost in unison.

"I thought so."

Eden placed her drink order. "A glass of white wine, please."

Natasha, the oldest at thirty-two, turned to Maria. "How's your birthday been so far?"

"It's been perfect. Chris and the girls made me breakfast in bed, but Mattie accidentally tipped over the coffee. The mattress has a big old stain now."

"Oh, no!" Katie laughed. "Poor Mattie. I bet she felt awful."

Then Maria showed them her glittering pink nails and told them how Chris had set her up for a pedicure and manicure as a gift. "He's such a good guy."

"He really is." Eden smiled despite the pang in her chest. Her birthday this year would be very different. "I'm so happy you're having a great day."

Their meals came quickly. Maria got her clam chowder. Natasha chose the halibut burger and a cup of chowder. Katie ordered the salmon burger. Eden and Anya, who was the youngest, both ordered fish tacos.

Eden raised her glass. "Happy Birthday, Maria!"

"Happy Birthday!" the others repeated.

They clinked glasses, and then dug in.

The conversation ranged widely during dinner. Natasha's job at the Alutiiq Museum, where they'd just had a ceremony to repatriate old Alutiiq remains. Maria's oldest starting kindergarten in the fall. Katie's resolution to remain single and her new backyard chickens. Anya's latest awful dating app experience.

"Then he replied, 'I'm going to show you what you've been missing.'"

Natasha made a face. "Ew! He doesn't even know you. How can he know what you're missing? What an ego."

"Right?"

"You dodged a bullet there, sis." Katie dipped a French fry in ketchup.

"Why are you still trying to meet men online?" Maria dabbed her lips with a napkin. "The good ones don't hang out there."

Anya rolled her eyes. "I know."

Eden had never used dating apps, and she wasn't sorry. "What did you message back?"

"I told him what I was really missing was decent men without big egos. He called me a bitch and blocked me."

It was then Eden saw him.

Sean walked in with Trey, his gaze missing her. He wore a dark blue button-down shirt with faded denim jeans, his gaze moving to the stage where the Outriggers were getting ready for their set. He and the others took a table in the back, close to the pool tables where he and Justin used to play each other.

"Eden?"

"Oh, sorry."

"I asked how you're doing." Natasha looked worried. "Any more trouble with dear, beloved Cousin Mila?"

Eden had kept her sisters up to date on Mila's nonsense via group texts. "Thankfully, not. Not since Crab Fest."

Maria had finished her clam chowder and was perusing the dessert menu. "Mom told me you and Maverick were sick with scarlet fever."

"Scarlet fever?" This was apparently news to Natasha and Anya.

"We're better. Sean, Justin's best friend, stayed with us. He took us to the doctor and then watched over Mavie so I could sleep. He gave him his medicine and even changed his diaper. I can't remember when I've been that sick."

"Sean?" Maria's eyebrows rose. "I remember him from your wedding. He was the best man. Isn't he the hot guy you were staring at just now?"

"Was I staring?"

"Yes," her sisters said together.

Eden couldn't help it, her gaze drawn to him once more.

Four heads turned.

Katie's voice took on a husky tone. "Oh, my."

"Will you excuse me for a moment? I just want to say hi."

"This is my birthday party, and I say go for it," said Maria.

Natasha seemed to find the whole thing funny. "Why are you wasting time with us?"

Then it was Anya's turn. "Run, girl."

Eden was already out of her chair and on her way.

SEAN PERUSED the menu even though he knew it by heart. He and Justin had hung out here during their off hours, playing pool, throwing darts, shooting the shit with other Coasties. He'd come here a lot less often since Justin's death.

Trey nudged him. "Incoming. Eleven o'clock."

Sean looked up—and stared.

Damn.

Eden was walking straight toward him, looking good enough to eat.

She wore a short black dress that made the most of her curves. Oh, yes, it did. The fabric clung to her body from her breasts to the flare of her hips. He knew it was wrong, but he couldn't stop his gaze from raking over her from her bare shoulders to that hint of luscious cleavage to those long, smooth legs.

Desire warmed his blood, scattered his thoughts, left his brain blank.

She reached the table before he'd gotten a hold of himself. "Hey."

He swallowed, stood. "Hey."

Trey stood, too, and pulled out a seat for her. "Good to see you, Eden."

She sat, her hair sliding over one soft shoulder. She was wearing makeup, her eyelids shimmering light brown, her lips glossy and red. "It's my sister Maria's thirtieth birthday, so we're here to celebrate."

"Happy Birthday to her." Sean had met her sisters at the wedding, where they'd stood with her at the altar. "You're looking *much* better. I mean, you always look great. But you look better than you did. I... uh... you were really sick and..." Sean got a sharp kick to the shin from Trey under the table, and his brain started working again. "How do you feel?"

Her lush, red lips curved in a sweet smile. "I feel much better. Thank you again for all you did to help us."

"I hear you had scarlet fever." Trey grimaced. "Nasty stuff."

"Poor Maverick still has bright red cheeks. The pediatrician said that should go away in a few more days. He's back to being his happy little self."

"Good." Sean did his best to act normal, the urge to touch her, kiss her, and carry her out of this place overwhelming. "Happy I could help."

"How have you been?"

"Good. Fine. Okay. Yeah."

Trey looked like he was trying not to laugh. "We've kept pretty busy. A surfer broke his leg and ended up on a tidal rockpile. We got him before he was washed out to sea. There was also a case where a fisherman caught himself in the eye with his hook."

Eden winced. "Oh, God."

This time it was Sean who kicked Trey under the table.

Trey's grin vanished. "Sorry. That was probably TMI."

On the stage, the Outriggers broke into their rendition of "Footloose," quickly filling the dance floor. Then the server was there to take their orders, all of them half-shouting to be heard above the band.

Sean ordered a salmon burger and a beer, while Trey went for the steak.

"Nothing for me. I'm actually sitting at the table with my sisters."

"Oh, right." The server smiled. "I recognize you now."

While the band went from number to number, they talked about little stuff, the conversation landing on everyone's favorite topic—the weather.

The Outriggers ended one song to applause and then launched into their rendition of Marvin Gaye's "Let's Get It On," which quite possibly was the very last song Sean needed to hear at the moment.

Trey was still talking about the weather. "They're saying we're in for a major storm system next week so—"

Eden stood, held out her hand to Sean, invitation in her eyes. "Dance with me."

Sean had just taken a drink and almost choked. "I... uh..."

Trey kicked him again—hard this time.

Sean shot him a look then stood and took her hand, his skin seeming to ignite at the touch. He led her onto the dance floor, where only a handful of couples remained, slow dancing. "Everyone's watching us. Your sisters are staring."

Eden came easily into his arms, rested her palms on his shoulders. "Let them."

Sean ought to have refused her, but he hadn't. So, he closed his eyes, drew a breath, and gave in to the moment, savoring the soft feel of her body against his, inhaling the sweet scent of her skin. "You smell so good."

She rested her head against his chest in a way that was

unmistakably intimate, unleashing an answering pull inside him.

God, he wanted her.

Worse, he was beginning to think she wanted him, too.

He rested one hand on the curve of her hip, splayed the other across the bare skin of her upper back, the contact setting him on fire. He nuzzled her ear, breathed her in, felt her shiver.

What the *hell* was he doing? Eden was Justin's wife.

No, she was his widow. She was alone now.

Justin is gone.

And just like that, Sean found himself balanced on a razor's edge, torn between past and present, right and wrong, duty and desire.

Did she know what she was doing to him?

All too soon the music ended, and she took a step back and looked up at him. There, in her eyes, he saw the same desire, the same need.

She took another step back, stood on her tiptoes, and pressed a timid kiss to his lips that he felt down to his bones. "Thanks for the dance."

Thinking he'd walk her back to her table, he took her left hand in his. Then he felt the warm gold of her wedding set. He raised her hand, turned the white gold band with his thumb, the sight of it bringing reality back into focus. "I remember handing this to Justin to slip on your finger at your wedding. Thanks for the dance."

Then he released her hand and walked back to his table, leaving her on the dance floor.

EDEN SETTLED Maverick in his crib, drew his blanket up to his chin. Spending an evening at his Baba's house with his cousins had worn him out. She turned off the light, left his door open a crack, and walked to the kitchen to pour herself a drink.

What had she done?

She hadn't known Sean was going to be there, and she certainly hadn't gone to his table to ask him to dance. But the way his gaze had moved over her had been as intimate as a caress. Desire had been written on his face so plainly that her sisters had seen it from across the room. Eden had found it hard to breathe, her belly in flutters. And so, she'd asked him to dance.

She knew now that Sean cared for her. She knew he was attracted to her. Any doubts she'd had about that were gone.

The way he'd held her... The heat in his eyes afterwards...

It had left her shaken—and wanting more.

Had he meant to touch her engagement ring and wedding band, or had that been an unhappy accident?

I remember handing this to Justin to slip on your finger at your wedding.

Afterwards, she'd stood alone on the dance floor and watched him walk away, wanting desperately to call him back or go after him. But she'd known better. Asking him to dance, kissing him in the middle of the pub—she'd pushed him.

You'll be lucky if you see him again this summer.

She took off her heels, mixed herself a rum and coke, and sat at the table, her gaze falling on her rings. She'd melted when Justin had surprised her at the beach with the half carat oval solitaire. The moment he'd slipped the wedding band on her finger had been one of the happiest of her life. She'd sworn in the days after his death that she would never take the rings off her finger. But she hadn't known she'd one day have feelings for Sean.

She set her drink down, drew a breath—and slipped the rings from her finger. Maybe she could wear them on a chain or put them on her right hand. "I love you, Justin, and I miss you so much. But I have to keep living. I know that's what you'd want."

She set the rings down, blinked back her tears, and got to her feet, suddenly needing air. She carried her drink outside to the front porch. The air was rich with the scent of the sea, a light rain beginning to fall. She took one deep, slow breath after the other, her emotions in turmoil.

The rain fell harder, fog concealing the mountaintops.

It's raining as hard as a cow pissing on a flat rock.

That's what Justin would've said.

In the distance, she heard an approaching car engine. Someone was probably coming home from their duty shift.

She sipped her drink, her mind fixed on Sean, her body still aroused from their dance.

Headlights through rain. A familiar vehicle.

Sean pulled into her driveway, climbed out, and walked through the rain to the foot of her stairs, stopping when he saw her. "Eden?"

"Sean."

"Please tell me what's going on." Rain soaked his hair, ran in rivulets down his skin, desolation on his face. "I know you miss Justin. I miss him, too. You're probably lonely as hell, especially at night. You miss having him in your life and in your bed. I get it. I really do. But I can't fill that gap. He was my best friend."

Eden's temper flared, making her splutter. "You... you think I'm just trying to fill the empty space Justin left behind?"

Sean came no closer but stood in the rain. "I don't blame you. You loved him so much, and you *should* have had a lifetime together. If I'd done my job right—"

"What happened *wasn't* your fault."

Sean changed the subject. "You're still grieving for him,

and it's hard. I understand. Either way, I can't be a substitute for the man you love. One day, you'd regret it."

And then she understood.

He didn't believe her feelings for him were real. He thought her attraction to him was just some strange phase of mourning, nothing more than a widow's loneliness.

Men could be *so* dumb.

"Is it hard to believe that I could come to care for you when you've been here for us every day since his death?"

He took one step toward the porch and then another. "Eden, it's too soon. You can't really mean that."

"What makes you think you know more about my feelings than I do?" She spelled it out for him. "I took you fishing so we could have time alone together, but you refused to kiss me then. I thought you weren't interested. I didn't plan any of that tonight. It just happened. But I don't regret it because now I know the truth."

"What's that?" He took another step toward her.

"You want me, too."

He shook his head. "Justin was my best friend."

That wasn't a denial.

"He was my husband, the man I loved. I'll never forget him. But my heart is strong enough to love and honor the man he was and care for you at the same time."

Sean walked up the steps in slow, deliberate strides to stand before her, soaking wet, his chest rising and falling with shaky breaths, his gaze locked with hers.

She'd never seen him like this—on the edge, vulnerable, at a breaking point. She touched a finger to his cheek, caught a rivulet of rainwater. "You're drenched."

"I know." He cupped her cheek with his other hand, traced her lower lip with his thumb, the heat in his eyes making her shiver. "Damn it, Eden."

Then he lowered his lips to hers.

Chapter Eleven

Even as his lips brushed over hers, Sean told himself he wasn't going to kiss her. He *wasn't* going to kiss her. He was *not*...

Ah, hell.

He gave in to the thrumming in his chest, slid his fingers into her hair, and claimed her mouth, tasting rum and sugar. She whimpered then gasped when their bodies met, and some part of Sean remembered that he was soaking wet. He was probably getting her wet, too, and making her cold. And still, he didn't stop.

She slipped her arms behind his neck, melted against him, her breasts pressing against his ribcage, her body warm. Hunger he'd tried so hard to ignore hit his bloodstream, his cock going hard, straining against his fly. He traced the curve of her lower lip with his tongue, nipped it, sucked it into his mouth, wanting to devour her.

She sucked in a breath, shivered. "*Sean.*"

But he wasn't finished.

He angled her head, and claimed her mouth again, teasing her tongue with his, blood racing hot through his veins. She drew him closer, answered his teasing with strokes of her own, her fingers curling in the hair at his nape.

From somewhere nearby, came the sound of a garage door opening.

Shit.

If they were seen kissing…

He released her, stepped back, trembling from head to toe, whether from the chill or from desire, he couldn't say. "I should go."

"Don't be silly." She took his hand, her fingers threading easily with his. "Come in and dry off before you get hypothermia. We can talk."

Sean should have said goodnight. He should have walked to his vehicle and driven back to the barracks, but he didn't. Instead, he followed her inside, his mind reeling.

But she was right. They needed to talk.

"I'll put water on to boil for tea." She smiled. "You know where the towels are. Just toss your wet stuff in the dryer."

While she busied herself in the kitchen, he removed his boots and damp socks, then walked to the bathroom and undressed, wet down to his skin. He took a bath towel from the cupboard near the door and dried off. As he rubbed the towel over his hair, he caught his reflection in the mirror.

Do you know what you just did, buddy?

Hell, no. He'd gone off the edge of the map tonight.

But *damn*.

In his twenties, he'd dated lots of women, wasting far too many hours on dating apps. He'd had more than a few first kisses in his life. But nothing could compare to what he'd just experienced with Eden. Their kiss had lasted only a few minutes, but it had rocked his world.

He wrapped the towel around his hips, grateful that his erection was gone. It would have been hard to have any kind of seriously conversation while pitching a tent.

Now what?

Hell, he didn't know.

Eden said she had feelings for him. She thought she wanted him. But Justin had been gone for only five months, and this was so sudden.

Or was it?

Hadn't Sean felt it, too—this growing attraction?

He had, and Eden knew it.

But he couldn't get involved with her. Justin had been his best friend, and if Sean had done his job right, Justin might still be here. So, what was Sean supposed to do now?

Just keep your dick in your ... towel.

He gathered his wet clothes from the tub where he'd dropped them, opened the bathroom door, and walked around the corner to the laundry room. He tossed them in the dryer, set the time for forty minutes, and pushed START.

"Do you need help?" she called to him.

"I work on complicated avionics equipment, and I have used one before. I'm sure I can figure it out." He chuckled to himself, then turned and saw her.

Geezus.

She stood in the hallway, wearing a smile and her sleep shirt and bathrobe, part of a sleek thigh showing, her feet bare. "I had to change out of the dress. You got it wet."

Yeah. He really ought to have gone back to the barracks. "Sorry."

She turned toward the kitchen. "There's tea steeping on the table."

Sean wasn't sure he needed to be any warmer, but he didn't say that. "Thanks."

He followed her to the kitchen, aware of everything about her. The way her hair moved side to side while she walked. The swing of her hips. The silky curves of her calves. The hint of perfume that followed her.

She set two mugs on the table, a smile on lips that he could still taste. "I promise not to spill it on you this time."

How could she be so damned calm when his entire world had just turned upside down? Maybe he needed to work on his kissing game.

Not tonight, buddy, and not with Eden.

She poured the tea, her gaze moving over his body before she looked into his eyes. "The last thing I expected to happen tonight was for you to show up on my doorstep. Why did you come? And why did you stand there in the rain?"

How could he answer without digging the hole deeper?

"After tonight, I needed to understand what's going on. I wanted to sort this out before it goes any further. As for why I stood in the rain... Hell. I didn't trust myself to be close to you."

EDEN SAW in Sean's eyes that he meant what he'd just said, his words giving her belly flutters. "That sounds serious. What did you think you'd do?"

He leaned against the counter, arms crossed over his bare chest in a way that made all of his delicious muscles shift, his gaze meeting hers. "I was afraid I'd kiss you, and I was right."

His honesty melted her heart. "I'm glad you did."

"It shouldn't have happened."

But she couldn't have this conversation, not with him standing there looking like Adonis of the Skimpy Towel. She couldn't keep her gaze off him—or ignore how he made her feel. "Let me get you a blanket."

"I'm warm enough. You don't have to do that."

"Yes, I do. There's no way I can sit here and talk with you if you're half naked."

"Ah." His lips curved slightly, as if he were trying not to

smile.

She walked down the hallway to the closet and grabbed a throw. When she returned, she found him standing near the table, his gazed fixed on something, his brow furrowed with concern.

Her rings.

"Thanks." He took the blanket, wrapped it around his shoulders. "You took off your rings. Isn't it too soon for this—for any of this?"

She sat across from him, sipped her tea, tried to put her emotions into words. "In the first weeks after Justin's death, I swore I'd never take them off. I couldn't imagine having feelings for another man. Then you happened."

"I didn't *happen*. We've known each other for almost four years."

"We've known each other as Justin's wife and Justin's best friend. But now he's gone, and I've come to see you in a different way."

She told him how much every one of a hundred small kindnesses he'd shown her had mattered, each building on the last. His support at the memorial service. His help with the paperwork. His willingness to listen when she spoke about Justin. His interest in Alutiiq culture. His willingness to go with her to Crab Fest. His kindness to Maverick.

"It was a gradual thing, but it didn't really hit me until Crab Fest. I felt confused, upset. I was afraid I was betraying Justin, so I talked to my grandmother about it."

He arched an eyebrow. "You talked with your grandmother about me?"

Eden nodded. "She invited me to go foraging for docks, but she really wanted to talk with me about Mila. Afterwards, I told her I had feelings for you, and that I thought you felt the same way. I felt so torn, and I knew she would listen."

"What did she say?"

"She reminded me that life is short." Eden left out the hanky-panky part. "She said that having feelings for another man didn't mean I was forgetting Justin. Then she said Justin would want me to be happy and that the best way for me to honor him was to live a full and happy life."

Sean reached across the table, took her hand, his fingers warm and strong. "He *would* want you to be happy. I know he would. Your grandma is a wise woman."

"She is."

"I have no doubt that you'll find love again. You'll meet someone and have a good life. But I can't be that man."

"Why not?" She tried to make him understand. "Like you said, I've known you for four years. You and Justin were friends for a reason. You're different, yes, but you're both good men. I *trust* you. You're not some rando on a dating app who lied in his profile and is actually an alcoholic who hates dogs. If you could hear the stories my younger sister Anya tells, you'd understand. As we women of Kodiak say, the odds are good, but the goods are odd."

"I can't argue with that last part. As for the rest of it, I want to be here for you. I want to help. But we can't be more than friends, and you know why."

"Because you were Justin's best friend." She fought not to roll her eyes. "Where is it written that a man can't get involved with his best friend's widow?"

He said nothing but watched her through troubled blue eyes.

Then Eden told him about her walk on Jewel Beach. "It was our special place, and now that water—the Gulf—it's Justin's grave. I started telling him how good you'd been to us, how I knew you cared about me and how I cared about you. I guess I felt like I needed his blessing or something. And then something washed over my boots."

"What was it?"

"I'll show you." She stood and retrieved the little piece of precious sea glass from the basket on the kitchen counter. "It's red sea glass in the shape of a heart. Red sea glass is rare. I've collected sea glass since I was a little girl, and it's the first time I've found any."

Sean took the piece of sea glass from her, turned it over in his hand. "Wow. I wonder how long it was out there and where it came from. A red heart. What are the odds? And this just washed up right then?"

Eden nodded. "I bent down, picked it up, and when I saw what it was, I knew Justin had answered me. He wants us *both* to be happy."

Sean set the little piece of glass on the table. There was a pensive frown on his face now, but he said nothing.

"You think I'm being silly."

He shook his head. "No. There's more to this world than we can see."

Eden picked up the tiny red heart. "Earlier tonight, you said you thought I was just using you to fill the emptiness in my life—"

He shouldn't have said that. "That's not how I meant it. I was worried that you were on the rebound and lonely and that I just happened to be here."

"It's okay. The truth is that my emotions *have* been all over the place. But I do know one thing for certain."

"What's that?"

Eden took his hand. "I care about you, Sean, and you care about me, too. When I'm with you, I feel happy and *alive* again."

SEAN TRIED to take in what she'd shared with him. She cared for him. She trusted him. She found him sexually attractive.

Well, he returned those feelings in spades.

In fact, he had to admire his own self-control for not dropping the blanket, peeling off her bathrobe, and kissing every lush inch of her sweet body.

You're the very image of restraint, sitting here in your towel, man.

But where she saw reasons for them to give this a try, he saw only obstacles.

He drew his hand away. "I *do* care for you, Eden. You're right about that. You're beautiful and fun and smart. But it's not that simple."

"Why not?"

"First off, a man doesn't hit on his best friend's widow—not in the military."

"You keep saying that, but I don't care what anyone else thinks. When I started dating Justin, Coasties told him to stay away from local women because we're all just looking for a man to get us off the island."

Sean remembered hearing about that from Justin. "Some people are idiots."

"Exactly. My ancestors have lived here for thousands of years. In two years, most of the Coasties here today will be stationed somewhere else."

"Including me." He let that sink in. "My CO is pushing to advance me. If they do promote me, they'll almost certainly transfer me somewhere else."

"But you can ask to remain here, right? That's what Justin did."

"I can, of course." Sean had already planned to do that. He loved living on the island—and he didn't want to be far from Eden and Maverick. "But you know how it works. In the end, I have to go wherever they send me."

Her gaze dropped to the table. "Orders, not options. I know."

"I'm single for a reason." He knew this wasn't news to her. They'd joked about it while Justin had been alive. "Life in the military is hard on families. You know the lifestyle. Long hours. Round-the-clock duty shifts. Never knowing when you'll be called in. Risky SAR and medevac calls. I don't want to put a woman through that."

"I know what you do for a living. Does it scare the hell out of me at times? Of course. Is it a deal-breaker? I wouldn't be much of an Alaskan if it was. I was proud of Justin for the work he did, and I'm proud of you, too."

Sean said it as clearly as he could. "We *can't* be together."

He saw the hurt on her face—and hated himself for it.

"So, what do you want me to do? Should I go back to treating you like Justin's best friend, try to forget that I have feelings for you, and pretend that amazing kiss never happened?"

He willed himself to say the right thing. "That's probably for the best."

She gave him a withering look. "I've played poker with you, remember? I can tell when you're bluffing. You want me, too. I felt it when we danced together—the way you held me, the way you nuzzled my hair. And I sure as hell felt it in that kiss. Your heart was pounding—and so was mine."

Shit.

"Eden, I..." Somehow, he'd lost control of this conversation. "I'm not bluffing. Life isn't just about what I want. I have a duty to the Coast Guard. One day soon, my job will take me away from here."

"But you also get some choice. What do *you* want, Sean?"

That was one hell of a question, but the answer was easy.

He wanted *her*.

From the laundry room came the buzz of the dryer.

"It sounds like my clothes are ready. I should probably get back to the barracks."

Chapter Twelve

June 12

EDEN BUNDLED Maverick into his rain gear—pants, hooded jacket, boots—then slipped into her own boots and jacket. "Let's go for a little walk, okay?"

"We go to the beach?" He was putting new words together every day now.

"Not today. The waves are too high."

Last night's rain had only been the leading edge of a major storm. Her neighbors would probably think she was crazy heading out into this weather. But this was Alaska. If she kept Maverick indoors every time it rained, snowed, or was cold, they would rarely leave the house. It was her job to teach Maverick to feel at home outdoors, no matter what the conditions. As her grandparents had taught her, there was no such thing as bad weather, only the wrong clothes.

Checking to make sure she had her keys, she took Maverick by the hand and led him out the front door. The moment they left the cover of the porch, cold rain lashed their faces.

Eden laughed. "That's cold, isn't it?"

Seeing her reaction, Mavie's shocked distress transformed into laughter. "Wainy cold."

"Yes, the rain is cold, isn't it?" The wind was even colder. "Let's go."

She led him out to the sidewalk and down the block, heading toward the trail to Old Woman Mountain. She had no fixed goal in mind. This was about getting fresh air and teaching Maverick to enjoy being outdoors in all weather.

And it might help take her mind off Sean.

After that dance and the kiss— *oh, my God, that kiss!* —she'd thought they were about to turn a corner in their relationship. She'd known from the moment he'd touched his lips to hers that he wanted her. She'd felt undeniable proof of that in his jeans and the racing of his heart. It would have been a new beginning for both of them. But he'd put on the brakes with all of his talk about duty and being Justin's best friend.

Life isn't just about what I want.

Eden had gone to bed weighted down by sadness and loneliness—and buzzing with sexual frustration. But if that's how Sean truly felt, there was nothing she could do. She didn't play games, and the last thing she wanted him to do was betray his own beliefs.

A few feet ahead of her, Maverick discovered a small puddle next to the sidewalk and did what Eden would have done at his age. He stepped into it and stomped his feet, laughing in delight as the water splashed around him.

"Splash! Splash!" If it hadn't been raining so hard, she'd have taken a photo to send to her family and Justin's. "You're a little duck."

When Maverick had gotten his fill of jumping in the puddle, they continued to the trailhead, where Mavie had room to run and explore. He picked up interesting rocks, oddly shaped pieces of bark, a weather-worn stick, and a small empty crab shell.

He held up the shell. "See, Mommy?"

"Oh, look at that!" She knelt beside him. "That's an empty crab shell. I bet an eagle sat in that tree to eat it and let the shell fall to the ground when he was done."

When she looked up, she saw that the treetops were swaying ominously. Their roots weren't deep, and every big storm caused trees across the island to topple. Every once in a while, someone was killed. Not wanting to be caught in a blow-down, she took Maverick's hand again.

"Let's head home for some lunch. Are you hungry?"

As they neared the house, she heard it—the whir of a helicopter. There in the distance was a white-and-orange H-60 returning to base, ambulances waiting on the tarmac. It was the peak of the fishing season, and with thirty- and forty-foot seas, the Coast Guard would be busy.

Stay safe, Sean.

When they got home, Eden removed Maverick's rain gear and was happy to see that he'd stayed warm and dry and was cheerful. Creating good memories outdoors was the best way she knew to teach children to love nature. "Let's have some lunch."

She made grilled cheese sandwiches, chopping Maverick's into bite-sized squares, and placing them on his plate with apple chunks. "Here you go, buddy!"

She kissed the top of his head and sat beside him to eat her own lunch, talking with him about the day's adventure. By the time his tummy was full, he was falling asleep in his highchair. "Come here, sweetie."

She picked him up, carried him to his crib, and tucked him in for his nap.

Then she walked to her bedroom closet, took out her

Fire and Rain

VHF radio, and set it up in the living room to monitor Channel 16.

"...amplifying information, over?"

Eden thought that was Spurrier. Justin had flown a lot of SAR cases with him.

"Rescue Six-Zero-Three-Two, Sector, that's a negative. We haven't had contact with the Sea Dog since their original call, over."

"We don't know whether they had survival suits or a raft. If the boat sank, they're in real trouble." That was James again, talking to the crew. "You've got door speed."

"Cabin door open. Vis is so poor I can't see much, even with the IR goggles."

Eden's pulse picked up. That was Sean.

"I'm going to circle around. I don't see anything, and we've passed the boat's last reported—"

"Mark! Mark! Mark!" Sean cut him off. "We've got at least one PIW about two hundred yards off at our five o'clock. The survivor has a strobe."

Eden let out the breath she hadn't realized she'd been holding. They'd found someone in the water. But was the person still alive? Were there others?

She shouldn't sit here listening to this. It would only upset her.

And yet knowing Sean was out there made it impossible to stop.

SEAN GRABBED the strap and dragged both Trey and the survivor into the cabin. Then he worked to free Trey so he could start treating the man, who was clearly in bad shape. "The Wiggy's bag is ready."

"Thanks, man." Trey turned to the survivor, shouting to

be heard over the noise of the helo. "Were there other people on board your vessel?"

The survivor struggled to speak. "Th-three...m-m-more..."

"We've got three more PIW," Trey told James. He took off the man's life jacket and cut through his survival suit and the clothes beneath it. "Do they have strobes?"

The man nodded, his eyes closing.

"We're looking for them." Sean moved back to his position by the door, his infrared goggles on the water.

Three heat signatures. Three tiny dots of light amid fog and rain and churning seas. It might actually be easier to find a needle in a haystack.

Then he saw them. "Two strobes, low one o'clock. We're almost on top of them."

Spurrier brought the helo around. "I see them."

Sean prepared the cabin for another hoist. When it came to severe hypothermia, seconds mattered. "You want to use the strap again?"

It would be hard for Trey to put a semi-conscious person in the basket in rough seas. But using the strap meant leaving one survivor alone in the water, something no one wanted to do.

Trey got himself back into the strap. "I don't think we have a choice."

Sean did the safety check. "Safety check complete."

"Begin the hoist."

"Swimmer is leaving the cabin." Sean lowered Trey to the water once more. "Swimmer is in the water. Swimmer is okay."

Sean saw both survivors grab hold of Trey, their panic putting the hoist at risk. "It looks like the survivors are in a panic."

Trey seemed to calm them down. Then his voice came over the radio. "I'm sending them both up together."

"Roger that." Sean waited for Trey's thumbs-up. "Survivors are in the strap. Survivors are on their way up. Survivors are outside the cabin."

Sean again dragged them inside. But the two young men didn't know their way around rescue gear, and they started to panic when he tried to take them out of the strap, legs and arms thrashing. "It's okay. You're okay. I need you to move into those two troop seats so I can retrieve the swimmer. Stop struggling!"

"I d-don't w-want to f-fall out!"

"You won't fall out if you calm down and let me remove the strap."

Trey was out there, his second time in the water on this mission. His survival suit would keep him safe—but only for a while.

The survivors seemed to calm down at the sight of their friend, allowing Sean to remove the strap and prepare for the final hoist of this evolution. He checked the strap again. "Ready to retrieve our swimmer."

"Roger that."

Sean leaned out the cabin door, scanned the surface of the water—but Trey was gone. Adrenaline punched through him. "I don't see our swimmer anywhere."

"How in the hell did he end up there?" Spurrier banked the helicopter. "He's a hundred yards out at our nine o'-clock. And it looks like he's got our fourth PIW."

The first survivor they'd rescued almost sobbed with relief. "M-my s-son."

When the aircraft was in position, Sean lowered the strap a third time. In a matter of minutes, Trey was back in the cabin with a teenage boy, who was barely conscious.

"Closing cabin door. Crank the heat." Sean and the others would sweat their asses off, but their comfort was not what mattered.

Zeke answered. "You got it."

Then the helicopter pitched, spun, tossing Sean against the closed door.

What the...?

Were they going down?

"A big gust just caused a loss of tail-rotor effectiveness," Spurrier said. "We're getting the hell out of here. Sector, this is Rescue Six-Zero-Three-Two. We recovered zero-four survivors from the water and are RTB. They're all severely hypothermic. Please have EMS standing by."

"Rescue Six-Zero-Three-Two, Sector. You are RTB. Calling EMS."

Sean went back to helping Trey, getting men out of their wet things and into the Wiggy's bags, handing Trey what he needed. Another O2 mask. A blood pressure cuff. Several heat packs.

"D-did we j-just almost crash?" one of the survivors asked him.

Sean shook his head. "That was just a little gust of wind."

Trey met Sean's gaze, neither of them willing to tell them the truth. If James and Zeke hadn't regained control, they might well have gone down. "Sean here, our AET, has survived a helo crash."

Oh, great.

The two survivors in the troop seats gaped at him.

Sean nodded, tried to play casual. "The helo went down. I swam out and got picked up twenty minutes later."

And it was the worst fucking day of my life.

"D-damn!" said one of the young men. "Y-you all are b-badasses."

"I-is my boy g-going to m-make it?" asked the first man they'd rescued.

Trey, who was working on the kid, didn't respond.

Sean answered for him. "We're doing all we can. EMS will be waiting for us when we get back to base."

Sean took over first aid for the three other survivors so that Trey could devote his time to the kid. By the time they landed, the boy's condition had improved. "EMS is standing by. Do you want the boy to go first?"

Trey nodded. "And then his father."

One by one, the survivors were transferred onto gurneys and rolled to the waiting ambulances. Then, at last, Sean stood with Trey on the tarmac.

"You scared the shit out of me. You just disappeared. Care to warn us next time?"

Trey nodded. "Sorry, man. I caught a glimpse of the kid's strobe and went for it. I didn't realize until I had him how far I was from my previous position."

"I'm glad you found him. Great work today."

Trey grinned. "Thanks, Flo."

"Eat me."

It seemed to Eden that the Coast Guard launched one rescue after another through the course of the afternoon, mostly for mariners in distress. She knew everyone on base must be exhausted. The local news station was reporting trees down across the island, and the city of Kodiak had lost power for a time. But by evening, the worst of the wind had died down, a light rain falling, the fog settling in.

Eden turned off her VHF and made pan-grilled salmon with rice and salad for supper, using the last of the nettle pesto. Maverick loved salmon and talked about their walk while they ate—the puddles, the rain, and the crab shell. Eden was glad it had made an impression on him.

After supper, she did the dishes, and they played for a

while. Then it was time for Maverick's bath and stories. They snuggled together on the sofa as she read his favorite books—one about an orca searching for his pod, the other about the animals of Alaska, and one about the Aurora Borealis.

"You're good at naming all the animals now, aren't you?"

Maverick nodded, bottle in his mouth, his favorite blankie clutched close to his chest.

She held him on her lap and sang to him, songs her mother had sung to her. "*Cikmia, cikmia, Agyangcuk...*"

Twinkle, twinkle little star...

Eden didn't speak her Alutiiq ancestors' tongue well. For that matter, she didn't speak Russian, either, apart from *grandma* and *grandpa*. Still, she wanted to pass on what she knew to Maverick, who soaked it all up like a sponge.

When he was asleep, she carried him to his crib. She was about to slip into her pajamas and settle down with a glass of wine and a new novel when her phone buzzed with a new text message. It was Natasha.

```
You make it through the storm okay?
```

```
                    We did. How are you?
```

```
Everyone's fine. Mom had lost power for a
while.
```

```
                         Is it back on?
```

```
Yes, just a few minutes ago.
```

```
                        Good! Stay safe!
```

Eden was about to undress and put on her sleep shirt

when her phone buzzed again. Thinking it was Natasha, she picked it up, tapped the message—and stared.

```
Call off the police, or more members of
your family will get hurt.
```

She didn't recognize the number and replied, more than a little irritated.

```
Who are you? What are you talking about?
You've got the wrong number.
```

Not that it would be okay for them to threaten someone else, whoever they were.
Another message.

```
I'm talking to you, Eden. Unless you're
stupid, you'll do as I say. Tell the cops
to stop the investigation.
```

Chills skittered down her spine at the use of her name, her mind racing. The investigation? What investigation?
The investigation into the explosion that killed Justin.
The realization knocked the breath from her lungs, and Eden sank to the bed. She typed a quick reply.

```
Who are you? I have no control over the
cops. I haven't talked to them.
```

The reply was immediate.

```
Bullshit. Tell them to back off, or what
happens next will be on YOU!
```

Eden wanted to tell this person to go to hell, but what if he was serious?

She blocked the number, went to her closet, and took down her shot gun. Next, she grabbed a box of shells and loaded five. She'd learned to shoot as a child on hunting trips with her father and grandfather and knew how to use firearms.

With the shotgun loaded, she checked her doors to make sure they were locked, closed all of the blinds, and called the base police. The voice on the other end of the phone promised to send someone right away. And so, Eden waited, fear simmering into rage.

How dare some son of a bitch threaten her and Maverick? How dare they intrude into her life and try to scare her? And what was going on with the investigation that someone thought they needed to come after her?

She ignored the urge to call Sean. If he wasn't in the air, he was probably getting some much-needed sleep. Besides, she wasn't his problem. He'd made it clear that they were just friends, and she didn't want to bother him.

A knock at the door made her jump.

"It's Coast Guard police, Mrs. Koseki."

She set the shot gun aside and hurried to the door, peeking out to be certain.

Who else would it be? Didn't they say they were on their way?

She opened the door and found two uniformed Coastie police officers in their ODUs and black body armor—a man and a woman—and a second man in jeans and a parka with some kind of carrying case in his hand. "Thank you for coming so quickly."

The officers introduced themselves.

"I'm Officer Andy Briggs and this is Officer Rachel Vasquez."

Fire and Rain

Rachel reached out, shook Eden's hand. "We're very sorry for your recent loss."

"Thank you."

Then the tall man in street clothes flashed a duty badge. "I'm Special Agent Chase Santee from the Coast Guard Investigative Service. I'm leading the Coast Guard's investigation into the drug operation that resulted in the death of your husband."

Chapter Thirteen

EXHAUSTED, Sean walked back to his locker to stow his gear bag. He wanted nothing more right now than a hot shower and sleep. And the hot shower was optional.

In the locker room, he found James leaning back against his locker, arms crossed over his chest, gaze downturned, eyes closed, a troubled expression on his face.

James' eyes opened and his head came up. "Good work out there today, McKenna."

"You, too." Sean opened his locker, shoved the bag inside. "Thanks for keeping us in the air. That gust sure got my adrenaline going."

"Yeah, me, too." James grabbed his jacket from the bench. "How's Eden?"

"She and Maverick were fine when I last saw them."

He'd been part of five SAR flights in the past twenty-four hours. It had been as grueling a shift as any he could remember, apart from the one that had nearly killed him. The upside was, of course, that staying busy had kept his mind off Eden—and that kiss.

"Then I guess you haven't heard."

Fire and Rain

Sean closed his locker. "Haven't heard what?"

"Walcott told me. Base police and an agent from CGIS went to her place a little while ago. Some asshole sent her threatening text messages related to the drug investigation. They told her to get the cops to back off or they'd hurt her—or something like that."

"What?" Sean's fatigue vanished. "How long ago was this?"

"No more than an hour. She and the boy are fine, as far as I know."

"Thanks, Spurrier." Sean bolted out the door, calling back to James. "Get some rest!"

He hurried to his barracks, changed into jeans and a T-shirt, and threw a few things together in his duffel bag. Two changes of clothes. Toiletries. His Glock 19M. Two loaded mags. His pocket holster. Then he went out to his vehicle and made the short drive up Aviation Hill to Eden's place.

There were two vehicles parked in Eden's driveway. He parked on the curb, shouldered his duffel, and walked across her lawn and up the stairs. He knocked and came face to face with the CGIS agent.

He held out his ID. "Sean McKenna, a friend of the family."

"Chase Santee, CGIS."

"Sean?" Eden appeared behind Santee. "He's a friend."

Santee stepped back, let him inside.

Two Coast Guard police officers he recognized stood near the table, where a large laptop sat running some kind of program. A shotgun he recognized as Eden's leaned up against the wall beside the table. What the hell had happened?

"Hey, Vasquez. Hey, Briggs." Sean dropped his duffel by the door just as Eden stepped into his arms. "Are you okay? Where's Mavie?"

It felt too damned good to hold her.

She stepped back, and he saw lines of stress on her pretty face. "I'm fine. Mavie's asleep. I'm so glad you're here."

She quickly brought him up to date about the threatening messages. "Agent Santee wanted me to unblock the number to see if he'd call so they could trace his location. So far, no calls. Just more threatening messages."

"We were just about to wrap up here." Santee walked back to the table, closed a laptop. "I've gotten what I can from your phone, Eden. I've cloned it, which means that I'll be able to monitor your calls, texts, and voicemail. If he calls—we're assuming it's a *he*—we'll do our best to pinpoint his position. We'll know exactly what he's saying to you."

"But that means I can't block the number, right?"

"You can turn off your phone or give it to me to keep temporarily and get something cheap with a new number if that makes you feel safer. We'll still get any calls or texts. Here's my card. Call if you have any questions. I'm sorry this happened, but we'll do all we can to keep you and your family safe. Hopefully, we'll have this wrapped up in a few weeks."

Eden took the card. "Thank you."

Vasquez also handed Eden a card. "We'll set up extra patrols of the neighborhood. In the meantime, I suggest you stay close to base. Don't go anywhere alone, and that includes going out on the water."

Eden shook their hands. "Thank you all."

Briggs moved toward the door. "Sorry for your trouble, ma'am. McKenna."

Then Sean and Eden were alone.

"Why didn't you call me?"

"I thought you'd be asleep. How did you hear?"

"Spurrier was in Walcott's office when base security notified him."

She glanced at his duffel bag. "Is that your gear?"

"I thought I'd stay the night—if that's okay." He glanced

at the shotgun. "I know you can defend yourself, but I don't want you to be alone."

"Of course, you can stay. And thanks."

"I'm so sorry this happened, Eden." He wanted to rip the man's lungs out through his ass. "I have no doubt that CGIS will find him."

She nodded, but he could see worry in her eyes. "Are you hungry?"

He shook his head. "I'd just like to look around outside, make sure everything is locked tight, and then hit the rack. I can sleep on the sofa."

She smiled. "You've done that more than a few times. I'll get it ready."

Sean took his firearm out of his bag, slipped it into his pocket holster.

"You came ready to play rough."

"Better ready than sorry." He walked outside and made his way around the house, which was actually a duplex with living quarters separated by garages. He checked her windows, the garage door and looked for any sign that anyone was around.

Nothing.

Back inside, he found a sheet covering the sofa. Two pillows were stacked at one end, and a blanket was neatly folded at the other.

Eden appeared, wearing her bathrobe. "Can I get you anything else?"

"No. I'm good. We can talk in the morning."

"Thanks, Sean." Her gaze was soft with gratitude. "I'm not sure whether I'd sleep at all tonight without you here. I'm not really sure I'll sleep anyway, actually."

"Try. I'm right here."

"Sleep well." Eden grabbed her shotgun and disappeared down the hallway.

With that, Sean stuck his firearm on a high shelf where

Mavie couldn't reach it and turned off the lights. He took off his T-shirt, stretched out on the sofa—and was instantly asleep.

EDEN STOWED her shotgun out of Maverick's reach in the closet, slipped out of her bathrobe, and crawled between the covers, those messages running through her mind.

Why would this person think *she* had the authority to call off an investigation? This went far beyond her and Justin. The DEA and FBI were involved. Ironically, she knew more now than she had this morning, but only because of those text messages. But she couldn't call Agent Santee or the DEA and FBI and tell them to stop.

At least Sean was here.

She'd felt a surge of relief when she'd heard his voice. He was the last person she'd expected to see after what had happened Saturday night—and after such a grueling shift. But he'd heard she was in danger, and he'd come anyway, armed and ready.

That idea wrapped itself around her like a warm blanket, helping her to relax.

She closed her eyes and began to drift.

She thought she heard Mavie call out for her and opened her eyes to find it was already morning. She didn't want to wake Sean, so she climbed out of bed and walked to Mavie's bedroom only to find his crib empty. Her pulse picked up. "Maverick?"

No answer.

She ran out into the hallway, her heart hitting her breastbone when she saw the front door ajar. "Maverick!"

There were no pillows on the sofa, no sheet, no blanket.

Fire and Rain

Where was Sean? Had he taken Maverick out to play? If so, why hadn't he left a note?

She ran to the front door. "Maverick!"

She didn't see him anywhere.

She slipped her feet into her rainboots and ran outside, looking on the side of the house and in the back, shouting his name, but there was no sign of Maverick.

Call off the police, or more members of your family will get hurt.

Terror left her mouth dry, made her pulse pound against her eardrums as she ran through Aviation Hill, calling for Maverick, thoughts chasing through her mind.

Had he been kidnapped? Had he gotten outside somehow and been taken by a bear? Was he lost in the forest?

God, no!

He was her baby, her little boy. He was the only part of Justin she had left.

Tears filled her eyes, ran down her cheeks, and…

Eden jolted upright, found herself in her own bed. It was still nighttime and dark.

It was just a dream. Just a dream.

But there were real tears on her cheeks.

She got out of bed and walked quietly to check on Maverick. He lay in his crib, safe and sound, his blankie tucked beneath his chin.

A shadow fell across the floor. "Eden? Are you okay? I heard you crying."

"I had a nightmare. I just had to see if Maverick was safe."

Sean walked up behind her, rested a big hand on her shoulder. "He's all cozy and fine. Hey, you *are* crying."

"It was awful, Sean. I woke up to find him gone and the door open. You weren't here, and I couldn't find him anywhere. I ran up and down the streets, calling for him. I was terrified."

"That was a really bad dream. But I *am* here, and your baby is safe."

She stroked Maverick's downy head, and she and Sean left his room.

Out in the hallway, Sean drew her into the shelter of his embrace. "You're trembling."

She sank against his bare chest, his warmth enfolding her. "He's all I have left, Sean. I don't know what I'd do if I lost him, too. Sorry I woke you."

"You're not going to lose him." He stroked her hair. "Do you need a drink—Scotch, wine, warm milk and honey? I make a mean hot toddy."

She thought for a moment about suggesting he sleep in her bed, but only so she could feel safe and fall asleep, of course. But that would be devious—delicious and devious. She stepped back, resting her palm against the middle of his chest. "You need to get some rest. I'll just read until I'm ready to try sleeping again."

He ran a finger down her cheek, and his gaze fell to her lips. For a moment she thought he was going to kiss her, but the moment passed. "I'm right out here if you need me. No one will get past me."

She could have thanked him and gone to her room right then, but she didn't. "I hope you're comfortable."

"Are you kidding?" He gave her a lopsided grin. "I could probably sleep on the floor. Or maybe leaning against the wall."

She found herself smiling. "I really am sorry I woke you. I hope you get back to sleep. Goodnight."

"Goodnight, Eden."

She walked into her bedroom, climbed into bed, and picked up the book on her nightstand. But there was no way she could read—not after that nightmare and not after being held in Sean's arms. Her gaze kept moving to the door, part of her wishing that Sean would come to check on her and stay. After an hour or so, she finally quit trying to read, closed the book, and turned off her bedside lamp.

But it was a long time before she fell asleep again.

June 13

SEAN OPENED his eyes from a dead sleep to find Maverick's face inches from his.

Maverick held a little finger to his lips. "Ssh. Sawn seepy."

"I *was* sleeping." Sean sat up. "Good morning, buddy."

"Maverick! I told you to be quiet and let Sean sleep." Eden hurried in from the kitchen wearing jeans and a T-shirt and scooped up her boy. "Sorry, Sean. You can go lie down on my bed if you want. You'll be able to shut the door."

"What time is it?" He had no idea.

"Almost seven-thirty." She carried a squirming Maverick to the table and put him in his highchair. "I made coffee. I thought we could both use some."

Coffee.

Thank Christ.

"That sounds incredible. Thanks." He stood, folded the blanket and the sheet, then retrieved his handgun and slipped the holster into his jeans. In the kitchen, he found a dish of scrambled eggs and a plate of sausage. He snuck a piece of sausage and ate it with his fingers. "This smells delicious. Venison?"

"Natasha's husband, Craig, took down a buck last November." Eden prepared a small plate for Maverick and carried it to the table. "He smoked it at my uncle's place and gave some to everyone in the family."

"Nice." Sean made a plate for Eden and handed it to her,

then poured himself a mug of coffee. "Sit down and eat. I can serve myself."

"Okay." She smiled, but he could see dark circles beneath her eyes.

"Did you get any sleep?" He carried his plate and coffee mug to the table and sat across from her with Maverick to his left.

"It took me a while to get back to sleep."

Despite his fatigue, it hadn't been easy for him to sleep again, either. Sexual tension had gnawed at him, the sensation of holding her against his bare chest imprinted on his brain, her scent in his head. Even now, he felt the pull of her.

"You should have let me make you that hot toddy." Sean knew only too well what it was like to have nightmares. "Any more dreams?"

She shook her head. "No, thank goodness."

"I'm glad." Without thinking, he reached across the table and took her hand. "I can head into town and get you a new phone if you want—a cheap flip phone, just something to use until they've caught this guy."

"Thanks. I would really appreciate that."

They ate the rest of their breakfast, keeping the conversation light. Then Eden dressed Maverick and set him to play in front of a *Thomas and Friends* DVD, giving her and Sean uninterrupted time to talk.

She told Sean in greater detail what had happened yesterday. He kept his temper in check but found himself wanting to hunt this bastard down. Not only had this son of a bitch frightened Eden, but he'd seemingly also been part of the drug ring that had gotten Justin and David killed.

"Agent Santee said he doesn't think prosecutors will be able to charge anyone with Justin's or David's deaths because everyone responsible for the explosion died that night. I guess the investigation is just about drug trafficking."

Fire and Rain

"It doesn't really seem fair, does it?" He caressed the back of her hand with his thumb, the contact feeling somehow essential.

She turned her face toward the window, morning sunlight on her skin. "Not really. If the people who died in the explosion were cooking meth to pay off their drug debt to some dealer, doesn't the dealer bear some guilt? They were probably afraid for their lives and ended up killing themselves—and my husband."

Sean remembered the three people on the boat, people whose faces he hadn't quite been able to make out, people who'd almost killed him. "I have a hard time feeling compassion for them. They could have warned us. They might have saved their own lives if they'd been truthful. Instead, Justin and David are gone, and I spent three months recovering."

Her gaze met his. "I hadn't thought of that. What if they'd just warned you?"

"We might have handled it differently." Or maybe it would have been like his recurring nightmare where, no matter what he did, Justin and David always died.

Again and again, they died.

Eden squeezed his hand. "You okay? You just got a far-away look in your eyes."

He broke eye contact and released her hand. "Sorry. I was just remembering."

"No, I'm sorry. So much of our time together has been focused on my situation. But you survived an explosion and a helo crash and were badly hurt. I've been selfish."

"No, you haven't. I'm fine."

"Are you?"

"Yeah." He stood, picked up their plates. "Thanks for breakfast. How about I clean up these dishes and we head into town to get that phone?"

She took the plates from him. "How about I do the dishes while you take a shower? Then we can get the phone."

"Do I reek?" He raised his arm and sniffed beneath it.

Okay, so a shower wasn't a bad idea.

She laughed. "I just thought you might want one. You came here straight from a long duty shift last night still in your ODUs. There's a towel hanging in there for you."

It touched Sean that she'd thought of that. "Thanks, Eden."

She carried their dishes into the kitchen, giving him a smile that put a hitch in his chest. "I'll have more coffee ready when you're out."

Chapter Fourteen

EDEN WRESTLED Maverick into his car seat. "I know you're hungry, sweetie. We'll go home now and have some lunch, okay?"

They'd gone into town, where Eden had bought a small, prepaid flip phone. Then they'd taken Maverick to play at one of the city playgrounds before stopping at the base commissary to buy groceries. Sean had picked up a few things, too.

By the time Maverick was buckled in, the bags were loaded and Sean was pushing the shopping cart back to the corral. Eden started to climb into the driver's seat, but her gaze caught Sean's backside, which looked incredible in jeans.

Good grief!

She knew women who would pay money for this view.

A car pulled into the parking spot next to her, and Dalton Leavitt got out.

She smiled. "Hey, Dalton. How are Angela and Noah?"

He ignored her and strode toward Sean, who was now on his way back to the vehicle. "You lied to me, McKenna. People saw you on the dance floor with Eden. They saw you two kiss, and your car was parked in her driveway all night at least a couple of times. Now you're shopping together, a happy little family?"

Eden gaped at him, stunned.

Sean kept walking, his expression hard. "Mind your own business, Leavitt. I don't owe you or anyone else an explanation."

Dalton stepped in front of him, blocking his path. "Did you go behind Justin's back? Did you sleep with Eden before he died, or did he leave her to you in his will?"

"What the *fuck* did you just say to me?" Sean's fists clenched, and he looked angry enough to kill.

Oh, God!

"Shut your mouth, Dalton Leavitt!" Her face hot with rage, Eden darted over to the two men and pushed in between them, glaring up at Dalton. "How *dare* you? Sean was like a brother to Justin. He almost *died* that night trying to save him. Not only are you insulting us, but you're also insulting Justin's memory."

"It's okay, Eden." Sean's voice was unnaturally calm. "Dalton was on his way inside."

Dalton didn't budge. He looked surprised and amused at her outburst, grinning down at her. "People saw you slow-dancing and kissing the other night."

By now, others had stopped and were watching.

"We danced *once*—and I gave him a little thank-you peck on the lips. What business is that of yours? You're a worse gossip than my little sister. You should apologize—to both of us."

Dalton's face flushed an angry red, his smile gone. He opened his mouth as if to speak but said nothing.

From the back seat came a little voice. "Mama?"

"Let's go, Eden." Sean rested a hand on her shoulder. "Maverick is hungry, and I think Dalton has said all he has to say."

Dalton glared at him. "I outrank you."

"I don't think that will cover falsely accusing me of adultery with my best friend's wife." Sean's voice was as smooth and cold as ice. "But if you want to continue this conversation in Walcott's office, that's fine by me. Should I set something up?"

Dalton's gaze dropped to the pavement. "No."

"I didn't think so."

Dalton turned and walked away.

Eden climbed into the vehicle, pulse still pounding. "I'm sorry, Mavie. We're going home now. Do you want mac and cheese for lunch or chicken and stars?"

But Maverick only cried.

Sean took the passenger seat, his expression tense.

It was a quick drive back, and neither Eden nor Sean spoke.

Eden seethed. How dare Dalton! He'd turned one dance and a little kiss on the lips into accusations of an affair. It was absurd. Eden had never even looked at Sean in a sexual way when Justin had been alive. She'd known he was hot, but she could appreciate male beauty without wanting to get into a man's pants.

She pulled into her garage and parked, glancing over at Sean. His jaw was set, his brow furrowed. She couldn't blame him for being furious. "I'm sorry, Sean. That was my fault. If I hadn't—"

"You grab your hungry kiddo and let me carry in the groceries."

She climbed out, grabbed her handbag, then took Maverick from his car seat and carried him inside. "I'll make lunch now. Do you want some crackers?"

She set her handbag on the counter, put him in his highchair, and poured fish crackers on the tray. "There you go."

While Maverick nibbled crackers and Sean carried in her groceries, Eden quickly made mac and cheese. "Here, buddy."

Sean set a package of diapers on the floor. "I'm going to head back to base. I've got a few things I need to do."

"You're not going to punch Dalton, are you?"

Sean's lips quirked in a hint of a smile that didn't reach his eyes. "No, but I thought for a minute you would."

"God, I wanted to."

"I could tell." He held up his phone. "I've got your new number. Call the police if anything happens. Otherwise, I should be back in a couple of hours. Keep your doors shut and locked."

"Thanks, Sean—for all of this."

"You're welcome. See you later." He glanced at Maverick, and his gaze softened. "He's falling asleep in his lunch."

Maverick's head was nodding, little spoon still in his hand, cheese on his face.

"I think we wore him out."

"I guess so." With that, Sean turned and let himself out the front door.

SEAN PUT AWAY the things he'd bought at the commissary, still so on edge and angry that he inadvertently slammed his closet door. Thinking that exercise would help him burn off this rage, he dressed out and walked over to the training pool for his least favorite swim workout—interval training.

He focused on speed and efficiency, racing his own best time, pushing himself hard. But even exertion couldn't cut through the turbulence in his mind.

Did you go behind Justin's back? Did you sleep with Eden before he died?

Sean ought to have laughed it off. Before that dance, that

kiss, he'd never touched Eden in a way that was sexual. He'd certainly never slept with her. But instead of ignoring Dalton, he'd come perilously close to throwing his Coast Guard career away with a fist to the bastard's smug face.

What the fuck was wrong with him?

Eden.

He wanted her. No, he *craved* her.

Dalton had reacted exactly the way Sean knew his fellow Coasties would if he and Eden got together. He had no doubt that Dalton would share his malicious bullshit, and word would make it around base in a matter of days, maybe hours. And then life at Air Station Kodiak would get... interesting.

It wasn't that Sean had thin skin. He didn't much care what Dalton and the others thought of him, but operational readiness and station morale were vital for mission success. He didn't want to compromise either. But if they insulted Eden...

Oh, *hell*, no.

He'd kept his fists to himself today, but he wasn't sure what would have happened if Eden hadn't stomped over, put herself between them, and told Dalton what to do with himself. As angry as Sean had been, he'd still appreciated how fearless—and cute—she'd looked yelling at a man who stood a foot taller than she did.

Of course, the crazy part of it was that Sean wanted to do exactly what Dalton believed they were already doing. He wanted to take off her clothes, run his hands over her soft skin, explore her entire body. He wanted to kiss her and taste her. He wanted to bury himself inside her and fuck her until neither of them could walk.

Way to torture yourself, man.

Sean tried to channel all of that unspent sexual tension into his last lap, giving it everything he had, then he rested against the edge of the pool, catching his breath.

Maybe it would be better for both of them if he *didn't* stay at her place. He could cool off and get over his need for her, and his vehicle wouldn't be parked in her driveway to fuel rumors. Eden was just off base, after all—close enough for a rapid police response if there were an emergency. She had her shotgun, and she knew how to use it.

She's also five-foot-two and has a toddler to protect. Do you really want her to face a dangerous assailant alone?

Just the thought put Sean on edge.

It most likely wouldn't come to that, but those messages worried him. Whoever the sender was, he was a drug dealer and had Eden's cellphone number. He'd threatened her by name. He'd already been indirectly involved in Justin's and David's deaths.

He's a killer.

Then Sean remembered her tear-stained face after her nightmare last night. She'd gone into Maverick's bedroom just to make sure her boy was safe.

He's all I have left, Sean. I don't know what I'd do if I lost him, too.

Sean couldn't let that happen. It wasn't just the promise he'd made to Justin. He cared about Eden. He cared about both of them.

If anything happened to either of them...

Sean climbed out of the pool just as two new rescue swimmer candidates entered, followed by Chief Allen, the chief aviation survival technician. If they made it through their training, they'd be recommended for AST A-school—rescue swimmer school.

Sean greeted Ed with a nod. "Hey, Chief."

"Hey, McKenna. Glad to see you back in action, man."

"Glad to be back."

"Get in the water!" Ed shouted to the candidates. "I want twenty laps in twelve minutes. Give me an all-out effort. Go!"

Sean showered in the locker room, dressed, and headed

Fire and Rain

back to the barracks to grab a few things he'd forgotten before he headed up the hill to Eden's. He stuck his laptop with its charging cable in his backpack, tossed in his phone charger, and opened his dresser drawer to get a clean pair of boxers. His hand bumped something—an unopened box of condoms.

He stood there, looking at it, arguing with himself.

Better safe than sorry.

True. But there were so many ways to be sorry.

He closed the drawer, locked up, and left the barracks, backpack slung over one shoulder.

EDEN LIFTED Maverick out of the tub and wrapped him in a warm towel. "Let's dry you off and get you into your jammies."

She picked him up and carried him to his bedroom, glancing over her shoulder to find Sean sitting on the sofa, still on his laptop. He'd been closed off since he returned, and she knew he was still angry at Dalton. She couldn't blame him. They hadn't had a real conversation since then, not with Maverick around.

She finished drying Maverick, then picked him up and carried him to his room, where she set him on his changing table and combed his damp hair. "You look so much like your daddy. He had beautiful brown eyes, just like you do."

She put him in a nighttime diaper, zipped him into his pajamas, and set him on the floor. "Pick out some stories, okay? It's story time."

"Stowy time," he repeated in a sing-song way.

Maverick walked over to his little bookshelf, chose a few books, and ran out of the bedroom on tiny feet, as if story time were something that demanded swift action. Laughing to herself, Eden followed him down the hallway, only to watch him clamber into Sean's lap, books in hand.

Looking bemused, Sean closed his laptop and set it on the end table, then settled Maverick in his lap. "What have you got there, buddy?"

"Books!" Maverick held them up.

"That's okay, Sean. I'll…"

Sean looked up, a lopsided grin on his face. "It's okay. I'm happy to read to him."

Eden settled on the sofa beside them, listening as Sean read Maverick's bedtime stories and patiently answered his many questions. She wasn't sure what she'd expected of Sean, but he surprised her, doing different voices for different animals, even the orca, making Maverick laugh.

When story time was over, Eden gave Maverick his bottle and blankie and carried him to his crib. She stood there for a time, humming to him, rubbing his back until his eyes were closed. She shut his bedroom door behind her and walked back down the hallway to find Sean on his laptop once again. Was he trying to avoid talking to her?

She walked to the fridge. "Want a glass of wine or maybe something stronger?"

He closed his laptop and stood. "Scotch?"

"You got it." She took down a white wine glass for herself and a tumbler for Sean and poured them each a drink. "Here."

"Thanks." He took the tumbler, tossed it back.

"Another?"

"Yeah." He poured himself a double, but this time sipped.

"Are you okay? You've seemed really tense all evening. Dalton really got under your skin, didn't he? If I hadn't asked you to dance—"

Sean frowned. "Don't worry about it."

She rested her hand on his arm. "How can I not worry

after he went off on you like that? What if he spreads rumors on base and makes your job harder?"

"It's not your problem." He walked away from her.

"Like hell it's not. You're part of my family, Sean. When someone I care about is hurting, it matters to me."

"You have enough on your shoulders without listening to me whine."

Eden set her wine down on the counter. "I'm not some delicate flower. I'm strong enough to have my problems and to care about yours, too. You're clearly upset, so why not talk about it? I can take it."

"You want to talk about it?" He slammed his tumbler down on the counter with so much force that it made her jump, closing the distance between them in two long strides, rage on his face. "Dalton thinks I'm fucking you, and you know what? That's exactly what I want to do. But I can't, Eden. Justin was my best friend, and I came home that night, but *he didn't*."

And Eden understood.

She raised a hand to his cheek. "You truly believe his death was your fault, don't you?"

He jerked his head away, took a step back, clearly not wanting the comfort she offered. "It's the job of the AET to keep the rescue swimmer safe. Instead, I watched Justin *die*. One minute he was on deck, trying to help the victim ... and the next there was nothing but flames."

The anguish in Sean's eyes almost broke her heart.

Eden had never asked him for details of that terrible night. She hadn't wanted him to relive it, and she hadn't been sure she wanted to know. As unbearable as it was to imagine Justin dying in a few seconds of agony, it was terrible to think that Sean was carrying a weight that wasn't his.

"You almost died, too."

But Sean didn't seem to hear her.

"If I had yelled at him to abandon ship... If I'd just held onto that hoist line..." He squeezed his eyes shut, his right hand a fist. "Two men died because I failed."

"You broke your arm, tore up your shoulder, and suffered second-degree burns trying to hold onto that hoist line. What more could you do? You're not God, Sean." She took a step toward him. "Besides, you and I both know that Justin would *never* abandon ship and leave an unconscious victim behind. There was never anything you could have done."

She saw the moment her words hit him, the moment he began to understand. His eyes flew open, and he gaped at her as if he'd never once considered the fact that Justin might have made a choice that night.

Then she stood on tiptoes, cupped his cheek, and raised her lips to his.

Chapter Fifteen

Sean stood at an emotional edge, his heart thrumming, his mind caught between the words Eden had just spoken and the warm feel of her lips against his.

You and I both know that Justin would never abandon ship and leave an unconscious victim behind. There was never anything you could have done.

Nothing he could have done.

Almost unable to breathe, he slid a hand up Eden's spine, inhaled her scent, leaving control of the kiss to her. It was enough right now just to take it all in.

She teased his lips with hers, then nipped his lower lip with her teeth and soothed the bite with her tongue, sending a jolt of heat through him, rousing desires he'd tried so damned hard to ignore. He drew her closer, ducked down to answer her kiss with his own, taking his time, getting a feel for her, the heat in his blood building.

A voice in his head reminded him that he shouldn't be doing this. She was Justin's widow. But he ignored it.

He drew back for a moment, slid his fingers into her hair, tilting her head so he could look into her eyes. "*Eden.*"

Then he claimed her mouth with his, taking control this time, tasting her, teasing her, until they were both breathless and he was hard as a rock. He tilted her head back even more, lowered his mouth to her throat, and felt the thrumming of her pulse against his lips, her whimpers and the goosebumps on her skin urging him on.

She drew back, looked up at him through those big eyes, and gave him a seductive smile that he felt to his bones. Then she took hold of his fly, freed his erection, and dropped to her knees.

"Eden, you don't..." Whatever he was going to say became a quick inhale as she grasped him, stroked him, and took him into her mouth. "*Geezus.*"

She explored him with her tongue, lips, and hand, tasting him, nipping him, stroking him, her gaze still locked with his. He'd never experienced anything quite like this—the raw intimacy of looking into the eyes of a lover as she gave him pleasure. She clearly saw the effect she had on him, and he saw how much she enjoyed that.

She withdrew her mouth for a moment. "Does this feel good?"

"Just... yeah... mmm. But, Eden, you don't—"

This time, she took him all the way into her mouth, working up a rhythm, moving hand and mouth along his length from aching head to base, adding a twist now and again, teasing the most sensitive part of his cock with her tongue.

He reached down, adjusted her grip just a little and.... "Just ... like ... *that*. Hell, *yes*."

He tried to hold still for her, fought not to buck his hips, his fingers sliding into her silky hair. But, *damn*, she knew what she was doing, and it felt so *fucking* good, and she was so damned beautiful. He felt his balls drawing tight, his self-control fraying as her mouth and tongue and fist drove him headlong toward orgasm.

"Stop, Eden, sweetheart." He withdrew himself and gripped the base of his cock *hard*, fighting to relax so he wouldn't come like some randy college freshman. With his free hand, he brought her to her feet then tucked himself back into his boxers, his rigid dick looking straight up at him. "I don't want this to end like that."

She gave him a wickedly sexy smile, threaded her fingers through his. "Come to bed."

He followed her back to the bedroom, watched as she turned on her bedside lamp then drew down the covers, his body humming with need for her. When she turned toward him, he undressed, pulling his shirt over his head, tugging down his jeans and boxers to free his erection once more, his feet already bare.

She took a step toward him, her gaze raking over him, her brow furrowing, a look like hunger on her face. She ran her hands across his pecs and abs and over his obliques, making his cock jump. "You are such a pretty man."

"Pretty?" He chuckled. "I'll show you pretty."

Pulse thrumming with excitement, he dragged her against him, making her gasp. Then he caught hold of her T-shirt and drew it over her head, tossing it onto the floor. She stood there, looking up at him from beneath her lashes, a pink satiny bra cupping her full breasts. He brushed the mound of one breast with his fingers, saw her tense, heard her little intake of breath. He turned her to face away from him, lifted the silken weight of her dark hair over her right shoulder, and undid the clasp, letting the bra fall to the floor, freeing her for his touch.

And his heart beat faster.

He ducked down, kissed the satiny skin of her shoulder, reaching around with both hands to cup her. He nearly moaned, the weight of her breasts more than filling his hands, their velvety, dark tips growing pebbled, her skin like silk. It turned him on just to touch her.

She leaned back against him, resting her head against his chest while he played, her eyes drifting shut. But the more he teased her, the more she began to squirm, her hips shifting as he drew her nipples to peaks and grazed their tips with his palms. "Mmm."

He slid one hand down the smooth skin of her belly, unfastened the fly of her jeans, and slipped his hand inside to touch her, thick curls tickling his palm. "You're wet."

She whimpered as he found her clit and stroked it. But her jeans didn't give him the room he needed. With both of his hands, he yanked her pants down—and found himself staring at the twin mounds of her bare ass.

Damn.

She was wearing a thong.

He couldn't resist but kissed and nibbled one plump ass cheek and then the other, gratified by her quick intake of breath. Then, both of them naked at last, he turned her to face him. "God, Eden, you are *so* beautiful."

Her breasts were full, her waist narrow, her hips rounded. She didn't shave or wax, her thatch of dark curls completely natural just like everything else about her. Aching for her, he watched as she took two steps to the bed and stretched out on the sheets, her dark hair fanning across her pillow.

Then she reached for him. "I want you, Sean."

HER HEART TRIPPING, Eden feasted on the sight of Sean—all of that lean muscle, the hard length of his cock, narrow hips, powerful thighs. He stretched out on the bed beside her, propped up on an elbow, and began to explore her with one big hand, his expression almost worshipful, as if she were something precious and holy.

"I love your breasts." He palmed one of her breasts, lowered his mouth to the tip.

Eden's eyes drifted shut, and she arched off the bed as he sucked her nipple into the heat of his mouth and teased it with the tip of his tongue. Little barbs of pleasure darted from her breasts to her belly, sharpening her need for him. "*Yes.*"

He moved from one breast to the other, licking her, suckling her, nipping her with the edges of his teeth. She slid her fingers into his hair, giving herself over to the erotic thrill, savoring the torment. It had been so long, so long since she'd felt like this—vibrantly alive, on fire, reckless with need.

He skimmed a hand over her ribcage, her belly, the curve of her hips. "You're so soft—like silk."

Then his mouth returned to her breast—and his free hand began a slow slide down her body, his touch striking sparks off her skin. Anticipation shivered through her as he came closer to touching her where she burned hottest, his fingertips now skimming over her pubic hair. But just when she thought he was going to answer her need, his hand moved to her inner thigh, his fingers tickling her sensitive skin, heightening her arousal, making her wait.

And, oh, she loved it.

Even so, she moaned in protest and spread her legs for him, opening her eyes in time to catch the way his brow furrowed at the sight of her, his gaze fixed on her. Then at last, he cupped her again, applying pressure *right* where she needed it, one finger teasing her clit, flicking it, stroking it, caressing it in maddening little circles.

He kissed her forehead, blue eyes dark. "Show me what you like."

She reached down to guide him, whimpering when he got

the hang of it, her eyes drifting shut again. "That feels ... *so* good."

But he was only getting started.

He lowered his mouth to one aching nipple, picking up where he'd left off, the combined sensations deliciously erotic, the tension inside her building, desire making her frantic.

When he stopped, her eyes flew open. "Don't stop now."

"Patience." He stood, grabbed her ankles, and dragged her slowly toward the edge of the bed, a sexy grin on his handsome face.

It was so freaking *hot*—feeling his strength, watching his muscles in action as he drew her closer to the edge, seeing the sexual hunger on his face.

It gave her belly flutters.

She wondered for a moment whether she was close enough to her nightstand to grab a condom out of the drawer. Then he dropped to his knees, and her mind went blank, excitement shivering down her spine.

His gaze on hers, he rested her feet on his shoulders, parted her, and, without breaking eye contact lowered his mouth to her, tasting her with a few slow licks.

She sucked in a breath, her fingers sliding into his hair again. "*Sean.*"

At first, he seemed to indulge himself, teasing her with lips and tongue and gauging her responses. She let her knees fall wide open, her body thrumming with need. Then he covered her clit with his mouth—and sucked.

"Oh!" She gasped, her hips jerking, the sensation erotic and intense.

He chuckled, put his left forearm across her hips to hold her still, then lowered his mouth to her again.

Eden whimpered, her back arching, her fingers fisting in his hair. "*Sean*... oh, God... What are you...? *Ooh!*"

She'd never felt anything like this, whatever he was doing

with his lips and tongue unleashing a flood of sweet pleasure that drove her closer and closer to the shimmering edge.

Without breaking his rhythm, Sean teased the entrance to her vagina with a finger, circling her, probing, enticing her.

"*Yes*, please... Now!"

Another chuckle. Then he slipped a finger inside her, then two, thrusting deep, stroking her, keeping up the rhythm of both mouth and fingers.

"You're so... *good* ... so good... so... I...need... *Ah*!" Eden was lost in sexual bliss, the sounds coming from her throat uninhibited, raw, and blatantly carnal as pleasure carried her higher and higher, every muscle in her body tense.

Then climax hit her, and she came with a cry, arching off the bed, a tide of pleasure washing through her, buffeting her with wave after wave of ecstasy.

He stayed with her until her orgasm had passed, leaving her breathless. She opened her eyes, watched as he situated himself between her thighs, her gaze meeting his.

His expression was strained, his cock jutting upward. "Are you sure, Eden?"

Her heart melted at his thoughtfulness. "I want you."

She wrapped her thighs around him, reached down, and guided him into her, moaning as he buried himself inside her, stretching her, filling her completely. "*Oh, yes.*"

Then he began to move, thrusting into her with strong, silky strokes that rekindled the ache inside her. She fought the impulse to close her eyes and instead watched him. It turned her on to see *him* so turned on, to see on his face the pleasure it gave him to be inside her. His jaw was tight, his chest rising and falling with each breath, perspiration beading at his temples, his abs flexing as he drove himself into her.

Then his eyes drifted shut. "*Geezus*, Eden. You feel *so* good."

Slippery friction. The rocking of the bed with each forceful thrust. Pleasure building inside her.

He opened his eyes, caught her watching him—then reached down to tease her clit.

And just like that she was hurtling toward the edge once again, orgasm claiming her in a rush of bliss. But this time she wasn't alone. Body shaking, Sean withdrew from her and finished himself, groaning through gritted teeth as he came on her belly.

SEAN FLOATED SOMEWHERE between heaven and earth, his body replete, his mind empty. Eden's head rested against his chest, her fingers trailing along the ridges of his abs. He could still taste her, her scent all over him, the aftershock of bliss not yet faded.

"Are you okay?"

He was so strung out on her that it took him a minute.

He grinned. "I just made love with the most beautiful woman on Kodiak Island, and it blew my mind."

"That's not what I meant. Are you okay?"

"I know." He tried to put his emotions into words. "Earlier today, I yelled in Dalton's face that I wasn't sleeping with you, and now I am. I went against military norms and broke a promise to myself. More than that, I just had sex with you in the bed you once shared with my best friend. I ought to hate myself."

"Please don't. You don't deserve that."

"I only said I *ought* to hate myself, but the truth is, I don't."

"What do you feel?"

He thought for a moment, tried to put a name on it. "Happiness."

But it was more than that. Eden had offered him absolution, and he'd taken it. For the first time in five months, he felt ... *peace*.

"What you said earlier about Justin not leaving an unconscious patient behind—I never thought about that. It was my job to keep him safe. I told him to get out of there. Since then, I've hated myself for not doing my job. I believed that if I'd tried harder and called to him to abandon ship sooner, he might still be here."

"That's survivor's guilt talking. You did all you could, Sean. Justin made a choice. Even the Coast Guard report states that you followed regs and did all you could. In case you've forgotten, you came close to being killed that night, too."

Sean remembered those terrible hours after the explosion —the shock of it, the disbelief, the pain, the grief. "As they were rolling me to the ambulance, my last thought before I lost consciousness was of you. For some reason, I had it in my head that *I* was the one who would have to tell you that Justin was dead. I guess I was really out of it. But just the thought of having to tell you, of having to face you, nearly broke me."

"Oh, Sean, I'm so sorry." She rolled onto her belly, one palm on his chest, her beautiful eyes looking into his. "I'm so glad you were spared having to do that. You *never* had any reason to worry that I might blame you. When I heard you'd been badly injured and were in a Life Flight plane to Anchorage, I asked my family to pray for you. I was terrified I'd lose you, too."

"Thanks. I didn't know." But what about her? Eden had just had sex with a man other than Justin for the first time since his death. "How are *you*?"

"I'm happy." She smiled down at him. "Is it strange to be with you in this bed? A little. But I've spent five long months sleeping alone and reminding myself that Justin will never come home. Now, I'm with the hottest AET on Kodiak Island, and he's fan-fricking-tastic in bed."

Yeah, that didn't hurt Sean's ego one bit.

He smoothed strands of dark hair off her cheek. "To be fair, there are probably fewer than twenty AETs at Air Station Kodiak. That's like being the hottest guy in the hardware store."

She laughed, the sound like liquid sunshine. "What I said holds. You're the hottest—and you're incredible in bed. That thing you did with your mouth when you were going down on me. What was that?"

He chuckled, palmed her bare ass. "That, sweetheart, is a closely guarded secret."

"Is that so?" She gave him that smile, the one that made his pulse skip, and began to kiss and caress him, her breasts swaying enticingly as she moved. "I have ways of making you talk."

"Show me." He couldn't resist fondling her, his cock half hard again.

Eden teased him to fullness with tongue and hand before taking him into her mouth again. But this time she tormented him, driving him mad, bringing him to the brink of orgasm again and again only to stop and make him wait.

He moaned in frustration, his cock aching, one hand fisted in the sheets, the other in her hair. "Okay. You've got it. I'll tell you, you cruel woman. It's all in the lips. I just treat your clit like a nipple."

She stared at him as if amazed. "Really?"

"Really."

She sat up, reached into the top drawer of her nightstand, and took something out—a condom. She tore it open with her teeth, rolled it down his length, and straddled him, taking him slowly inside her. "And the truth shall get you laid."

Sean might have laughed, but she began to move, riding

him, the erotic motions of her hips carrying them both over the edge once more.

Afterwards, they lay together, arms around each other, bodies languid as the fever of sex cooled into drowsiness.

Then Eden spoke in a sleepy voice. "Should we send Dalton an email?"

Sean laughed and drew her closer. "To hell with Dalton."

Soon, they were both fast asleep.

Chapter Sixteen

June 14

EDEN WOKE to Sean's kisses, warmth sliding through her as she remembered last night. "Is it morning already?"

"It's only five. Go back to sleep. I need to report for duty by six."

She moaned in protest and rolled over to face him. "Can't you just call in and tell Captain Walcott I want you to stay in my bed all day?"

Sean chuckled, the sound warm. "I don't think he'd take that well."

"Probably not." Eden got up with Sean, slipped on her bathrobe, and admired his ass before he drew up his boxers. "Damn. I like that view."

He grinned. "Don't worry. You'll see it again."

"I hope so." She walked with him to the front door. "Are you sure I can't make you a cup of coffee or a quick breakfast?"

He slipped into his jacket, then drew her into his arms. "No need. I'll grab something at the cafeteria."

She looked up at him. "Be safe today, okay?"

"You, too. Please don't go anywhere by yourself."

"I won't."

He leaned down, kissed her. "I really hate to go."

"I hate it, too."

"I'll see you tomorrow." He opened the door, and she watched him walk down the steps, dawn turning the overcast sky pink.

Eden waited until he'd driven away then walked back to her bedroom, memories of last night making her smile. The sex had been *so* good, her body still glowing. But more than that, Sean had opened up, let himself be vulnerable with her about Justin's death and the guilt he'd been carrying. He'd been honest and unguarded, and that meant everything to her.

And then it hit her.

She was happy. Eden was genuinely happy.

Too full of excitement to sleep, she took a shower, dressed, and then took the sheets off her bed to wash them. Arm full of bed linens, she found herself standing at the foot of the bed, glancing around the room. She'd shared this room with Justin from the time she was four months pregnant until the night he'd died.

The wedding photo on her chest of drawers. His clothes in the closet and dresser drawers. His favorite fishing hat hanging on the coat rack he'd made from an old ski. The box with all of his Coast Guard ribbons. The case that held the folded flag from his memorial service.

Past and present collided, and she sat on the edge of the bed.

She had loved Justin with her whole heart. She loved him still. She had no intention of erasing all signs that this used to be *his* house. The idea made her heart hurt. But was it fair to expect Sean to share this space with her, to sleep here, to make love to her in this bed, when the space was still Justin's?

She stood, walked to the laundry room, started the load, then made coffee. She'd finished her first cup when Maverick surprised her by walking into the kitchen. "Well, good morning, buddy. You climbed out of your crib. It's time to get you a big boy bed, isn't it?"

Time was passing. Life was changing. Eden needed to keep up with it somehow.

She got up from the table, scooped him up. "Let's get you out of that wet diaper and have some breakfast."

By the time Maverick was dressed, fed, and settled with his little wooden train set, Eden knew what she needed to do. She sent a text message to her sisters.

```
Sean spent the night here with me last
night. I need your help sorting through
Justin's things. Can any of you come over
today?
```

Immediately, her phone blew up.

```
OMG! I've got swim lessons with the kids
this morning. Maybe later?
```

That was Natasha. Katie was next.

```
I have to work, but I want to hear all
about it!
```

Then came Maria's reply.

```
I knew it! Good for you! We're about to go
out on our boat. Maybe tomorrow?
```

But it was Anya's answer that made her laugh.

```
What?!? I am so here for this. I want all
the deets!
```

Twenty minutes later, Eden sat with Anya, the two of them sipping lattes and enjoying the pastries that Anya had picked up from a coffee shop on the way.

"I would have brought Mila to help," Anya teased. "We know how enthusiastic she was to do this. But Charlie got laid off, and she's upset."

"What?" Eden hadn't heard this.

"She doesn't want anyone to know, but I overheard Mom talking to Aunt Evelyn." Anya nibbled at her pastry. "Charlie got laid off and is looking for work in Anchorage and Deadhorse. Mila is afraid she's going to have to get a job. She's never worked before."

"I can understand why she's overwhelmed and afraid." Eden might not like Mila, but she didn't want her to be unhappy. "I hope Charlie finds a new job soon."

Anya had apparently said all she cared to say on that subject. She leaned closer. "Tell me everything."

Refusing to share intimate details, Eden gave Anya an overview of the past few days. But that wasn't enough for her sister.

"Oh, come on! At least tell me whether the sex was good?"

Eden couldn't keep the smile off her face. "It was *incredible*."

"So, he protects you, reads stories to my nephew, and f-u-c-k-s like a god. What's the problem?"

"Come." Eden led her to the bedroom. "Look."

Anya glanced around. "Sean is going to feel like he's having an affair with you in some other man's bedroom."

Eden might not have put it that way, but she definitely understood what Anya meant. "I can't face sorting through this alone. Can you help?"

Anya drew her into a hug. "Of course. We all knew this day would come eventually. You and I can get started—after I finish my pastry."

"Thanks, baby sister."

SEAN HAD HOPED to get a moment with the commander, but it had been a busy morning with two cases before lunch, one to deliver mechanical parts to a stranded container ship and the other a medevac of a woman with chest pain from Akhiok to a waiting ambulance in Kodiak. And still Eden had never left his mind, not for a moment.

He walked from the operations center to the cafeteria, trying to keep the smile off his face, his body humming with sexual energy. There was just something about Eden that made her different from any woman he'd known. She was authentic, spirited, fun—and that was outside the bedroom. In the bedroom, she was everything a man could want.

I'm with the hottest AET on Kodiak Island, and he's fan-fricking-tastic in bed.

Chuckling to himself, he entered the cafeteria, grabbed a tray and silverware, and chose the beef tacos. He spotted James and Zeke at a table with two other pilots. Trey was sitting with Dalton, Matt, Amanda, Rock, and Kai, so Sean went to join them. He wasn't looking for trouble, but he also wasn't going to walk on eggshells.

Trey looked up, grinned. "Hey, Flo."

But the others said nothing, Dalton giving Sean side-eye.

Then Dalton stood, picked up his lunch tray. "Let's go somewhere else."

The rest of the new AETs got to their feet, looking torn but following his lead, leaving only Trey, who didn't look surprised.

"Sorry, man. Dalton has been running his mouth all morning about how you're getting it on with Koseki's widow. I'd tell him to shut his piehole, but he outranks me. He said something about the two of you getting into it in the commissary parking lot."

Sean ought to have known. "He walked up to me, accused me of sleeping with her, and then asked me if we'd had an affair behind Justin's back."

Trey gaped at Sean. "What the *fuck*? Everyone knows how tight you and Justin were. There's no way you would have gone after his woman. What did you say to that?"

"Not much." Sean couldn't help but grin. "Eden gave him hell. I thought she was going to punch him."

Trey must have seen something in Sean's expression. "So, the two of you aren't...?"

"We weren't at the time." Sean left it at that.

"At the *time*?" Trey frowned. "Dude, that was yesterday."

Sean poured hot sauce on his tacos. "Things change."

"That explains the mood."

"What mood? I don't have moods."

"Clearly, you haven't spent much time with yourself. You had a smile on your face when you walked in." Trey grinned, leaned closer, his voice dropping to a whisper. "You and Eden?"

"If you tell anyone..." Sean took a bite and chewed, the flavors of cumin, chilis, tomatoes, and beef bright on his tongue.

Trey got an innocent look on his face. "I won't say a thing."

"I'm going to talk to Walcott as soon as I'm done here. I don't want the situation with Dalton to impact mission readiness."

Trey nodded. "Good thinking."

Sean let it go, and they talked about other things. The

storm system expected to blow through later this week. The new H-60 that had been flown in from Seattle. The upcoming wilderness survival training Trey was taking next week.

After lunch, Sean made his way to Captain Walcott's office to find Walcott on the phone. He turned to go, but Walcott motioned him inside.

"We were happy to assist, and we're glad to know there was such a good outcome. Thanks for calling. You're welcome." Walcott ended the call. "Remember the fisherman with the hook in his eye?"

Sean sat. "How could I forget?"

"Doctors were able to save his sight."

"I'm glad to hear it."

"But that's not why you're here, McKenna. Shut the door."

Sean did as he was told.

"I've heard the scuttlebutt about you and Eden Koseki. Is there any truth to it?"

"She and I are in a relationship, sir, but there's absolutely *no* truth to the rumor that she and I were involved before Justin's death."

Walcott frowned. "Who said that?"

"I prefer not to say, sir. I'm not here to get anyone in trouble. My concern is for mission readiness and morale."

Walcott nodded, the frown fixed on his face. "That's okay. One of my officers reported Leavitt this morning. He was convinced there was no truth at all to the rumors, but you're saying the two of you *are* involved?"

"There wasn't any truth to it until very recently, sir. It wasn't something either of us saw coming."

"No, I imagine it wasn't." Walcott drew a breath, and Sean knew he had much more important matters on his mind. "You're not breaking any regs. Your relationship does fly in the face of norms, however."

"It does, sir, but I don't know what to do about that. I won't let Dalton's attitude impact the performance of my duties."

"How did Dalton find out?"

"He saw my car in her driveway overnight and made assumptions. At that point, she and I were just friends. I stayed at her place twice—when she and Maverick had scarlet fever and after she got those threatening messages."

Walcott nodded. "I remember. So, this really *is* recent."

"Yes, sir." Sean wasn't going to give him details.

"God knows, Eden Koseki deserves some happiness after all she's been through. You, too, McKenna. Please continue to be discreet. As for Leavitt, he's transferring to Miami in two weeks, so it shouldn't be a problem."

The SAR alarm went off.

The operations duty officer's voice came over the speakers. "Now put the ready helo online. Now put the ready helo online."

Sean stood.

"They're playing your song, but thanks for coming to me."

"Yes, sir." Sean left Walcott's office and jogged toward the locker room.

WITH ANYA'S HELP, Eden sorted through Justin's belongings. It wasn't easy, memories ambushing her at every turn. The T-shirt he'd worn to the hospital the night Maverick had been born. The fly-tying kit she'd gotten him for his birthday last year. His favorite flannel shirt that was worn through at the elbows.

She packed most of his clothes into bags to take to St. Mary's, and some she set aside for Sean and Maverick. "Mavie might like wearing something that belonged to his father when he's older."

Natasha arrived after lunch, bringing extra boxes and her two daughters, Summer and Willow, who played with Maverick. "I've got one question, Eden. You've slept with this man once. You can't possibly know where this relationship is headed. Are you doing this for him—or for you?"

Eden understood Natasha's concern. "I'm doing it for both of us, I guess. Whether things work out with Sean or not, I need to do this."

By midafternoon, Eden had worked her way to the back of the closet where Justin had kept some of his Coast Guard gear. She carried out a waterproof bag, set it on the bed, and looked through it. "I wonder if Sean could use this stuff. It might..."

She felt something made of paper and pulled out a white legal-sized envelope. On the front in Justin's neat handwriting was one name.

Sean.

"What's that?"

"Something for Sean. I guess Justin didn't get the chance to give it to him."

"Are you going to open it?"

Eden shook her head. "It's for Sean. I'll let him open it."

Anya looked disappointed "Girl, you have more self-control than I do."

"We *all* know that." Natasha secured a box with tape.

Eden wanted them to understand. "Justin knew Sean longer than he knew me. They had their own relationship, and I respect that. They were like brothers. I can't open something that Justin meant for Sean."

She set the envelope on her dresser and got back to work, clearing out the closet and sorting through everything she'd found there. By late afternoon, a dozen boxes and as many bags cluttered the living room and porch.

Fire and Rain

"I need to get home and make dinner." Natasha glanced at the time on her phone. "Chris should be home soon. St. Mary's drop-off site is closing in a half an hour. I'm going to load as much of this into my SUV as I can and drive it down. Willow, Summer, can you help me carry boxes out?"

"Thanks so much for your help, Tasha." Eden gave her sister a hug.

"My brave little sister. You really are brave, Eden. I was happy to help."

They packed Natasha's SUV as full as they possibly could, and she set out, leaving Maverick to cry for his cousins.

Eden scooped him up. "You'll see Summer and Willow again, Mavie."

Anya surveyed the mess. "You know what you should do?"

"I feel certain you're about to tell me."

"Rearrange the bedroom furniture. Give the place a whole new look."

"I don't know. That seems like a lot." It had been a long day and an emotionally draining one, too. "I think I'll just order pizza and get the place put back together."

"Forget pizza. Katie's on her way with sushi—and a few other things."

That sounded mysterious.

"You've been plotting behind my back."

"You know it."

Eden made Maverick a simple supper of mac and cheese with salmon for extra protein. He had missed his afternoon nap and was cranky. "Here you go, Mavie."

Katie arrived ten minutes later, carrying in the food and a large shopping bag from Target. "Hey, Maverick! Aren't you a cute little macaroni mess?"

While Eden set the table and took the sushi out of the bags, Anya filled Katie in on everything they'd done and then took her back to see the bedroom. Eden didn't think much of it until they returned and Katie informed her that she and Anya would rearrange the furniture if Eden felt too tired.

"I mean, come on." Katie sat, picked up her chopsticks. "It's a new start, a new beginning. Why not go all the way? You won't have to lift a finger. Anya and I will do it all."

Anya looked up from her California roll. "We will?"

Buoyed by her sisters' enthusiasm and humor, Eden tried to relax and just enjoy their company. After they'd eaten, they all walked back to the bedroom, where Katie and Anya got to work, carrying everything out into the hallway, then vacuuming and putting the furniture into place one piece at a time.

Eden, whose job it was to offer feedback and snuggle Maverick, found herself laughing at her sisters' unintentional antics. Anya did a face plant on the mattress while trying to lift it from the bed. Katie found a spider in one corner and let out an earsplitting scream. Then the two of them got stuck in the doorway trying to decide who should go first while carrying out her chest of drawers.

Eden hadn't laughed this hard in a very long time.

But then it was time to give Maverick his bath, read him stories, and put him to bed, so her sisters finished putting the room back together without her. When Mavie was asleep in his crib, Eden ventured a peek at her bedroom.

The bed, which was still unmade, stood against the far wall with a nightstand on each side. Her big chest of drawers stood where the bed had been. Everything was neatly arranged, the jar where she kept her favorite bits of sea glass sitting in the window where it caught the evening sunlight.

"Wow. It's so different. I love it. Thank you."

"There's more room to walk, for one thing." Anya demonstrated by walking around the bed. "See?"

"I'll get the sheets out of the dryer and make the bed."

"Don't bother. We've got a gift for you." Katie jumped up

off the mattress. She dashed out of the room and returned with the shopping bag. "This is from all of us."

"It's heavy." Eden opened it to find a duvet with an aqua blue cover and matching high thread-count sheets. "Thank you! This is wonderful."

Anya beamed. "A new guy in the bed means new bedding."

Eden smiled. "Is that proper etiquette these days?"

They enjoyed a glass of wine together, and then it was time for her sisters to go. Eden thanked them, gave them each a hug, and waved to them as they drove away. Then she went back inside, found the piece of red sea glass, sank onto the mattress, and let her tears come.

Chapter Seventeen

IT WAS mid-afternoon when Sean drove up the hill to Eden's place, the idea of seeing her again making his heart beat a little faster. They'd had a quiet night on base with no SAR calls, so he'd been able to sleep and work his regular daytime shift. Now, showered and shaved and packing that box of condoms, he was free to be with Eden until six tomorrow morning.

She hadn't once left his thoughts, memories of their night together on a loop in his mind. This was new for him. Most of his relationships back in his dating app days had been one and done. But he couldn't get Eden out of his head. She was like a fever in his blood.

He pulled into Eden's driveway and found her outside playing ball with Maverick. He parked, climbed out, and watched.

"Hit the ball, Mavie." Eden gave Sean a smile then tossed a small plastic baseball.

The ball landed in the grass and rolled, but that didn't stop Maverick. He ran over to where it lay in the grass and whacked it squarely with his bat.

Sean chuckled. "Well, he hit it."

Fire and Rain

Eden pointed at Sean. "Look who's here."

Maverick turned, dropped the bat, and ran toward Sean, a smile on his little face, reaching for Sean. "Sawn!"

A strange warmth blossomed in Sean's chest, and he scooped Maverick up. "Hey, buddy. Are you playing baseball with your pretty mama?"

"I hit a ball."

Sean grinned. "You sure did."

Eden picked up both ball and bat and walked over to them. "How was your shift?"

"Not bad." Sean could see she was about to put her arm around him, so he stepped back, set Maverick on the ground. "We should go inside first. I need to grab my bag."

Eden led her son toward the door. "Let's get a snack, Mavie."

Sean followed, duffel slung over his shoulder. He left the duffel bag on the floor by the door and walked to the kitchen, where Eden opened a piece of string cheese and handed it to Maverick, who dashed off, cheese stick in hand.

Sean drew Eden into an embrace, held her close. "I've wanted to do that all day."

"I missed you, too. How was your shift?"

"We had a few calls during the day, but the night was quiet."

She tilted her head back and smiled up at him. "Does that mean you're well rested and full of energy?"

"*So* full of energy." He gave a little thrust of his hips. "You're all I can think about."

She smiled. "I like that. Can I get you something to drink—tea, water, soda?"

"I'll get it." He took a glass from the cupboard and filled it with ice and water. "How was your day?"

"It was hard—and good." She sat at the dining room table. "My sisters came over yesterday and helped me sort through

Justin's things. I saved some stuff for you, me, and Maverick, and the rest went to St. Mary's."

Sean hadn't expected this. He sat next to her, took her hand. "Are you okay?"

She nodded, a sad smile on her face. "It wasn't easy, but it was time. I found something he intended to give you." She stood, walked to the bedroom, and returned with an envelope. "I found it in his helicopter survival kit. He must have forgotten it was there or misplaced it."

Sean took it from her and was surprised to find it unopened. "You didn't read it?"

Her answer was simple. "It's not for me to open. It's yours."

He turned it over, the sight of Justin's handwriting a punch to the gut. Then he opened it, the first words another blow.

If you're reading this, it means I'm dead. I hope I was strong and true to my oath in the end and made you, my fellow Coasties, and Eden proud.

Sean's throat grew tight, Justin's words reopening a pit of unresolved grief inside him. He read on, his vision blurring. He blinked his tears away, determined not to lose it in front of Eden, whose grief was deeper. When he came to the end, it hit him hard—and made him smile.

He looked up, saw Eden watching him from the kitchen. How like her *not* to stand over his shoulder or demand that he read it aloud. She gave him space, and he liked that. "Justin really did think of everything. I'd like to read part of it to you."

"Okay." She drew a breath as if steeling herself.

Sean skimmed to the bottom, swallowed hard.

Hold it together, man.

He read aloud. "One day, I hope Eden will start dating again. I hope she'll meet a man who cares deeply for her and Maverick and any other children we might have had in the meantime. Whoever this guy is, please don't beat the shit out of him. Eden is a good judge of character. She married me, right? I hope you find someone, too, my friend. Don't live your life alone. You'll miss out on so much happiness if you do. Semper Paratus. Stay cool, brother."

Heart aching for the friend he'd lost, Sean read the letter silently once more, some part of him clinging to every word. He heard a *sniff* and looked up to find Eden smiling, tears running down her cheeks.

"See?" She came to stand behind him and wrapped her arms around him. "He wants us both to be happy. *Please* don't beat the shit out of yourself."

EDEN HAD THAWED out some halibut and made fish tacos for supper. Sean insisted on doing the dishes. When he was done, she asked him if he would mind taking a walk with her and Mavie on Jewel Beach. "I've been stuck inside since getting those messages. The tide is coming in, but we'll have a good couple of hours."

"I suppose that's safe enough. It's technically on base." He turned away from her, drew something from inside his jeans, and she heard what sounded like the racking of a slide.

"Are you carrying?"

"Of course." He slipped the pistol back into its hidden holster. "I'm not taking any chances with your safety."

A light rain had begun to fall. While Sean moved his vehicle out of the driveway, Eden dressed herself and Maverick in rain gear, complete with fisherman's hats, and grabbed their buckets. Then she secured Maverick in his car seat. "We're going to the beach, Mavie. Here's your bucket."

He took his little pail from her. "Sheshell!"

"Yes, we're going to find seashells."

Sean climbed into the passenger seat. "What's with the buckets? Clams?"

She smiled. "Not today. Treasure."

He raised an eyebrow. "Treasure. Huh."

"You'll see."

"I talked to Captain Walcott today, told him what was going on."

This surprised Eden so much that she slammed on the brakes, stopping at the end of the driveway. "You told him? Everything?"

"I had to do something. Dalton is flapping his jaw to anyone who will listen. When I went to sit with him and the new AETs, they all got up and left the table. While I don't care what people think, I don't want it to disrupt the unit."

"What a jerk! I should have punched him while I had the chance. What did Walcott say?"

"He told me to be discreet and thanked me for coming to him. I made it clear I wasn't there to rat out Dalton, but someone else had already reported him. I just didn't want this to cause strife on base. The SAR alarm went off and cut the conversation short."

Eden took her foot off the brake, backed into the street, and drove toward base. "Is he going to kick Dalton's butt?"

Sean chuckled. "No idea. He said we both deserved happiness after all we've been through."

She took Sean's hand, squeezed it. "Well, he's right about that."

The officers at the gate recognized both of them, gave their IDs a cursory glance, and waved them through. Eden parked as close to the beach as she could, then climbed out, got Maverick out of his car seat, and grabbed both buckets. "Let's go find treasure, Maverick."

It felt so good to be outdoors. Eden inhaled the fresh sea air, let the sound of the surf wash over her, savored the bite of

Fire and Rain

the rain on her face. The past couple of days had been good, but they'd also been hard. And now Justin's letter to Sean...

Eden had been able to hear Justin's voice in every word Sean had read.

Sean walked beside her, Maverick between them.

Eden knelt, pointed. "Look, Maverick. A sand dollar. You won't see many of these around here."

"See, Mommy?" Maverick picked up the sand dollar, held it out for her.

"I see." She repeated the name. "You can tell it's not alive because it's white."

Sean bent to look, his hair damp from the rain. "I didn't know that."

"Dollah." Maverick dropped the sand dollar in his little pail and moved on.

Soon, a cracked butter clam shell joined the sand dollar. Then Eden found her first piece of sea glass. She scooped it out of the pebbles. "Lavender-colored glass is fairly uncommon. It comes from a specific kind of bottle made in the late eighteen-hundreds."

Sean took it, examined it. "This has been floating around in the ocean all this time?"

"Isn't that fun?" She took the piece, dropped it into her bucket. "It's treasure."

Sean seemed to get into it after that, walking alongside her, handing her bits of sea glass that he spotted among the pebbles or pointing Maverick toward some interesting find—a seagull feather, an antique Japanese fishing float, a rather large shark's tooth.

"Look how big this is, Mavie."

"Toof?"

Sean placed it gently on Maverick's upturned palm. "It's a shark's tooth."

As she watched the two of them, a niggling worry she

hadn't realized she was carrying surfaced. Sean had told her and Justin many times that he never planned to be a father. And yet he wasn't some dude bro who was afraid of changing diapers or spending time with small children. Instead, he was good with Maverick and so natural.

Don't worry about it.

After about an hour, the rain began to fall harder. It was almost bath time for Maverick anyway, so they walked back up the beach and uphill to her vehicle. When Maverick almost slipped in the mud, Sean picked him up.

"What did you think? Do you like my idea of treasure hunting?"

"I don't think I've ever gone anywhere just to be there and explore. It was fun and relaxing. I see why you enjoy it so much. But next time, I'm bringing my own bucket."

Eden laughed. "You just want that shark's tooth."

He grinned. "You know it."

SEAN READ Maverick his bedtime stories, gratified by the boy's laughter at his silly voices. Then he stood in the hallway, listening while Eden rubbed Maverick's back and sang him a lullaby, the tenderness of it hitting him in a soft spot he hadn't known he had.

I hope you find someone, too, my friend. Don't live your life alone. You'll miss out on so much happiness if you do.

A year ago, Sean would have brushed off Justin's words. He'd been single for thirty years, and it had worked well for him. He'd moved from one duty station to the next without having to worry about uprooting a wife and kids. He'd spent his free time doing whatever he felt like doing—surfing, fishing, sea kayaking, sky diving, or just catching up on sleep.

But so much had changed since Justin's death.

Fire and Rain

In the past week, Sean had changed Maverick's poopy diapers and given him medicine. He'd read him bedtime stories using funny voices and had gotten a kick out of every little giggle. His heart had lit up when Maverick had come running, arms outstretched, to greet him earlier. And he'd just spent two hours on a beach in the rain finding interesting things for Maverick and Eden to put in their buckets—and he had *enjoyed* it.

You left out the part where you slept with Eden.

Yeah, there was that.

You're in love with her.

The thought hit Sean like a ninety-knot headwind, his pulse skyrocketing, adrenaline hitting his bloodstream.

No. No way.

He strode to the door then stepped outside onto the porch where he stood in the darkness, sucking in deep breaths, his pulse still racing, rain falling from a starless sky.

How could he fall in love with her so quickly? Five months ago, she'd been the wife of his best friend, and now he was in love with her? What the fuck?

He wasn't an impulsive man. It made no sense.

Except that it made perfect sense. He'd never had inappropriate thoughts about her before Justin's death, but he'd spent every day since he'd met her thinking how lucky Justin was. He'd tried dating women in Kodiak, but none of them had held his interest.

Had he subconsciously been comparing them all to Eden?

Sean leaned against the railing, eyes closed, listening to the sound of the rain. He'd always imagined falling in love would be more like a lightning strike, a sudden attraction to a woman who ticked all of his boxes—single, beautiful, independent, successful in her own way, sexually compatible, and not the least bit interested in having children.

Well, Eden was beautiful, independent, and incredible in

bed, but she was already a mother. She had an entirely different idea of what constituted success, one that was simpler and more about living in the moment than climbing a career ladder. And like the slow, steady rising tide, she'd gotten into him, filling him in places he hadn't known were empty.

The door behind him opened.

Eden came to stand beside him, and for a moment they stood together in silence. Then at last she spoke. "I've always loved the rain."

I love you, Eden.

Sean thought it but didn't say it. He put his arm around her shoulders. "Let's go inside."

He locked the front door behind them and walked with her to her bedroom, his fingers laced with hers.

She motioned to the room. "We rearranged it. It was time for a new start."

"Nice." In truth, he'd barely noticed.

The only thing he could see was Eden.

He cupped her face between his palms and kissed her, deep and slow, drinking her in, cherishing the feel of her lips against his.

Eden. *His* Eden.

Every inch of her seemed sacred to him as he undressed her, exploring her secrets by touch and taste. Soft skin. Beautiful full breasts with their dark, pebbled tips. The heat between her thighs. The fire in her blood.

She was life. She was his salvation. She was a miracle.

She undressed him, too, the two of them standing naked together at last. Hands caressed, teased, stroked, seeking always to please. Then she took one of the condoms from the box he'd set on the nightstand and rolled it down his erection.

He drew her onto his lap, his hands on her hips. She wrapped her legs around him and took him inside her. He yielded control to her, the two of them face to face as she rode him, bringing them both release. They lay in a tangle afterwards, looking into one another's eyes, Sean's heart almost too big for his chest.

She smoothed a hand over his pecs. "You might want to run for the door."

"Why is that?"

"I think I'm falling in love with you."

Sean brushed a strand of hair off her cheek. "I'm not going anywhere."

Chapter Eighteen

June 23

EDEN AND SEAN buckled into their seats on the float plane, their gear already stowed in the small baggage compartment.

The pilot, who said his name was Grit, climbed into his seat, put on his earphones, and got the plane into the air, soaring over Kodiak Harbor before turning inland. He smiled back at them. "Is this your first time in Alaska?"

"I was born on Kodiak Island, and Sean flies with the Coast Guard." Eden realized she'd probably just ruined the pilot's plan for in-flight conversation. "But this is our first time to Uganik Lake. Can you tell us about it?"

Sean glanced over at her, suppressing a grin, his fingers twining with hers. "What kind of fish will we find there?"

The pilot seemed relieved. "I hear it's great for Dolly Varden trout. This time of year, you might be able to catch sockeye and chum, too. You'll just have to compete with the bears. A lot of people fly up there to hunt bear."

While Grit talked about brown bears and asked Sean about his work as a Coastie, Eden watched the landscape below them—the ocean to their rear, the city of Kodiak below, mountains ahead. She'd left Maverick with Natasha and had rented the cabin for two days so she and Sean could be alone together. Dating with a toddler had its cute side, but she wanted them to have a chance to focus on one another.

She'd chosen this place because she didn't want to take him to a cabin where she and Justin had stayed. She wanted the area to be new to both of them, a spot where they could make their own memories.

It was only a thirty-minute flight, and they soon landed on the lake, the pilot bringing the plane to a halt just off the pier. Sean climbed out and turned to help Eden.

Grit left their bags and fishing gear on the pier, where a skiff with an outboard motor was tied off for their use. "I'll leave you to it. Hope the fish are bitin' for you. Thanks for flying Island Air."

Sean shook his hand. "Thanks for the lift."

They stepped back and watched as the pilot moved onto the lake and took to the sky. And then at long last, they were alone.

Sean glanced uphill toward the cabin, looking ridiculously handsome in his aviator shades. "Let's get settled."

Eden shouldered her duffel bag and fishing rod. "It's beautiful here."

They walked uphill a short distance to the two-room cabin. It looked exactly like the photo—a simple structure with windows, a deck, and a few Adirondack chairs. Firewood stood neatly stacked in a nearby woodshed on one side.

"So far, so good." Eden unlocked the door.

Inside, it was clean and cozy. A woodstove sat in one corner, while a wooden table with bench-style seats stood in the middle of the front room. There was a sink, too, with an old-fashioned pump handle that drew water from an outdoor tank. In the back room were bunk beds against one wall and a full-sized bed against the other, all with homey quilted coverlets.

Eden wrapped her arm around Sean's waist. "It's perfect."

He kissed the top of her head. "I'll get a fire going."

While he went out to get firewood, Eden arranged their gear—fishing and boating stuff in the main room and personal items in the bedroom. By the time she had organized everything, Sean had a roaring fire going in the wood stove.

"Ready to go catch dinner?" She grabbed her fishing rod.

He closed the woodstove's door and dragged her against him. "How about we test the bed instead? We can catch fish later."

Her fishing rod landed on the floor as they kissed and stumbled their way to the bedroom. They fell across the bed in a tangle of limbs, hands sliding beneath clothing, undoing zippers and clasps, hungry for skin. Eden raised her bottom off the bed as Sean yanked down her jeans, his erection free. She would have spread her legs for him, but he drew her to her feet, turned her to face away from him, and bent her over the bed, nudging her feet apart with his.

He palmed her bare buttocks with big hands. "God, I love your ass."

She wiggled her butt to tease him, looked back at him over her shoulder, saw an expression of raw hunger on his face. "I want you inside me."

"Hold that thought."

She heard a condom wrapper tear, looked back to watch him roll it on his erection, her inner muscles tightening in anticipation. Then he moved in, teasing her with the head of his cock before burying himself inch... by slow inch... inside her.

They moaned almost in unison, Eden arching her lower back to take all of him.

Then he began to thrust, going easy at first. "God, I love this view."

Eden loved the silky strokes, the sweet stretch.

Then Sean reached around to play with her clit, stroking her inside and out. Oh, he knew her body well now, knew just what she needed. Each thrust rocked her, made the bed hit the wall, the tension inside her quickly blossoming into gold.

Then he changed it up, following three quick, short thrusts with a deep slow one, using his cock to hit that secret place inside her. It felt so good, so incredibly good. He kept up the rhythm until she found herself hovering on that bright edge.

She came with a cry, heard him groan her name as he finished with several deep, powerful thrusts. After a moment, he withdrew, tossed the condom, and they sank, laughing, onto the bed, their jeans still around their ankles.

Sean kissed her. "I'm hungry."

"Then you'd better get moving." Eden smiled. "Your dinner is still in the lake."

SEAN HELD EDEN CLOSE, tracing the curve of her spine with his fingers. The two of them lay together, naked, having chosen sex for dessert. He couldn't remember the last time he'd felt so relaxed, so at peace. He didn't want it to end.

They'd taken the skiff out on the lake and had caught five good-sized Dolly Varden. While Sean had cleaned the fish, Eden had foraged for greens and berries in the forest behind the cabin. Then she'd fried the fish on the woodstove, and they'd eaten a meal fit for a king, while she'd given him a master class on fishing flies. With one appetite satisfied, they'd gotten naked and sated the other.

Did she have any idea how incredible she was?

When are you going to tell her you love her?

Sean was working on that. It shouldn't be hard, but it was. He hadn't expected to fall for Eden. He hadn't seen it coming. Some part of him just wanted to make certain this was *real*.

Coward.

Sean broke the silence. "I've never met a woman like you."

She tilted her head back so she could look up at him. "What do you mean?"

"Well, for starters, you fish, hunt, shoot, and pilot a boat as well as any man."

"So can a lot of women in Alaska."

Sean knew that was probably true. "Can they also forage for dinner, cook on a woodstove, and tell the history of a random piece of glass on the beach?"

She smiled and stretched like a contented kitten. "Native Alaskan women can."

He stroked her hair, tried for once to put his emotions into words, and ended up babbling. "God, Eden, you drive me out of my mind. I want you even when you aren't around. I can't quit thinking about you. Everything about you turns me on—your smile, the way your hair moves, your eyes, that sound you make when you're about to come. There's no other woman in the world who can say that."

She raised her head, turned onto her belly. "What sound do I make—?"

Footsteps.

"Did you hear that?"

"Yes." Sean jumped out of bed, reached for his pistol. "Stay here."

She got up, grabbed her shot gun, and followed. "It's probably wildlife."

"Eden, you should..." He turned to tell her to get back into the room, but the sight of her holding a shotgun naked did something to his brain. "...stay behind me."

"If I stay behind you, I can't shoot."

Naked and armed, they walked out to the main room, the only light coming from the glass pane in the door of the woodstove.

More footsteps—heavy, awkward ones.

It sounded like a drunk was stumbling around on the cabin's deck.

Sean had heard of campers and hunters in remote cabins being attacked by strangers. It was rare, but it happened. He moved toward the window when a strange bawling sound came from the other side of the door.

"Bear cubs." Eden raised her voice and bonked the locked door with the butt of her shotgun. "Hey, baby bears! This is our house! Go find your mama! Skedaddle!"

The sound of scrambling. A cub bawling and... silence.

Sean drew back the curtains. In the moonlight, he saw two brown bear cubs running toward their mother, who stood on her hind legs near the edge of the forest, sniffing the air. "She can smell us."

Eden came up beside him. "She can smell us—and the fish we fried."

"Damn, she's big. They seem a lot smaller from a helicopter."

Eden seemed to find that funny. "You think? The cubs are so cute."

"Their mama is the size of a small car. We'll have to take firearms and bear spray when we go out tomorrow." Sean let the curtain fall back into place, took Eden's shotgun, set both of their firearms on the table, then drew her into his arms. "Please follow my lead in crisis situations. I know you can hit a target, but I'm the one with military training. If those footsteps had belonged to bad guys instead of bears..."

You could tell her that you love her and want to keep her safe.

"I hear what you're saying, and it means a lot to me that you would put yourself between me and danger. But I already lost Justin. I can't lose you, too."

"I won't let that happen." He kissed her, soft and slow. "I'll stoke the fire. You head back to bed."

She took her shotgun and walked to the bedroom, giving him a glorious view of her bare ass, long hair tumbling down her back. He added more wood to the stove, checked to make sure the door and windows were secured, then followed her.

EDEN SAT NEXT to Sean on the deck, watching the sunset over the lake, the two of them holding hands and sipping whiskey from paper cups. A soft breeze blew, carrying the scent of cedar and Sitka spruce, the last rays of the sun turning the clouds pink.

She looked up at the summit of the mountain across from them. "It's hard to believe that just a few hours ago, we were up there."

They had hiked to the summit after a lunch of trout, which they'd cooked over a fire on the edge of the lake. The climb had been a real workout, especially in areas where the undergrowth was dense or the slope was steep and slippery with vegetation. Then Sean had caught a sockeye for supper, and they'd feasted on the deck.

"That view was incredible." Sean had taken photos, including a selfie of the two of them with the lake and most of Kodiak National Wildlife Reserve behind them.

It was the first photo of them alone together.

But would this last? Were they truly a couple?

Did Sean care for her the way she cared for him?

Eden tried not to worry about it. "I never expected this."

"What?"

"You."

Sean smiled. "Yeah. Me neither."

"The night Justin died, I thought I would never laugh again, never love again, never be happy again. I couldn't even imagine it. It was like half of me was ripped away. I was no longer whole, but somehow my heart kept beating. I told myself that Maverick was the only thing that mattered now. I knew I had to somehow find a way to keep going for his sake."

"And you did, Eden. You were so strong."

Eden laughed. "Says the man who watched me cry my way through an entire box of tissues—twice."

He squeezed her hand. "Hey, you were entitled to those tears."

"I didn't believe it was possible for me to love anyone again. Now it's almost six months later, and I'm with you watching the sun set over this beautiful lake."

He ran his thumb over her knuckles. "I never want to make you cry or cause you pain. But we both know I might get transferred to a new duty station—and soon."

Eden's heart constricted at the thought. "Have you gotten word?"

"No, not yet. I've already asked to remain here, but you know how that goes."

"Orders, not options."

"Exactly."

She willed herself to let that worry go and sipped her whiskey. "We have to enjoy the time we have. If I didn't understand that before Justin's death, I do now. Joy and tears seem to be a package deal, one following after the other just like sunshine and rain. I can't stop it, any more than I can stop the sun from setting. If we waste our time in the sunshine worrying about the rain, we'll miss the whole point of living."

He exhaled—a quick gust of breath—and looked at her as if he'd never seen her before. "I meant it when I said I've never met any woman like you. How did you get to be so wise? You're only twenty-eight, for God's sake."

"I come from a long line of very wise women."

"Yeah, I believe that."

Motion caught her eye, and she spotted the mama brown bear and her two cubs about a half mile up the shoreline. "Look. She's teaching them to fish—or trying."

One of the cubs rolled in the mud, while the other splashed in the water with its front paws, surely frightening all the fish away. Mama Bear looked back at them, an almost recognizable expression of frustration on her furry face.

Sean laughed. "She's got a long way to go."

Eden heard a telltale whine and got to her feet. "Time to go inside unless you want to be dinner for the state bird."

"Nah, I *hate* mosquitoes." He waved one away from his face.

She walked toward the door. "I brought a deck of cards."

"A deck of cards?" Sean headed down the stairs toward the woodshed.

"Strip poker."

"Oh, hell, yes. Deal me in. Have I mentioned I'm very good at poker?"

"Have I mentioned that I just want to get you naked?"

By the time Sean had the night's firewood stacked next to the woodstove, Eden had the bottle of whiskey, cups, and the deck of cards ready to go.

She shuffled the deck. "Jokers are wild."

As the evening passed and Sean won hand after hand, Eden found herself treasuring each moment, holding them in her heart. This was her life right now. The sun was shining on her, and she would revel in it.

Sean threw his cards onto the table—a straight flush. "You lose! Those panties have to come off, sweetheart."

She stood, gave Sean a little strip tease, baring herself a bit at a time, turning so he couldn't see, then taunting him with glimpses of the real estate between her thighs.

Okay, so they were both a little tipsy.

"Tease." He stood, scooped her into his arms, and carried her to the bed.

And there, he made the world go away, pleasure carrying them both to the stars.

Chapter Nineteen

June 25

THE FLIGHT back to Kodiak on Sunday afternoon went without a hitch. They loaded their gear into Sean's vehicle and headed toward Natasha's to pick up Maverick.

"I can't wait to see my boy."

"Me, too."

Eden fished her phone out of her backpack to let Natasha know they'd landed and were on their way. But the moment she turned on her phone, it lit up with messages from her sisters and her mother, all of them saying the same thing.

```
Big news. We're all at Baba's.
Come to Baba's.
When you land, we'll be at Baba's with
Mavie.
```

"Oh, God." A knot of dread settled in her stomach.

"Is something wrong?"

"I think so. We need to go to my Baba's house." She

replied in a group text to tell everyone that they were on their way, then gave Sean directions. "I hope she's okay."

"So do I." Sean glanced over at her, took her hand, eyes hidden behind his aviators. "I've wanted to meet her for a while now."

Eden told herself that her grandmother had lived a long and happy life. Even so, she wasn't ready to say goodbye. But at Baba's age, anything might happen. She might fall and break a hip, have a stroke, or just pass away in her sleep.

They turned the corner, and Eden saw a dozen cars she recognized parked along the road. "It looks like everyone's here."

The knot of dread grew heavier.

She climbed out, met Sean at the rear of the vehicle, the two of them walking toward her grandmother's home, holding hands. "My grandfather built this place. It started as a one-room cabin, but he expanded it as their family grew. There's a garden out back with an orchard, though it's pretty overgrown these days."

The door opened, and Natasha stepped out, holding Maverick by the hand. She pointed to Eden. "Who's that, Maverick?"

Maverick's face lit up. "Mommy!"

Natasha let go of his hand, and Maverick dashed toward them.

Eden scooped him up, hugged him tight. "I'm so happy to see you, Maverick. Did you have a fun time with Auntie Tasha, Summer, and Willow?"

Maverick nodded, a shy smile on his face.

Sean tousled Maverick's hair. "Hey, buddy."

They walked inside, Eden hit with a rush of relief when she saw her grandmother sitting in her recliner. Her mother was there, too, with Auntie Evelyn, who was crying. Then she saw him—Agent Chase Santee.

He stood, greeted her and Sean with a nod. "Eden. McKenna."

What was he doing here?

She had to know. "Is everyone okay?"

"We're all fine," Natasha reassured her. "But Agent Santee has news. Summer, Willow, sit on the floor to give Auntie Eden and Sean room on the sofa."

Summer and Willow moved, and Eden and Sean sat.

But something wasn't right. "What's happened? What's wrong?"

It was Agent Santee who answered. "Last night, the CGIS, DEA, FBI, Kodiak Police, and others executed arrest warrants on eighteen people associated with the drug ring behind the explosion that killed your husband and left you injured, McKenna. Those threatening text messages were the key to helping us solve this case. Thank you for reporting them."

Adrenaline made Eden's head buzz. "You... you found them?"

"We took seventeen suspects into custody, some of them here, some in Anchorage, and others elsewhere. One suspect eluded us and is now in the wind."

But Eden wasn't keeping up. "In the wind?"

Sean explained. "On the run."

"Here's the hard part." Agent Santee glanced at Aunt Evelyn, who let out a sob. "That suspect is Charlie Crane."

Eden gaped at him. "Charlie Crane—my cousin Mila's husband?"

"Yes, ma'am. He was the ringleader. The people who blew themselves up worked for him. Apparently, some meth they'd been supposed to sell on the island was stolen. They tried to make their own, knowing he'd kill them if they couldn't recoup the money."

It all came together. How terrible and needlessly tragic.

Fire and Rain

"And they killed themselves, Justin, and David in the process."

"Yes, ma'am." Agent Santee drew out his cell phone, read through a message, slid it back into his pocket. "Crane served as the contact for a bigger drug ring that operates out of Seattle. He used bush pilots and boats to transport drugs to dealers in villages across Alaska, then used that same network to get cash back to his bosses."

Eden's sisters nodded, while Auntie Evelyn wept. But Eden struggled to believe it. "I thought Charlie had a high-paying job in Prudhoe Bay. Why would he sell drugs?"

Maria handed Auntie Evelyn a box of tissues.

Agent Santee explained. "He *did* work in Prudhoe Bay, but he didn't earn nearly as much as his wife believed. He quit when he realized we were onto him and told her he'd been laid off."

Eden asked her next question. "Does that mean Mila didn't know?"

"No!" Auntie Evelyn snapped. "Of course, she didn't. Why would you think that?"

Eden's grandmother answered before Eden could. "None of this is Eden's fault, Evelyn. We all feel bad for Mila, but don't take it out on Eden."

Agent Santee answered Eden's question. "Mila didn't know. This came as a terrible shock to her, and she continues to cooperate with law enforcement. We've temporarily placed her and her children in protective custody."

Poor Mila!

"How awful for them." Eden couldn't imagine how wrenching this was for her, Nick, and Lina. The shock. The sense of betrayal. The humiliation. "I'm so sorry to hear this. What happens next?"

"One of the men we arrested told us Crane planned to steal a boat and head toward Homer where he has a buddy who can get him into Canada. We've alerted law enforcement throughout Alaska, as well as Canada. We will continue the hunt for him. I'd like to keep your phone if that's okay. Given the pressure he's under, I'd say there's a good chance he'll try to contact you again."

"That's fine."

"Is Eden safe now?" Sean needed to know.

Agent Santee seemed to consider this. "I would continue to be cautious until we're sure that the suspect is in custody or has been sighted far from Kodiak. If he shows up at your door, call the police immediately. Don't open the door for anyone you're not expecting. That goes for all of you. Charlie Crane is considered armed and dangerous—a killer."

Eden tried to pull herself together. "Thank you for all you've done."

"I'm truly sorry for how Crane's actions have affected this family. None of you deserved this. We will find Crane and put him away. If you have other questions, Eden, call or shoot me a message. I need to go."

A chorus of thank-yous followed Agent Santee out the door. Then there was only the sound of Auntie Evelyn's weeping.

It was Eden's grandmother who spoke next. "Sean, come sit over here so this old woman can get a good look at you."

Sean stood, shared a glance with Eden, a smile tugging at his lips. "Yes, ma'am."

"My grandma likes you."

Sean brought Eden's gear inside while she carried a sleeping Maverick. "You think so?"

"I know it. She said you have kind eyes."

Fire and Rain

"I liked the way she stood up for you." He set her stuff down near the door.

"She always speaks her mind."

"Like someone else I know." He waited while she put Maverick in his crib.

Sean had ordered a special toddler bed for Maverick, but it hadn't yet arrived.

Eden quickly returned. "I wish you didn't have to go."

"So do I. Lock the door behind me, and stay indoors." When she stuck out her tongue at him, Sean drew her close, held her tight. "I know that's hard for you, but hopefully they'll catch Charlie soon."

"You stay safe, okay?"

"I will." Sean kissed her. "See you tomorrow afternoon."

He turned and walked out the door. He hated leaving Eden and Maverick alone with Crane somewhere on the island. Hopefully, the bastard was making his way toward Canada as Santee's intel suggested. If not...

Desperate people did desperate, stupid things.

When he arrived back on base, he went first to the barracks to drop off his gear and change into his thermals. Then he made his way to the briefing and found Zeke and Trey already there, with Lt. Yamada as their operations duty officer once again.

Sean glanced at the time, saw that Spurrier was late. "Anyone talk to James?"

Zeke shook his head. "I haven't seen him all day."

This wasn't like him.

The door opened, and James walked in, unshaven, his hair disheveled, dark circles below his eyes. "Sorry. I overslept."

They got on with the briefing, focusing on a moderate low-pressure system expected to bring rain and forty- to fifty-knot winds to the Gulf and Shelikof Strait. A bigger system was headed their way, but that was almost ten days out and might not materialize.

After the briefing, Sean followed James, who hadn't yet settled into his duty room. "Hey, Spurrier, are you okay, man?"

James opened the door to his duty room and motioned for Sean to enter. "Yeah. I'm ... I just had a rough night."

"Sorry to hear it. I'll go and let you get some sleep."

"No, it's okay. I ..." He was quiet for a moment. "Do you still have nightmares?"

"I did for a while. I haven't had as many lately." The realization surprised him. He hadn't had a nightmare since he and Eden had gotten together. "I used to dream that I did something different, that I yelled at Justin to get off the boat sooner or raised the hoist line faster. But no matter what I did, Justin always died."

James' gaze was focused out the window, his jaw tight. "I keep reliving the crash—feeling the blast wave, losing the tail rotor, hitting the water... seeing that David was dead."

"Have you told anyone?" Sean and James had both been cleared to return to duty, but Sean certainly hadn't been completely honest about his nightmares.

"Yeah. Well, at first. I thought it would stop."

"But it hasn't, has it?"

James ran a hand through his hair. "Not really."

The SAR alarm sounded.

"Now put the ready helo online. Now put the ready helo online."

Shit.

"Maybe you should sit this one out, get some rest."

"Nah, I'm good. I just had some coffee. Once we get in the air, I'll be fine."

Sean clapped his shoulder. "Let's go."

This case took them to the southern end of the island off

Fire and Rain

Akhiok where two Alutiiq teens had reported their skiff taking on water. It was daylight, and conditions weren't bad.

"Cabin door open." Sean spotted them easily. "There they are, low two o'clock. Their skiff is listing hard to port. It looks like it could sink at any minute. They're both wearing life jackets, but not survival suits."

"Let's get them out of there."

James contacted them via radio. "Skiff taking on water, this is Coast Guard Rescue Six-Oh-Two-Three. Do you copy?"

While he worked to calm the two distressed teens, Sean went through the safety checklist with Trey, who would be lowered into the water off their starboard side. Trey would board the skiff and send them up one at a time in the strap. Then Sean would recover Trey.

"Swimmer's going out the door." Sean gave him a nudge, lowered him into the water, and watched for the thumbs-up. "Swimmer is okay. Swimmer is boarding the vessel."

Sean watched as Trey slipped the first survivor into the strap. "The first survivor is on his way up. What the...? The second survivor has taken off in the skiff. He's headed toward shore, I think, but he'll never make it."

He kept his gaze on Trey, who now treaded water in the skiff's wake.

"Skiff taking on water, this is Coast Guard Rescue Six-Oh-Two-Three. Your vessel is in imminent danger of sinking. You won't make it back to shore. Please throttle down, abandon ship, and let us bring you on board, over."

"Coast Guard, this is my uncle's boat, and he's gonna kick my ass if I don't bring it back like I promised."

Then a voice cut in. "Joel, this is your grandpa. Get off the boat. Your mother is standing here. You wanna break her heart?"

"I'm sorry," the boy said.

"It's gonna be okay, grandson. Just come home."

Sean's gaze was still on Trey, but he couldn't help but grin. Lots of people on the island followed the Coast Guard on their VHF radios at home, and this time one of them had become part of the rescue. "I'm lowering the strap to pick up the swimmer."

He raised Trey into the cabin as James and Zeke brought the helo alongside the skiff once again. Then he lowered Trey into the water to rescue the second survivor. By the time poor Joel and Trey were both back in the cabin, the skiff had sunk.

As Sean helped Trey make the survivors comfortable, he met Trey's gaze. "Only in Alaska."

July 2

SEAN POPPED his head out of Maverick's bedroom. "It's done."

Eden finished washing the peanut butter and jelly off Maverick's face and hands and lifted him out of his highchair and onto her hip. "Let's go see your new bed, Mavie."

"A big-boy bed?"

"Yes, a new big-boy bed. You won't be sleeping in a crib anymore."

The thought hit her with an unexpected pang. Her baby was growing up too fast. He'd be two next month.

Sean stood in the hallway, a big grin on his face. "Okay, Maverick. There's your new big-boy bed."

Maverick's little face lit up the moment he saw it. "Fietwuck!"

Eden set him on the floor, swallowing the lump in her throat as he ran as fast as his little legs could carry him to the bed. The foot of the bed was the front of the truck, with a built-in wooden shelf for books, toys, and stuffed animals. Wooden guardrails painted to look like ladders would keep Maverick from falling out.

"What do you think, Maverick?" Sean asked.

Maverick gave Sean an elated smile. "Fietwuck bed for me."

"That's right, buddy. I put your helmet and uniform right there. See?"

Maverick hurried over, put the helmet on his head.

"Can you thank Sean?" Eden had told Sean that she could afford it, but he'd insisted on buying it as an early birthday present.

"Tank you!" Maverick crawled into bed, helmet and all, and pretended to sleep, the smile on his face giving him away.

"You even got him a red comforter." Eden wrapped an arm around Sean's waist. "Thanks. This is perfect—all of it."

Sean's gaze was on Maverick, who was now pretending to drive the firetruck. "I love seeing him happy. What do you want me to do with the crib?"

The question hit Eden hard, put tears in her eyes. "I'm ... I'm not sure."

She turned and hurried from the room, not wanting to spoil the moment for Sean or Maverick, but Sean followed.

"Hey, are you okay?"

She walked to the kitchen, grabbed a tissue, dabbed her eyes. "I'm fine."

He raised an eyebrow. "No, you're not. What's wrong?"

"I was five months pregnant when Justin and I bought this crib."

"I remember. I helped him put it together."

"Right." Eden had forgotten that. "At the time, he and I talked about having two or three kids. If Justin hadn't died in that explosion, I'd probably be pregnant now. But those dreams died with him. It's hard to think of giving the crib away."

"Then don't give it away." Sean drew her into his embrace. "You should keep it. You're only twenty-eight. You've got time."

She sank against him, but his words left her feeling worse. He hadn't yet told her he loved her, and now it seemed he didn't think of their relationship as permanent. He hadn't said *we have time*. No, he'd said *you have time*. As if he knew he wouldn't be part of that future.

You knew he didn't want kids when this started.

Yes, she had, and she wouldn't shift the goal posts on him. Instead, she would be grateful for the time they had together.

She drew back. "If you could put the crib in the garage for now, that would be great. Thanks. I'll make us some lunch. How does clam chowder sound? I still have some frozen from this past spring."

"Sounds delicious."

While they ate, they talked over plans for the holiday. Sean had a duty shift on July 3, so Eden would spend the evening at Maria's with her sisters and all of the kids. Chris, Maria's husband, was a volunteer firefighter and put on a fireworks show for them every year. Then they would watch the city's fireworks, which started at midnight on July 4, from Maria's front yard.

"I'm sorry I'll miss it. It sounds fun." Sean finished his chowder. "That was delicious, by the way. Thanks."

"I thought I'd gas up the boat the next morning. After you've caught up on sleep, the three of us could go out fishing and grill something tasty for supper. We could even spend the night out on the water, maybe off Puffin Island."

"That sounds perfect. There's a low-pressure system arriving sometime that evening, so I'll get here as soon as I can." Sean took her hand. "Just be careful when you drive around town, okay? CGIS might have lost Charlie's trail, but that doesn't mean he's left the island."

Agent Santee had kept Eden and Sean up to date. Every time her phone buzzed, Eden hoped for the good news that they'd caught Charlie. "I'll be careful. I promise."

From the bedroom came the sound of sirens as interpreted by Maverick. "Wooooo! Woooooo!"

Eden couldn't help but smile. "He loves it."

"I had a feeling he might." Sean stood, released her hand. "I'll get that crib stored in the garage and put the tools away. Thanks for lunch."

"You're welcome." As Eden cleaned up the dishes, she willed herself to focus on the holiday and not worry about the future.

Chapter Twenty

July 4

"Mommy?"

Eden opened one eye to find Maverick in bed beside her. "Hey, buddy."

They'd gotten home from Maria's at one this morning, with Chris following in his truck just to make sure they were safe. Maverick had loved Chris' fireworks but had fallen asleep hours before the official Kodiak show. He looked fully rested and ready to take on the day.

Eden needed sleep, but she would have to settle for coffee.

She got up, started the coffeemaker, and pulled together a breakfast of scrambled eggs and toast, tuning into the morning news to hear the forecast.

"A low-pressure system is expected to move into the area by this evening, bringing seventy-knot winds and heavy rain."

Damn.

They probably wouldn't be able to spend the night on the boat, not with hurricane-force winds. Eden loved sleeping

Fire and Rain

while being rocked by gentle waves, not being tipped into the ocean. But that's just how it was.

In Alaska, people made plans, but weather was king.

She set a plate on Maverick's tray with his little fork. "We're going to go out on the boat with Sean today to catch fish. Won't that be fun?"

"Fishies?"

"That's right." She took her first sip of coffee and almost moaned.

Today was going to be a busy but fun day.

When she'd done the dishes, showered, and dressed, she started getting everything together for the trip. She kept the fishing gear organized and ready to go on a moment's notice. But she also needed to think about meals. She would need snacks, drinks, and something for dinner in case they got skunked and caught nothing.

She made a quick run to the grocery store, then came home and stowed the drinks and food in the fridge. By then, Maverick was hungry for lunch. She made grilled cheese sandwiches for both of them and sliced an apple to share, while Maverick chattered about the fireworks.

"Fiewook go boom!"

"They were loud, weren't they?"

Eden hadn't heard from Sean yet, so she imagined he'd had a busy night and was asleep. That gave her time to refuel the boat so they could head out when he got here. But she'd never gassed up alone with Maverick. She wasn't sure she could watch over him while also piloting the boat to the fuel dock and filling the tank.

She sent a quick text to Natasha asking if she could drop Maverick off for an hour and got a quick response. "Come, Maverick, let's go see Summer and Willow again."

It was a twenty-minute drive to Natasha's.

"I'll be back within the hour." Eden watched as Summer

and Willow welcomed Maverick, who was wearing his firefighter helmet.

"Sounds good. We'll be here when you get back."

It was a quick drive to St. Paul Harbor. Because it was a holiday, the place was buzzing, and many of the slips were empty. She walked to where the *Sea Nymph* was moored, clipped into her life jacket, and made ready to sail, excited to be out on the water again. It took about fifteen minutes and a small fortune to refill the tank, but that's why she and Justin had kept a special savings account for boat maintenance and fuel.

Save all winter, sail all summer.

She ran the blower to vent any gas fumes, then started the engine and piloted the boat away from the dock, slowing for a cuddy cabin that was towing a battered skiff. She'd just gotten underway when she heard a *thunk*.

It seemed to happen in slow motion.

The cabin door opened, and Charlie stepped out, pointing a pistol straight at her. He hadn't shaved or bathed for days, stubble on his jaw, his brown hair unkempt, a stench about him. "Hello, Eden."

Eden's mouth went dry. "What the hell are you doing here?"

"You've been ignoring my messages."

She would have reached for her phone, but he had the pistol.

Pulse thrumming in her ears, she did her best not to look afraid, her mind racing for a safe answer. "*Your* messages? That was you, Charlie? I thought you were just some rando, some pervert, and I didn't appreciate the threats."

"Well, you'd better listen closely this time. You're going to get me to Homer, or I'm going to decorate your dead hubby's wedding present with your brains."

In a blink, Eden went from fear to rage. "Can you imagine

Fire and Rain

Baba's reaction to you killing one of her granddaughters, your own wife's cousin? You'll be a murderer and not just a drug dealer and kidnapper. Let me go, or they'll come after you even harder. You must know that."

His jaw clenched. "Look. I had no idea those stupid bastards were cooking meth in a boat. I had nothing to do with the explosion that killed those two guys—"

"One of whom was family to you, Charlie. You *knew* Justin!"

"I didn't mean for him to die. If I could have stopped it, I would have. I don't want to kill you either. *Fuck*!" He closed his eyes and looked away, the barrel of the pistol sagging.

That was the break she needed.

She quickly lifted the flap and pushed the button to set off the EPIRB—Emergency Position Indicator Radio Beacon. She was the widow of a Coastie and knew her way around a boat. Justin had gotten every possible safety feature installed on the *Sea Nymph*. The EPIRB would send a signal to a satellite, which would transmit her distress call and location to the nearest Coast Guard station.

Any moment now, they would know right where she was.

But she'd forgotten about the EPIRB's automatic strobe. She tried to cover it, but the bright flash caught Charlie's eye. He rounded the console before she could take a single step, grabbed the unit out of its bracket, and hurled it into the ocean.

Then he took her by the throat and jammed the pistol to her temple, his breath foul. "*That* is exactly the kind of shit that will get you killed."

SEAN WAS in the shower when he heard a helo lift off. For once, he was glad not to be on it. He dried off and shaved his patchy beard, so eager to see Eden again that it almost made him laugh at himself. He remembered getting an email from Justin after his first date with Eden.

She's incredible. She loves to do all the things I do, and she's beautiful, too. If I had to conjure a dream woman out of the air, she'd be Eden.

Sean hadn't understood then. He did now.

He'd realized somewhere over the Gulf of Alaska last night that he needed to tell Eden how he felt about her sooner rather than later. He'd hurt her yesterday. She'd told him she'd wanted more children, and he'd been so taken aback by the realization that she might want to have kids with *him* that he'd answered like an idiot.

You still have time.

That made him sound like a dude who didn't understand basic biology—or one who had no intention of sticking around to do the job himself.

He'd never imagined he'd want to be a father. It meant added responsibility and a lot of complications to his already busy and complicated life. He'd seen how hard it was for Coasties burdened with families to move from place to place. Their kids transferred from one school to the next, never in one town long enough to make lifelong friends. When a person served in the military, their entire family served with them.

But Eden knew the score. She knew what it took to be the wife of a Coastie. And nothing about her or Maverick felt like a burden to Sean.

Yeah, love was a crazy thing.

Sean rinsed his face, put on a clean pair of boxer briefs, jeans, and a T-shirt. He'd started packing his overnight bag when his cellphone buzzed.

It was a text message from Agent Santee.

Get to ops now.

Fire and Rain

Sean's stomach knotted. He slipped on some runners, grabbed a clean pair of thermals just in case, and jogged over to the ops center to find Captain Walcott, Agent Santee, and a group of other CGIS agents clustered together.

"A short time ago, we got a signal off an EPIRB in Chiniak Bay. A helo was dispatched a short time ago to check it out. I heard the name of the boat over the radio and realized we have a situation. It's the Sea Nymph."

Sean's pulse picked up. "What?"

"I contacted Eden's family, and they said she went to the harbor to refuel the boat and planned to be back at her sister's house within the hour to pick up her son. She never showed. They tried calling and texting but got no response. They were about to report her missing."

Shit.

"There's more. The helo just recovered the EPIRB from the bay but saw no sign of any PIW or debris from the boat. It's a possibility that the boat sank. We've got a cutter on scene, and they haven't found anything either."

Christ.

Santee's words hit Sean like a body blow.

No. It couldn't be. Eden couldn't be gone.

Sean fought to focus. "You said Maverick was at her sister's place?"

Santee nodded. "Apparently, she wasn't sure she could safely pilot and refuel the boat alone with a toddler on board."

Thank God.

Walcott's gaze was on the charts. "We all know that Eden is smart and resourceful. There's a chance she tossed the EPIRB overboard to alert us that something was wrong. Crane told his buddies that he wanted to steal a boat and get to Homer, is that correct?"

Santee nodded. "I've since learned that he knows nothing about piloting watercraft. He couldn't tell the prow of the boat from his asshole. He might have abducted Eden to pilot the boat for him. We've alerted the station in Homer. They're waiting for an FBI team with a hostage negotiator. They'll deploy if and when we locate the Sea Nymph. We've also put out an alert to all boats, asking anyone who sees the Sea Nymph to report its location. There are a lot of people on the water today. Someone is bound to see them."

Independence Day was the busiest boating day of the year.

Sean wanted to punch something. "So, our plan is for the rescue helo to continue to search the area where the EPIRB was found until they hit critical fuel levels and have to return. Then we'll wait to see if anyone reports seeing the Sea Nymph. Failing that, we'll have a welcoming committee waiting for him near Homer. Is that right?"

"If you've got any other ideas, right now is the time to share them." Santee waited while Sean ran options through his mind.

"We could calculate where the boat might be now by using the time of the EPIRB signal and the craft's average miles per hour. Then we could send out another helo."

Captain Walcott shook his head. "With this storm heading our way, we can't afford to exhaust our SAR resources without knowing where she is. If she's still on the boat, this is a hostage situation, and that's not part of our mission at Air Station Kodiak. Until or unless we hear that the boat has been spotted and is in trouble, there's nothing else we can do."

Sean had to clench his teeth to keep himself from saying something he'd regret. But he'd never felt more helpless in his life.

EDEN WATCHED the charts on her screen and went as slowly as she could, trying to keep her speed under thirty miles per hour and fighting not to give in to despair. Had her sisters reported her missing? Had the EPIRB sent its signal? Did Sean know she'd been abducted?

At least Maverick was safe.

She'd gotten over her fear of Charlie—for now. He needed her to pilot the boat. It was the storm that scared her. She'd never piloted a boat through open ocean in seventy-knot winds. And if they made it to Homer, what would happen then? What was to stop Charlie from killing her when he no longer needed her?

There was a small Coast Guard station in Homer. Did Charlie know that?

The thought gave Eden hope. But she needed to find a way to signal the station. If only Charlie would go back inside the cabin, she could call over the radio, give them her location. But he sat on the seat to her left, keeping an eye on her and periodically checking the screen to make sure she was headed in the right direction.

She kept up the conversation, focusing on their family ties. "You should have seen Auntie Evelyn when she heard what you'd done. She couldn't stop crying."

"She cries over everything."

Eden laughed, deliberately steering close to a fishing trawler. "That's true. We all did our best to comfort her. But her daughter and grandchildren are in protective custody, and she can't see them. I'd say that's a good reason to cry, wouldn't you?"

"Shut up! And stay away from other boats!"

She ignored him. "I saw Nick and Lina at Crab Fest. I can't believe how tall Nick is now. I feel terrible for them. They're going to grow up without a father, just like Maverick. Everyone on the island knows what you did. Can you imagine how hard it will be for them at school, or are you too busy thinking only of your—"

"I said *shut up*!"

"What's the matter, Charlie? Actions have consequences. When we do stupid things, it hurts those who love us most—our families. I'm part of your family, Charlie."

"Yeah? My wife never liked you. She thinks you're stuck up."

"Baba says Mila is just jealous."

"Jealous—of you? You have *nothing*. You don't even own your house."

"No, but I don't need money. I have Kodiak Island. It feeds and shelters me, just like it fed and sheltered my ancestors for thousands of years."

"My wife likes the finer things."

"Right now, your wife has nothing."

Charlie lunged out of his seat, pressed the barrel of his pistol to her forehead. "If you don't shut your damned mouth…"

She had to force herself to stand her ground and meet the rage in his eyes. "What? You'll shoot me and pilot the boat to Homer yourself?"

"Fuck you, bitch. I never liked you, either."

She willed herself to smile. "I *used* to like you. I never could have imagined that you'd sink so low."

He glared into her eyes but backed off. "If you don't watch your mouth, I'll give you to my buddy when we reach Homer. He'll slit your throat. I've seen him do it. Then Maverick will be an orphan."

"What will you tell Mila? What will she say to Baba?"

"Look, they shouldn't be coming after me. I told you to make the feds back off, but you didn't. So, this is as much your fault as anyone's."

Eden laughed, a shrill, terrified sound. "I thought your texts were from some crazy person. I didn't even know they were investigating you until they arrested all your cronies. It's not like I control the Coast Guard or the DEA."

Ahead of them, dark clouds filled the sky, the waves double the size they'd been twenty minutes ago. She was grateful for the boat's windshield and hardtop because it sheltered her from most of the rain and sea spray. But nothing would save them if they went into the frigid water without survival suits.

"See those clouds? We're supposed to get seventy-knot winds and heavy rain. We should pull into a cove somewhere and—"

"No! We keep going."

"You've never piloted a boat. You know nothing about it. Do you know what kind of waves we'll face out there? We're talking hurricane-force winds. Look. The swells are already picking up. We're far beyond the protection of Chiniak Bay now."

He looked out over the water. "Do your job right, or we'll both die."

"If you're okay with dying, why run? Why not commit suicide by cop or just shoot yourself? If you think freezing to death in the water is an easier way to go, you're wrong."

Then inspiration hit.

"At least let me stop and get you a life jacket." Mind racing, she came up with a justification. "If a Coast Guard vessel sees you without one, they'll pursue us."

"Fine."

"It's going to get choppy without me at the helm."

"Make it fast."

Pulse picking up, she throttled back and walked back to the storage compartment that held their ditch bags, waves buffeting the boat. Each bag held two strobes and two Personal Locator Beacons, a pocket-sized version of the EPIRB. PLBs worked in the same way but were used when people needed to abandon ship. That way if they were separated in heavy seas, the Coast Guard would be able to locate them even if they couldn't see them.

She opened the storage compartment and delved into one of the ditch bags, her hands searching. "Are you hungry? We have emergency rations."

"Like what?"

"Chips. Candy bars." She tossed him a Snickers, deliberately throwing it short.

He bent to pick it up, giving her a split second to act.

She turned on the PLB, closing the bag to conceal the flash, then pocketed a strobe with an Almond Joy, Justin's favorite candy bar.

"What did you just put in your pocket?" Charlie stood, pointed the pistol her way.

She closed the storage compartment and carefully drew the Almond Joy out of her pocket far enough for him to see what it was, using it to hide the strobe. "Are you going to shoot me over a candy bar? The life jackets must be over here."

She walked back to the storage beneath the rear lounger and took out a life jacket, tossing it to Charlie. Then she set the survival suits and the emergency raft onto the deck. "We really should put these survival suits on before we hit that storm."

"Quit fucking around and get underway."

All she could do now was pray that the Coast Guard arrived quickly—and hope that she could keep the *Sea Nymph* afloat when that storm hit.

Chapter Twenty-One

Sean stood in the hallway, listening to the radio traffic, and doing his best not to let the tumult inside him show. He didn't want the captain to doubt his ability to do his duty because Eden was involved. But he couldn't even be certain she was still alive.

He sat, buried his face in his hands, wishing to *fuck* that he'd told her he loved her. Now, he might not get the chance. If only he could trade places with her...

"How are you holding up?" Santee sat beside him. "I'm pretty sure she tossed that EPIRB into the water to get our attention."

"I hope so. In the meantime, he could do anything to her—beat her, rape her, kill her."

Santee shook his head. "I doubt he'll be able to whip his dick out on a pitching boat, and I don't think he'll harm her—not until he reaches Homer. That's where—"

"Air Station Kodiak, this is Sector Anchorage. We just got a distress beacon from a PLB registered to the Sea Nymph, and it's moving, over."

Sean's heart gave a hard thud. He shot to his feet and strode back into the office.

"Sector Anchorage, this is Air Station Kodiak, good copy. We're ready to receive those coordinates." Captain Walcott had taken over as operations duty officer. He frowned as he wrote down the information and checked the charts. "This location is in open ocean. They're moving east-northeast at a speed of about twenty-six knots, heading toward Homer."

That meant Eden was most likely on the boat and still alive.

Sean felt almost weak with relief. If she'd been in the water, there would have been no way they could have saved her. "Can we send a helo now?"

"A PLB alarm falls under our mission parameters, whether it's on a moving boat or in the water. But don't exceed those parameters." Walcott pushed the SAR alarm. "Now put the ready helo online. Now put the ready helo online."

Sean turned to Santee. "You coming?"

"Damned straight." Santee turned to follow him to the locker room.

Then James appeared, already dressed out. "I'd like to take this one."

Walcott studied him. "It's your day off."

"I know, sir, but Eden is one of ours. After what happened to Justin..."

Walcott nodded. "We treat all rescues the same. But, yes, she's one of ours, and she's already been through too much."

While James gathered intel on the weather and the flight route, Sean, Santee, and Trey quickly dressed out, Santee putting body armor over his survival suit.

Trey grinned. "Nice look."

"You're just jealous." Sean filled in James and Trey as they jogged to the helo, telling him about the EPIRB from earlier.

"That storm is bearing down on them. Santee is coming with us, and he's armed."

"Good." James gave a nod. "Let's bring Eden home."

They took off, a stiff headwind giving them translational lift, getting them airborne quickly.

Once they were en route, James spoke again, his voice sounding in Sean's headphones. "McKenna, you've been on the boat. What are we looking at?"

"It's a cruiser cabin. We won't be able to see inside the cockpit from above because it's covered by a hardtop." That part worried him. "There's a lounge area in the stern that's pretty open. The boat has radar and some antennas on the hardtop, but no outriggers or crane or anything to tangle up the hoist line."

Santee's rifle was pointed at the cabin floor. "Time for a tactical chat." He waited while James muted the cabin mic so that no one back at base could overhear the conversation, then went on. "Walcott okayed this mission because of the personal locator beacon, but you heard him. We can't exceed the parameters of a search and rescue mission. We are most likely heading into a hostage situation on rough seas. We all understand that, correct?"

"That's why you're here," James said.

Sean had his view on this. "Eden's safety should come first."

James cut in. "The safety of the helicopter and this crew are our top priority. I need to bring this bird home with all of you still on board. But regulations be damned. We won't return without Eden. Agreed?"

"Agreed."

They talked through various scenarios—if Crane came peaceably, if he threatened Eden, if he refused to let Eden stop the boat, if he endangered the helo in some way, if Santee had no choice but to use lethal force.

Sean was against putting a bullet through the *Sea Nymph*'s engine. The boat had been Justin's wedding present to Eden. But if that was their only option…

"What if he fires at the helo? It's not bullet proof. Or what if he shoots me when I'm being hoisted down to get Eden?" Trey was right to ask.

A rescue swimmer on a hoist line would make an easy target.

Santee answered without hesitation. "If he fires at us, I take him out."

"And you can do that with these waves and the wind?"

"Absolutely."

"You're cocky."

Santee grinned. "I'm confident."

James brought them all back to earth. "We need to face the possibility that we'll have to leave the rescue to the cutter. They have the boat's coordinates and are following its progress. We'll go until we hit bingo fuel levels, and then return to base. If we can't stop Crane from the air, they'll stop him on the water."

But Sean wasn't coming home without Eden.

"The ride is going to get bumpy," James warned them.

Within minutes, turbulence began to bounce the helo around, a vicious headwind slowing their progress, every minute that passed putting Sean more on edge.

"Got any barf bags back there?" Zeke sounded like he was about to lose it.

Trey handed one forward. Zeke was the first to lose his lunch, followed by Trey. But Sean wasn't bothered by the turbulence, and neither were Chase or James.

James checked in with Sector. "We'll be arriving on scene in zero-five mikes."

Sean closed his eyes and sent a prayer skyward.

Hold on, sweetheart. We're almost there.

Fire and Rain

EDEN FOUGHT to keep the bow up, slowing to about nine knots. She was exhausted, her hands and shoulders aching from gripping the wheel so hard. She was also freezing. The cockpit was open to the rear, allowing some sea spray and rain to get in, soaking her skin.

Charlie launched himself to his feet and staggered over to her, shouting to be heard above the storm, anger on his greenish face. He'd spent most of the past hour vomiting over the side. "Why are you slowing down?"

"I have to maintain control of the boat and keep the bow up. These are six- to nine-foot swells. If the waves crack the bow, we sink. If we take on too much water, we sink. Do you want to end up as fish food?" She took the next wave head-on.

"Make this thing go faster!"

"We can't! Do you want to reach Homer or not?"

He glared at her. "You're making shit up."

"I want to live as much as you do. *Don't* tell me how to pilot my boat! I can't babysit you and keep us afloat at the same time!"

He swore, backed off, leaving Eden to focus on the ship. She aimed the bow into each wave, trying to stay on course, resigned to taking Charlie to Homer.

She was certain the Coast Guard knew where she was, but she'd belatedly realized they wouldn't send a SAR team after her. They would leave rescuing her to a cutter crew carrying federal agents and maybe operatives from the Coast Guard's Maritime Security Response Team. That meant she had no choice but to face this storm and trust that help would find her in Homer.

Sean.

Would she see him again?

He must know she was missing by now and would be

angry and worried. She hoped he was with her family, but he wasn't the kind of man who'd find it easy to stand by and do nothing. That's why he'd gone into the Coast Guard in the first place. He was probably being a pain in Captain Walcott's butt.

Thomp-thomp-thomp

Was that her imagination, or was there a helo somewhere nearby?

She listened intently, but with the engine, wind, rain, and waves, it was hard to hear anything. She glanced over at Charlie, who sat in one of the lounge seats looking miserable. He didn't look like he'd heard anything. If he had, he'd be…

Thomp-thomp-thomp

As if out of a vision, an H-60 appeared ahead of the *Sea Nymph*, hovering at about fifty feet above the water. To Eden, it looked like an orange-and-white angel.

Charlie drew his pistol, jumped to his feet—but found it hard to stay upright. "You called them? I told you I'd kill—"

"No, I didn't call them." Eden tried not to look afraid, but she was.

Charlie was clearly desperate now, and desperate people did terrible things. "I don't believe you."

"How could I? You turned the radio off." Eden risked taking one hand off the wheel for a second to point. "See? It's still off. I don't know how they found us, but they did. It's over, Charlie."

"Like hell it is. Just keep going."

"That's crazy. We can't outrun them."

"No, but we can outlast them. They'll run out of fuel eventually."

"What would be the point of that? If they know where we are, they'll just watch us via satellite and have a cutter waiting for us in Homer."

Okay, so she'd made that up. The Coast Guard wasn't

going to tap military satellites to track the *Sea Nymph*, but she hoped Charlie didn't know that.

"I have to turn the radio on." Without waiting for his permission, Eden switched it on and took the handpiece. "Coast Guard helicopter, this is the Sea—"

The blow took her by surprise, pain exploding in her cheek and skull as her head struck the bulkhead. The handset slipped from her grasp as she slumped to the floor.

Charlie grabbed the handset. "We're fine here, Coast Guard. We don't need your help."

"Sea Nymph, this is Coast Guard Rescue Six-Zero-Three-Two, maintain current speed and course, and prepare to be boarded."

Charlie let out a primal shriek of rage through gritted teeth. "Coast Guard, get lost, or I'll blow Eden to hell."

Eden's head spun, and she cupped her cheek then touched a hand to the lump on her head. Blood. She struggled to stand. But no one was at the helm, so the boat was now at the mercy of the waves, pitching and rolling in the swells.

Then the helicopter veered off, disappearing above the clouds.

Eden's heart sank.

They'll send a cutter. They will *send a cutter.*

"Haha!" Charlie watched through the sunroof as the helicopter passed overhead, a wide grin on his face. He raised his middle finger at the sky. "Fuckers!"

Did he truly believe he'd won?

Eden grabbed onto the edge of the console with one hand and the pilot's seat with the other and fought her way to her feet, her thoughts and movements sluggish.

Charlie reached for her but stumbled backward as the boat pitched. "That was *your* fault."

"Don't you ever... take responsibility for anything?" She

took the wheel, tried to get the *Sea Nymph* under control once more, but could barely stay on her feet, much less pilot a boat.

Thomp-thomp-thomp

She turned in time to see the helicopter descend from the clouds until it hovered thirty feet above her stern. But this time, there was a man with a rifle leaning out of the cabin door.

James' voice came over the radio. "Sea Nymph, this is Coast Guard Rescue Six-Zero-Three-Two, prepare to be boarded."

Eden tried to get beyond Charlie's reach, but she was closed in on three sides. He grabbed her hair, dragged her painfully toward him, then wrapped a wiry arm around her throat. He forced her, stumbling, out into the rain, pistol against her temple.

Her mouth went dry, her heart slamming in her chest.

He used her as a shield, pointing his pistol at the helicopter. "Back off or—"

BAM! BAM!

Charlie cried out and fell backward, releasing her. Unsteady on her feet, dizzy with pain, she stumbled. But at that moment, a wave hit the boat, pitching Eden over the starboard gunwale and into the frigid water.

"PERSON IN THE WATER!" Sean's heart lurched to see Eden disappear beneath the surface. "Eden just fell overboard on the starboard side. She's not wearing a survival suit."

"Person in the water on the starboard side, roger."

Sean exhaled in relief when he saw her surface and look up at the helo.

Hang on, Eden.

No rescue had been this desperate or personal since the

night Justin had died. That water was only forty-six degrees, and she was only wearing a T-shirt and shorts. Twenty percent of people without survival suits died within the first minute from cold water shock. Those who survived the initial shock lasted maybe ten minutes.

Santee lowered his rifle. "Before we go after Eden, I need to make sure Crane is no longer a threat. He's still conscious and holding that pistol."

Below, Crane lay on the deck of the *Sea Nymph*, holding the pistol and rolling with the boat, his blood mixing with seawater.

They had talked this through and knew what to do. While Trey kept his gaze on Eden, Sean worked his way through the safety checklist and hooked Santee onto the hoist line. Santee left his rifle, but unholstered his pistol.

Sean willed himself to focus on his job. He conned the helo into position. "Forward ten and left. Hold. Agent is leaving the cabin."

"Roger that."

He gave Santee a shove out the door and lowered him a bit at a time onto the wildly pitching deck of the *Sea Nymph*. "Agent is on deck. Agent is okay. Retrieving the hook."

Santee recovered Crane's pistol, checked him for weapons, and cuffed him, then took over the helm, restarting the engine and moving the boat slowly forward.

"The Sea Nymph is moving again," Zeke said. "Should we match speed?"

"No," James said. "Follow the PIW. She's our priority. Let's not drown her with rotor wash."

Trey clipped into the hook. "Eden is now at our eleven o'clock. The waves are carrying her off, but she's got a strobe."

"I've got my eye on her," Zeke said.

"Preparing to send down the rescue swimmer to retrieve

the PIW." Sean started the safety check, but a sudden gust of wind sent the helo pitching.

Alarms shrieked.

Trey was tossed forward and slammed his knee into the door's lock stile and cried out. "Shit! My knee."

While James and Zeke worked to regain control of the helo, Sean dragged Trey away from the edge. "Are you okay, man?"

They needed to get Eden out of the water—*now*.

"I smashed my knee on the locking mechanism. I think it's broken."

"The swimmer is injured. He thinks he's got a broken knee."

Lines of pain on Trey's face told Sean it was serious. "I can't straighten it."

"Roger that." James muted the cabin. "What the hell do we do now? We've got a PIW, an injured asshole, and Santee, and no rescue swimmer."

Trey tried to straighten his knee once again, grimaced. "There's no way I can swim in rough water if I can't kick. Maybe Santee can get close enough to Eden to toss her a rope and pull her back on board."

Sean had a better idea. "Send me down. Drop me in the water. You know I can swim as well as any AST."

"Have you ever retrieved a survivor, McKenna?" James asked.

"No, but I've seen it done a thousand times." He quickly went over the controls with Trey, who already knew how they worked. Then he slipped into a vest and went through the safety check, his pulse picking up. "Lower me into the water. I'll swim over to Eden. Then send down the strap. Make sure to hold the line so it doesn't get caught by the wind. You *don't* want it hitting the tail rotor. Anything I should know?"

"That water is going to be colder than you can imagine.

The rotor wash will feel like a hurricane in your face. Some people think they're drowning when it hits them and panic. Just keep your head and hold onto Eden."

"Thanks, Trey."

"Sorry, man."

"It's not your fault." Sean scooted to the edge, nothing below him but thirty feet of air and churning ocean. It felt surreal. "Here I go."

"McKenna is leaving the cabin."

Sean felt himself fall, the cable catching him and lowering him steadily toward the waves. He looked for Eden, watched for that strobe, and saw her about fifty yards to the helo's starboard side. Then he hit the water and went under.

Even with the survival suit, it was a shock to the system, the water so cold it made his teeth ache. He surfaced, looked up to see Trey watching him and gave him a thumbs-up. Then he unhooked the hoist cable and swam in the direction where he'd last seen Eden.

But where was she?

Chapter Twenty-Two

EDEN WAS SO cold that her bones ached, her body shaking, her teeth chattering, saltwater stinging the cut on her cheek and the laceration on her scalp.

Just stay conscious. Stay alive.

She did her best to tread water, to stay on top of the swells, but the waves were relentless, crashing over her one after the other, carrying her far from the *Sea Nymph* and the helicopter. She couldn't even see the boat now. If she hadn't been wearing the life jacket, she would be lost.

The *Sea Nymph* had been her wedding present from Justin, and now she was going to lose it. Without a pilot, it would most likely founder and sink—another part of him that would rest in the sea. The thought put a hole in her heart.

When the next swells lifted her up, she caught a glimpse of the helicopter.

They'll get you out. They won't leave you here.

Unless they couldn't find her...

She'd heard Justin talk so many times about how hard it was to spot a human alone in heavy seas. A rescue swimmer could be only feet away and not see them because they were in a trough. That's how the personal locator beacons helped, giving the flight crew a precise location. But Eden had only the strobe. She had managed to fish the strobe out of her pocket and had clipped it onto her life jacket so that the light faced upward.

Could they see it? Did they know where she was? Would they find her before hypothermia took her or their fuel got low and they had no choice but to turn back and leave her?

A wave crashed over her... then another... and another.

She fought to catch her breath, kicked hard to stay on top of the water, but she knew she was slowly losing the battle. Her head throbbed, and the cold seemed to sap her strength with each passing moment. But she couldn't die here. She couldn't.

Maverick.

She saw his little face so clearly in her mind. She was the only parent he had. She couldn't die, not now.

My baby, my boy.

Tears blurred her vision.

Another wave and another.

And then it came to her. This had been Justin's life, jumping into frigid water to rescue people who would otherwise have no hope. Every day he'd gone to work, he'd done his best to save lives, with Sean on the helicopter to pull him back. Justin knew how cold it was. He knew. He'd flown so many missions. He'd always been a good swimmer.

Eden's mind began to drift, her thoughts unraveling into nonsense. At least she wasn't so cold now.

That's hypothermia.

Some part of her felt a jolt of alarm at that realization, but the thought faded before she could react.

A light from the sky.

She opened her eyes and saw him. "Justin?"

He was there in the water with her, dressed in his ODUs.

But he didn't seem to be wet. "Eden, you need to wake up. You need to stay alert. Can you do that for me?"

"I've missed you so much."

There it was—that smile she loved so much, lighting up his handsome face. "I'm here. I'll always be here. But you need to wake up, okay?"

"Justin, I—"

"Hang on just a little longer, honey." There was worry in his eyes.

"I'm trying, but it's so cold."

"Take care of our boy." He began to fade, a sad smile on his face. "I love you, Eden. I always will. Be happy."

"No!" She reached for him, stretching her arm in his direction and...

Then her eyes opened, and she saw someone swimming toward her.

Sean!

"Sean!" She cried out for him, but a wave crashed over her, carried her away.

But then Sean was there. She was so relieved and happy to see him that it didn't occur to her to wonder why he was in the water instead of the rescue swimmer.

He took hold of her life jacket, then caught her in a rescue hold, his strong arm encircling her. "I've got you, sweetheart. We're going to hoist you up. The rotor wash is going to make you feel like you're drowning, but you'll be okay. Just do as I say."

Another wave. Aching cold. A bright light.

A flood of rotor wash and sea spray that made her cough.

Sean slipped something around the two of them, bringing her face to face with him, holding her tight. She buried her face in the crook of his neck and held on as they were lifted out of the water and into the air.

Spinning, spinning. Cold wind. The thrum of the rotors. Sean's arms around her.

She raised her gaze to his but couldn't see his eyes behind his visor.

He ran a thumb over her aching cheek. "I love you, Eden."

"I l-love you t-too." But she was so cold and exhausted.

After that, she was aware of little. Hands pulling her into the cabin. Sean reassuring her, working to warm her. Trey pulling Charlie and Sean into the cabin. Charlie shouting for morphine. And then it all faded away.

SEAN HELPED GET Eden on a gurney, made sure she was covered by blankets, and pushed it toward the waiting ambulance. She was still unconscious, and Trey had said he was certain she had a concussion in addition to hypothermia. But at least she was alive.

"We'll take good care of her." An EMT took his place, worked with another to lift the gurney into the ambulance.

Sean stepped back, everything in him wanting to go with her.

But his job wasn't done.

He helped EMS get Crane onto a gurney and over to a waiting Life Flight plane headed for Anchorage. Then he went back for Trey.

"You didn't beat his face in, man." Trey chuckled. "I'm so proud of you—and a little disappointed."

"I think I regret that." It hadn't been easy, not when his fist would have looked so good smashing into Crane's ugly mug. He held out his hand, clasped Trey's. "You take care, Trey. Keep us posted. And thanks for everything."

"You did the hard work. You'd make a good AST, by the way."

"Thanks, but no thanks. That water is fucking cold."

He watched as the plane lifted off, James coming to stand beside him.

"Captain Walcott wants to see us before the debriefing."

"I bet he does." Sean was still wearing his survival suit, his hair wet, but he walked with James back toward the building. "Any word from Santee?"

"He's checking in every half hour."

Agent Santee had confiscated Charlie's cell phone and had decided to sail the *Sea Nymph* the rest of the way to Homer to find out who was waiting—and to take that person into custody. He was coordinating with the small Coast Guard station there, and other CGIS and FBI agents would be waiting to join in the fun.

The man was a crazy bastard and one hell of a shot.

James clapped Sean on the back. "She's going to be okay."

Sean nodded. "Yeah."

"How are you?"

"Seeing Crane with Eden and watching her fall overboard took a decade off my life."

Christ.

He'd been terrified that he was going to lose her.

"You did one hell of a job out there. I've never seen an AET change places with a rescue swimmer to save someone's life. I'm betting you'll get a medal out of this."

"A medal?" Sean laughed. "Nah. I'll be lucky if I still have a job."

Captain Walcott met them at the hangar door and drew them aside. "Spurrier, McKenna, well done. I listened in the entire time, which included a stretch where you muted your feed."

James explained. "We needed to plan and didn't want to clutter the radio."

"Right." Walcott stopped, lowered his voice. "Before we

go into this debriefing, I need you to know that there are two versions of what happened out there this afternoon. The first is that you responded to the PLB but went beyond SAR mission parameters, triggering a hostage crisis, breaking a few regulations, and somehow getting back with the victim, the suspect, and the flight crew alive."

Sean wasn't sure he much liked that version. "What's the other option?"

"The second version says you responded to the PLB, found the victim in immediate danger, and acted heroically in extremely unusual and difficult circumstances to save her life."

James nodded. "That's definitely what happened."

Sean agreed. "Yes, that's exactly what happened out there."

"Good." Walcott leveled his gaze at them. "The first version comes with potential unpleasantness and consequences."

Sean shared a look with James as they walked to the debriefing room, where they spent the next hour going over the mission in detail with Walcott and Chief Allen and answering their many questions. As the meeting went on, Sean grew impatient and tired, the after-effects of adrenaline hitting him in a way they hadn't since ...

The night Justin died.

But this time, there'd been a mostly happy ending.

How was Eden? Was her concussion serious?

Had she heard him say that he loved her?

"One last question." Chief Allen looked straight at Sean. "The fact that you were able to change places with Trey Nash on the spur of the moment and finish this evolution amazes me. Have you trained as an AST?"

"No, sir, but I worked with one of the best until he was killed." Sean's throat went tight. "I knew his job, and he knew mine. We were a team and flew more than a hundred missions together. After Trey was injured, I just changed the plan and moved ahead. There was no way in *hell* I was going to let Eden die."

"Well, I'm impressed, McKenna." Walcott's gaze shifted from Sean to James and back again. "I'm going to be putting you in for a commendation. You're dismissed. I expect you have somewhere else you'd rather be."

"Yes, sir. Thank you, sir." Sean left the room.

James stayed. "If you have a moment, sir..."

The door closed.

Sean wanted a hot shower and a meal. Then he would head to the hospital to see Eden.

Eden had just finished telling Baba, her mother, and her sisters the whole story when Sean stuck his head through the door. Everyone except Baba stood when they saw him, Anya's squeal making Eden's head ache.

"It's him! You saved our sister's life. Thank you!"

Sean seemed bemused. "The sister posse is here."

Still, Eden couldn't help but smile as Sean worked his way through a sea of hugging women to reach her side.

He leaned down, kissed Eden's forehead. "Hey."

"Hey." She took his hand. "I'm so glad you're here."

Anya moved a chair closer to the bed. "Here you go. Just pretend we're not here."

"Thanks, Anya." Sean sat, ran his thumb over the back of her hand, his gaze moving over her swollen cheek. "How do you feel?"

"My head hurts. Light bothers me, too. They said it's a concussion."

He glanced up at the lights. "I see you're keeping the lights dimmed. Are they giving you anything for pain?"

"Just acetaminophen." It wasn't doing much. "They're

keeping me overnight because I was unconscious for a while and because I also had hypothermia."

That had scared Sean as much as the head injury. "How's your core temp?"

"I think it's normal again, but I'm not giving up these heated blankets any time soon." She drew them up to her chin.

Her sisters laughed.

Then Baba stood. "I think we should let Sean and Eden have some time alone, yeah? I'm sure they have things they want to say to each other."

Eden's mother stood, too. "We'll be right downstairs if you need us."

Then, one by one, they all hugged Sean again, Baba going last.

She patted his cheek. "I knew you were a good man. You brought my granddaughter home to her family. That makes *you* family now."

"Thank you, ma'am." His response was so formal that Eden had to smile.

"You can call me Baba or Granny." Her grandmother left the room.

Then she was alone with Sean.

"You incredible, brave woman." Sean raised her hand to his lips, kissed it. "If you hadn't thrown that EPIRB overboard and set off that personal locator beacon, you'd have been stuck on the boat with him until he reached Homer."

"I didn't throw the EPIRB into the water. Charlie did." Eden told him everything that had happened from the moment Charlie had appeared out of the cabin until the helicopter had arrived. "When he threatened to shoot me and the helicopter disappeared into the clouds, I was afraid you'd decided to turn back. Then the helicopter reappeared at my stern, and I saw the man with the rifle leaning out. It meant so much just to know I wasn't alone anymore."

"I'm sorry we didn't get there sooner." His brow furrowed as he spoke, and she knew her time as Charlie's hostage had been hard on him, too. "The plan was to send a cutter with an FBI hostage negotiator to rescue you when you reached Homer. When the PLB signal came in, Walcott authorized a search-and-rescue."

"I'm so glad you didn't wait." Tears blurred her eyes. "Charlie kept talking about handing me over to his buddy. He said he'd seen this guy slit someone's throat before and said he'd have him do the same to me. I was sure their plan was to kill me and take my boat. I was afraid no one would find me in time."

Anger flashed through Sean's eyes, but when he spoke his words were gentle. "I am so sorry, Eden. If it had been up to me, we would have followed you from the moment that EPIRB signal came in, but I'm not in command."

"Orders, not options."

"Exactly."

Then Eden remembered what she'd wanted to ask him. "I must be remembering it wrong, because I thought *you* pulled me out of the water."

"I did." Sean explained how Trey had badly injured his knee and wouldn't have been able to swim. "There was no way I was going to leave you to die. We could have asked Santee to maneuver the Sea Nymph closer and try to throw you a line, but in heavy seas, you could easily have missed the rope or been injured. So, I traded places with Trey, left him on board to manage the hoist, and swam after you."

Eden was stunned. "Oh, Sean."

His face crumpled. "I couldn't see you. I couldn't see your strobe. Zeke put you in the Trakkabeam, and I just swam toward the light. I've never been more afraid in my life, Eden. If I'd lost you... God!"

Eden raised a hand to his cheek. "I don't think I had much

longer. Something happened, something I can't explain. I... I saw Justin."

Sean didn't laugh. "You saw him?"

Eden's throat went tight, and the tears came. "There was a light—it must have been the Trakkabeam—and then he was there. He was wearing ODUs and looked like himself. But he wasn't wet. He looked worried. He told me I needed to wake up and stay alert. He told me that he would always love me and asked me to take care of Maverick. Then he said, 'Be happy' and faded away. I reached for him. Then he was gone, and you were there, right where he'd been."

Sean got a strange expression on his face, and Eden worried that she'd hurt him. Sean had saved her life today, but it wasn't him she'd seen in her darkest moment. It was Justin.

"I'm sorry. I know it must be awkward to hear me talk about Justin, but—"

"No." He shook his head. "No, it's not that. I found you because you reached up. I saw your hand over the crest of a swell."

"You did?" A shiver went down Eden's spine. "Do you think..."

Sean smiled. "That you truly saw Justin, that he was really there? Well, he sent you that piece of red sea glass, didn't he?"

Eden nodded, smiled, happy that he understood. "I guess I had both of you working together to save my life today."

"We always made a good team." Then Sean's smile faded, a troubled expression on his face. "The whole time we were in flight, I kept kicking myself in the ass for not telling you sooner. I thought I might never get another chance to do it."

"To do what?"

Sean looked into her eyes. "To tell you how much I love you."

Eden's heart soared.

Chapter Twenty-Three

EDEN SPENT the next few weeks on total rest, while Sean and her sisters pampered her, took care of the chores, and watched over Maverick. She didn't pay much attention to the outside world, the abduction and those terrible hours of being in the storm with Charlie finding their way into her dreams. Of Agent Santee, Charlie's buddy in Homer, and the fate of her beloved *Sea Nymph,* she heard nothing.

Three weeks after the abduction, Sean got a call from Santee. He told Sean that he, together with the FBI and DEA, had, indeed, caught Charlie's buddy in Homer that day. Federal agents had interrogated him and Charlie and had used that information, together with data on the phones they'd confiscated, to bring down the entire network in a series of coordinated arrests.

"That's why there was nothing about it in the papers." Sean sat beside Eden on the sofa. "They kept it quiet because they didn't want to tip off the bad guys."

Eden's reaction wasn't just the anticipated relief at knowing it was over, but something much deeper she hadn't expected. "This gives Justin's death meaning."

Fire and Rain

"I had the same thought." Sean took her hand, the smile returning to his face. "Santee wanted me to tell you he thinks you're a badass, and he's right. I don't know many people who could have done what you did—figuring out a way to set off the EPIRB and the personal locator beacon, standing up to your abductor, and piloting the boat in heavy seas."

Eden hadn't felt like a badass. "I didn't have much choice."

"He also wanted you to know that, when they'd heard what had happened, the cutter crew in Homer decided to give the Sea Nymph a cleanup. He's arranged to have it towed back to the marina at no cost to you. It should be there later this afternoon."

Eden's heart lifted. "Oh, thank goodness!"

Life was slowly returning to normal—but not for everyone.

In the first week of August, Maria stopped by to tell Eden that Mila would likely lose everything as the federal government moved to seize all assets Charlie had purchased with drug money.

"They're going after everything—the house, the cars, their bank accounts, even Mila's jewelry. They'll take every dime he earned through selling drugs, and then charge him taxes on it, which Mila can't pay with the seized assets. And, Eden, she could owe millions. That's what Auntie Evelyn says."

Oh, God.

Eden couldn't imagine how devastated Mila must feel. Her entire life with Charlie had been a lie, and now she would probably lose everything. "How are Nick and Lina? This must be so confusing for them."

"They're having a really hard time."

Eden stood. "Let's stop by and bring some treats for the kids."

Maria stared at her. "Are you sure? You might not be Mila's favorite person."

"She's my cousin, and she's in trouble." Eden got Maverick ready to go, and they climbed into Maria's vehicle, picking up flowers for Mila and pastries for the kids along the way.

Auntie Evelyn opened the door and seemed surprised to see Eden. She glanced back over her shoulder. "I'm not sure she's going to want to see you right—"

"Who is it?" Mila stepped into the room and saw Eden, her dark expression turning darker. "Why are you here? Have you come to tell me what an asshole my soon-to-be-ex-husband is?"

Auntie Evelyn stepped aside, and Eden entered with Maverick and the flowers, Maria following with the pastries. "No, Mila, I came to tell you how sorry I am."

"Sorry? Why are *you* sorry? The bastard got your husband killed and might have murdered you."

"He did. But before that, Charlie deceived you and betrayed your trust."

Mila's chin quivered, and she burst into tears.

Eden handed the flowers to Auntie Evelyn and hurried over to Mila and wrapped her in a hug. "I'm so sorry, Mila. What a nightmare this must be."

Mila's arms went around Eden, and for a time, they stood there, Mila sobbing on Eden's shoulder, while Maria took Mavie, Nick, and Lina into the kitchen and gave them their pastries.

Mila stepped back, wiped the tears from her face. "Why are you being so nice?"

Eden smiled. "We might not be BFFs, Mila, but we're family."

While Auntie Evelyn made tea, Eden sat with Mila in the living room, listening as she shared a litany of fears.

"My attorney said I'll probably be able to keep our rental property because we paid that off before the rat bastard started dealing."

"It's a place to start over. It won't be easy, but you won't deal with this alone. Your family will be there for you, and the women in this family are strong."

Mila's eyes filled with tears. "I'm thirty-one with two kids. I'll probably spend the rest of my life alone."

Eden took her hand. "I don't believe that for a heartbeat. You're beautiful, Mila. Focus on yourself and the kids for now. The rest of it will fall into place."

Mila met Eden's gaze. "I'm sorry I've been a bitch to you. It's just... You're always so happy, and everything you do seems so ... effortless."

Eden remembered what Baba had told her that day on their walk. "You can never know the burdens another person is carrying, but I do know this. You've always been good enough just the way you are. You don't need a rich husband or a big house or four cars to be worthy of other people's love. You just need to be happy with yourself."

Mila's eyes filled with tears once more. "But who am I?"

"That's what you get to discover now."

It was late afternoon when Eden and Maria got ready to leave, and Mila seemed to feel better. "Thanks for the flowers, and thanks for stopping by. I'm really sorry about what Charlie did to you."

"That's not your fault."

When they'd gotten into the car, Maria turned to Eden and hugged her. "I overheard most of that. I am so proud to be your big sister. I'm starting to think you're the Baba of our generation."

Eden smiled, but she knew the truth. "I could never be as wise as Baba."

SEAN TRIED to fix the tie of his dress uniform. "I hate wearing this thing."

Most of the Air Station crew were already taking their seats, Captain Walcott, the Rear Admiral, and the Master Chief standing beside the dais, talking together while they waited for the ceremony to begin.

Eden batted Sean's hands away and took over for him, then lowered her voice to a whisper. "I love your dress uniform. You look hot. If we weren't in public, I'd show you how much I like it by taking it off."

"You're the hot one. God, I love you in that dress."

She finished, looked up at him from beneath her lashes, and ran her palms down the front of his single-breasted jacket. "Do you love me out of it?"

He could *not* get an erection—not now. "I love you even more out of it."

"I'll be sure to take it off later."

He couldn't think too much about that. "I see you all have front-row seats."

"Well, this involved our family, right? I just hope Maverick behaves."

"He'll be fine. I'll see you afterwards." Sean kissed her and walked toward the dais, putting on his cover as he went.

Captain Walcott drew him aside, introduced him to Rear Admiral Nicholas Marlow and Master Chief Petty Officer Phillip Halder.

Sean shook their hands. "It's an honor to meet you both."

"Have you seen Agent Santee?" Walcott glanced around.

"Right behind you, sir." Santee shook hands with the officers.

Then Captain Walcott walked toward the podium.

"Now come the speeches." Santee rolled his eyes.

Fire and Rain

They took their seats up on the dais, Sean's gaze finding Eden, who sat with Maverick on her lap, her sisters, mother, and Baba sitting beside her.

Captain Walcott introduced Rear Admiral Marlow, who talked about the things rear admirals always talked about—excellence, mission readiness, and the proud tradition of saving lives that was the hallmark of the Coast Guard.

Sean watched as Maverick pointed to the H-60 in the hangar, wriggled, and tried to get down. Clearly, the boy wanted a closer look. Sean would make sure he got it.

Applause.

The rear admiral took his seat, and then the Master Chief spoke about dedication, sacrifice, and those who distinguish themselves by going above and beyond.

More applause.

In the front row, Eden pointed to Sean, tried to get Maverick to settle down.

Maverick saw him. "Sawn?"

Sean waved to him discreetly.

Then Captain Walcott stood at the podium once again. "On Four July of this year, a violent drug dealer who was associated with the deaths of two of our own—Aviation Survival Technician Second Class Justin Koseki and Lt. Junior Grade David Abbott—abducted AST Koseki's widow at gunpoint in an attempt to evade capture."

Walcott told the entire story, giving Eden credit for her cleverness and courage, then focusing on Santee's actions that day. "Agent Santee hit a target area of no more than four inches on the deck of a rocking boat at a distance of approximately twenty yards while hanging out of the helicopter's cabin in turbulent weather. His marksmanship neutralized a dangerous criminal, saving Mrs. Koseki's life. For his courage and skill, the Coast Guard is proud to award Agent Santee the Silver Lifesaving Medal."

The room was called to attention, and Sean saluted along with everyone else while Santee walked up to the podium and endured the Master Chief pinning the medal onto his chest.

When he had returned to his seat, Captain Walcott went on, describing how Eden, injured and dizzy, had fallen overboard. "As the flight crew prepared to recover Mrs. Koseki from the water, the helicopter was hit by a gust of wind that temporarily robbed the aircraft of tail rotor effectiveness and injured the rescue swimmer."

Sean searched the rows of seated Coasties for Trey and found him near the back with his crutches. He grinned, gave Sean a thumbs-up.

Walcott went on. "At this point, there was one person in the water, one injured suspect on the Sea Nymph, and no rescue swimmer to recover either of them. Without hesitation, Aviation Electronics Technician Second Class Sean McKenna assumed the role of rescue swimmer—something I haven't seen in more than thirty years with the Coast Guard. AET McKenna recovered both Mrs. Koseki and the suspect, and the crew returned safely to base. For his heroism, boldness, and courage, the Coast Guard is proud to award Aviation Electronics Technician Second Class Sean McKenna the Silver Lifesaving Medal."

The room was called to attention again.

Sean stood, walked up to the podium, offered his best salute, and stood still while the Master Chief pinned the medal on his chest.

"Sawn!" Maverick's voice rang through the cavernous hangar.

Laughter.

Sean glanced out and his gaze met Eden's. There were happy tears on her cheeks and a smile on her lips, the Sister Posse applauding loudly as he made his way back to his seat.

Santee glanced at his ribbons and medal. "Nice rack."

Fire and Rain

Afterwards, there was a reception with cake, and Sean searched the room for James. None of the helos were out, so he ought to be here.

He walked over to Trey. "Have you seen Spurrier?"

Trey shook his head. "I haven't seen him for a couple of days."

Captain Walcott must have overheard because he walked over to Sean. "Lt. Spurrier resigned his commission. He'd fulfilled his service agreement and requested a voluntary separation, which was finalized a few days ago."

The news hit Sean like a fist to the gut.

"I understand your dismay. Spurrier was an excellent pilot."

But Walcott didn't understand at all. James was one of only two other survivors of that terrible night. He had understood.

Then Walcott stuck out his hand. "By the way, you made the cut. You're advancing in rank—and serving another tour of duty in Kodiak. I'll have the paperwork sorted by the end of next week. Congratulations again."

Still reeling but pleased with this news, Sean took Walcott's hand. "Thank you, sir."

Eden walked over with Maverick in her arms, concern on her face. "What's wrong?"

"I'll tell you later." He took Maverick from her, put his hat on Maverick's head. "Do you want to see the helicopters, buddy?"

Maverick pointed. "Copta!"

"That's what I thought."

EDEN WALKED ALONG JEWEL BEACH, holding hands with Sean, the two of them talking about the good news Sean had gotten today and enjoying the ocean air. Maverick walked ahead of them, filling his pail with treasure—the big shell of a geoduck clam, a marble, a twisted bit of copper wiring.

"See, Mommy?"

"That's a barnacle shell." She laughed as Maverick tried to say *barnacle*.

"Nucko."

Sean chuckled. "Good enough, kid."

"Are you going to be taking Dalton's place in avionics?" Eden knew that wasn't an assignment Sean had wanted.

"It looks like it." He nudged a piece of aqua-colored sea glass from the sand with the toe of his boot, which Eden picked up and dropped in her bucket. "On the upside, you won't have to worry about me as much, and I get to stay in Kodiak for now."

Eden had been so relieved to learn he wouldn't be transferred away. "Though I appreciate the fact you won't be flying as often, I also want you to be happy."

"I've got other priorities now, other things that matter more." He smiled, squeezed her hand, but she could see the sadness in his eyes.

She knew what was troubling him. "I'm really sorry about James leaving. You flew a lot of missions together, didn't you?"

More than that, James and Wade were the other two who'd survived the crash, and she could understand how that night had forged an unspoken bond between them.

"We did—dozens and dozens of missions. He insisted on flying to rescue you even though it was his day off. I think he felt like he owed it to you."

Eden couldn't help but feel touched. "He didn't need to do that."

"In his mind, he did, and I understand that. I also get that he might have been done flying. Most pilots come with an expiration date, but I think he left because the stress of living with the memory of that night was tearing him apart. I just wish he'd said goodbye. Walcott doesn't even know where he went. He just left base and ... disappeared."

"I'm sorry. Maybe he just needs to be alone for now."

They continued down the beach, gravel crunching beneath their boots, the conversation drifting to the medal ceremony and then Maverick's birthday next week.

"I can't believe my baby is going to be two." She watched as Maverick dug in the sand with a small stick, something she'd done so often as a child.

"It does seem like it happened quickly."

"I hope you get the day off so you can join us."

"I remember Justin saying there's always a ridiculous amount of cake when your family celebrates a birthday. Is that true?"

Eden picked up a bit of brown sea glass. "We all bake cakes."

"Everyone?"

"Well, my mother, my sisters, and I. We kind of compete for the tastiest cake."

Sean grinned. "So, you have *six* cakes at every family birthday party?"

"Yes—and every last crumb gets eaten."

"I get it. Okay." He chuckled. "I mean, what's a birthday for if not cake?"

"Exactly." Eden pointed. "It looks like Maverick has made some new friends."

A couple of seagulls checked him out, the spots on their feathers marking them as juveniles. He offered one a pebble, which it ignored. He tried to touch them, but they ran a short distance away, making him laugh. Soon, it became a game. He chased them, and they chased him back, Maverick squealing with laughter.

Sean drew Eden against him, wrapped his arms around

her, the two of them watching Maverick play. "I love this place—and I love being out here with the two of you. I want it to last forever."

Eden knew only too well that nothing lasted forever. "I wouldn't be here right now if not for you. You saved my life, Sean."

He kissed her hair. "No, Eden, you saved me."

Eden tilted her head to look up at him. "What do you mean?"

"After the crash, I was lost. The physical injuries were hard, but the emotional ones ... I felt broken. I had promised Justin that I'd watch over you and Maverick if anything happened to him. I didn't realize it at the time, but helping you took me out of myself and gave me a better reason to get up in the morning than physical therapy."

It was hard for Eden to think of those early days. "I hated seeing you in pain, knowing you were suffering, but I was so caught up in my grief. I wish I'd been there for you more."

"But you were." He seemed to search for words. "You showed me another way to live—foraging, treasure hunting, walking in the rain. More than that, you helped me get beyond the guilt I felt for not being able to save Justin. The biggest difference between me and James is that I have you. I love you, Eden, and I want to spend the rest of my life with you."

Eden's heart swelled to bursting. "I must be the luckiest woman on this earth. Both of the men I've loved are heroes."

About twenty feet away, Maverick plopped onto his bottom, and one plucky seagull chick ran over his legs, making him laugh harder.

"I love that sound. It's like ... music."

"Baby laughter is the best."

Sean took her hand, and they walked toward Maverick. "I think our boy is going to need a little brother or sister one day, don't you?"

Fire and Rain

Eden's heart soared. "One day."

"It's time to go, little man." Sean let go of Eden's hand and knelt beside Maverick, the seagull chicks scurrying away. "You found lots of treasure. Look at this cool stuff. Let's go home and have something yummy for supper."

While Sean brushed the sand off Maverick's pants and hoisted him onto his shoulders, Eden looked out toward the open ocean.

Rest, my love. All is well.

As they walked back up the beach, the sun broke through the clouds and turned the surface of the water to diamonds.

Thank You

Thanks for reading *Fire and Rain*. I hope you enjoyed Eden and Sean's story. Follow me on Facebook or on Twitter @Pamela_Clare. Join my reader's group on Facebook to be a part of a never-ending conversation with other Pamela Clare fans and get inside information about my books and about life in Colorado's mountains. You can also sign up to my mailing list at my website to keep current with all my releases and to be a part of special newsletter giveaways.

Also by Pamela Clare

Contemporary Romance:

Wildest Alaska Series
Fire and Rain (Book 1)

Colorado High Country Series
Barely Breathing (Book 1)
Slow Burn (Book 2)
Falling Hard (Book 3)
Tempting Fate (Book 4)
Close to Heaven (Book 5)
Holding On (Book 6)
Chasing Fire (Book 7)
Breaking Free (Book 8)
Take Me Higher (Book 9)
Bound to Fall (Book 10)

Romantic Suspense:

I-Team Series
Extreme Exposure (Book 1)
Heaven Can't Wait (Book 1.5)
Hard Evidence (Book 2)
Unlawful Contact (Book 3)
Naked Edge (Book 4)

Breaking Point (Book 5)
Skin Deep: An I-Team After Hours Novella (Book 5.5)
First Strike: The Prequel to Striking Distance (Book 5.9)
Striking Distance (Book 6)
Soul Deep: An I-Team After Hours Novella (Book 6.5)
Seduction Game (Book 7)
Dead by Midnight: An I-Team Christmas (Book 7.5)
Deadly Intent (Book 8)

Cobra Elite Series
Hard Target (Book 1)
Hard Asset (Book 2)
Hard Justice (Book 3)
Hard Edge (Book 4)
Hard Line (Book 5)
Hard Pursuit (Book 6)

Historical Romance:

Kenleigh-Blakewell Family Saga
Sweet Release (Book 1)
Carnal Gift (Book 2)
Ride the Fire (Book 3)

MacKinnon's Rangers Series
Surrender (Book I)
Untamed (Book 2)
Defiant (Book 3)
Upon A Winter's Night (Book 3.5)

About the Author

USA Today best-selling author Pamela Clare began her writing career as a columnist and investigative reporter and eventually became the first woman editor-in-chief of two different newspapers. Along the way, she and her team won numerous state and national honors, including the National Journalism Award for Public Service. In 2011, Clare was awarded the Keeper of the Flame Lifetime Achievement Award for her body of work. A single mother with two sons, she writes historical romance and contemporary romantic suspense at the foot of the beautiful Rocky Mountains. Visit her website and join her mailing list to never miss a new release!

www.pamelaclare.com

www.ingramcontent.com/pod-product-compliance
Lightning Source LLC
LaVergne TN
LVHW091512220625
814396LV00037B/381